D0483980

Chehak, Susan

Harmony

DATE DUE   18.95

JAN 0 9 1998		
2-5-98		
FEB 0 7 2001		
MAR 0 6 2001		
MAR 3 1 2001		

Books by Susan Taylor Chehak

THE STORY OF ANNIE D.

HARMONY

Harmony

Susan Taylor Chehak

Harmony

Ticknor & Fields
New York
1990

For information about permission to reproduce selections
from this book, write to Permissions, Ticknor & Fields,
215 Park Avenue South, New York, New York 10003.

Library of Congress Cataloging-in-Publication Data

Chehak, Susan Taylor.
Harmony / Susan Taylor Chehak.
p.   cm.
ISBN 0-89919-941-0
I. Title.
PS3553.H34875H37   1990   90-35957
813'.54—DC20   CIP

Printed in the United States of America

BVG 10 9 8 7 6 5 4 3 2 1

For my own big sisters, Debbie and Chris

Harmony

1

WHEN LILLY DUKE came to live with us here in Harmony, it was then that this place where I was born and brought up was for me forever and for all time changed.

She turned up at the old Duke cottage down by the south end of the lake, and she made herself at home there, just the same way that a starling will settle itself down into some other bird's abandoned nest. And then what had been predictable and snug about the town and the woods and the fields and the lake began to seem unfamiliar and strange, and what I had always believed was real and true became in some way skewed, different and new, and it was a long time before I was able to quite put my finger on just exactly how.

My sister Jewel would maybe say now that it was only me changing, and that was why, not anything that had to do with Lilly Duke. Jewel is older than I am, so maybe she should know better, but she has an irritating way of making things seem simpler than they are. She prefers to keep her ideas organized in her mind, and sometimes she can only see one face of a thing because she doesn't know how to turn it around and look on the other side for more.

But I know this. Harmony changed, and it was because of

what that girl brought to us that it did. Or maybe the truth is it was what she took away.

Nobody knew how she exactly got here. We hadn't heard that she'd be coming, and there wasn't anybody, either, who was a witness to it when she did. What happened was, one day Lilly wasn't here, and then the next morning she was. She didn't drive in, I do know that much, because she never did have a car.

She didn't come in on the bus, I don't think, either, with a suitcase hanging off one hand, her clothes smelling of diesel fuel and rumpled from the hours and hours of rolling straight along the roads, her face ashen with the exhaustion of it, her eyes gummy with the lack of sleep and staring out the grimy windows at the ditches and the trees and the houses full of families that were not hers.

It could have been she hitched a ride. That would make some sense, I guess. I could imagine Lilly Duke in the cab of a pickup truck, perched on the torn leather seat, her palms pressed up against the cracked vinyl of the dashboard, her nails chewed down to the nub, the veins thin and insubstantial on the backs of her hands, the thick scars across her wrists hidden by the frayed knit cuffs of the jacket that she wore over her dress. The driver's headlights might catch an outline of her standing all alone there in the gravel on the shoulder of the highway, the wind of passing cars and trucks whipping her already wild hair, and he would swerve and, kicking up a spray of sand, skid to a stop.

Her jacket flies open, the buttons missing or undone; her dress is too sheer, too short, its fabric tight across her shoulders, baggy at her breasts, its skirt blown back, clinging to her legs, outlining the twin stalks of her thighs as she runs to catch up to the waiting truck, struggles with the heavy door, steps up and scrambles inside.

The driver might have tried striking up a conversation, acting friendly, feeling sorry probably, protective maybe, fatherly. He might have offered her a smoke at first, then looked her over again, noticed the cinnamon sprinkle of freckles across her nose, thought twice, and handed her a Life Saver instead, or a stick of gum.

He would have thought she was too young to be hitchhiking all alone that way.

"Didn't your mother ever tell you?" he would ask her. "You're just lucky that it's me and not some psycho killer, murdering rapist."

Scaring her then with that. He would have been guessing probably she was some kind of a runaway. Domineering mother, alcoholic father, problems at home. He maybe tried to persuade her she should consider turning back.

"Your family's probably missing you bad, honey. Your mama must be worried crazy. I know I would be. If you were mine."

He could have asked her questions, offered some help, friendly advice.

"So, where you headed, girlie?"

Humming with the radio, changing the station when it came to the news. "Clear with a chance of showers. Wind out of the northwest. And, in Nebraska yesterday, Timothy Duke was sentenced to die . . ."

But Lilly would have gazed away, out the side window, watching the trees and telephone poles pass by, keeping herself to herself. Grateful for the ride, maybe, but reserved, reluctant, holding back, the way she could, looking off, avoiding any kind of eye contact, hardly answering him, only mumbling and nodding, wishing, I guess, that there was some way other than this so she wouldn't need a free ride, didn't somehow have to be sitting here, obligated like she was to this stranger who had had the heart to stop and give a seventeen-year-old girl a lift.

Most likely she was hoping that the driver would turn his attention away from her and back to the road again. Quit looking at her, stop studying her face, give up on trying to guess what she was, and who. She would have leaned over, finally, touched his arm, startled him with the flurry of her fingers, and pointed straight ahead, at the sign by the road that says HARMONY, and she would have whispered, "Here. Please. I'll just get out right here."

Then what? He drops her off at the side of the highway in the middle of the night and drives away, leaves her standing there alone with the woods all around and the moonlight glimmering down from behind a skim of clouds?

Of course, what doesn't reconcile, what can't fit in with what I'm guessing could have happened is the part about the baby, C.T. Because naturally he was there; she had him with her, three months old already by that time, bundled up in a blanket, held in her thin arms, his head as big as hers, pressed against her shoulder, propped awkwardly in the shallow bowl of her lap.

What could a truck driver think about that? Would he leave Lilly and the baby, too, that way then, alone in the dark, on the shoulder of the road? Would he listen and then do what she told him? Obey her when she said, "Here. You can just let us off right here?" Would he lean over and pull the door shut after her, glance in his rearview mirror, swing back out onto the roadway and, without a second thought, drive off, a different destination on his mind, a wife and kids of his own waiting for him, warm and cozy, somewhere up ahead?

Well, it doesn't seem quite likely that the same man who would take the time to stop for her in the first place could all of a sudden turn out to be as heartless and cold as that. Picking her up and then dropping her down again, without asking for some of the why or what for. Without making an attempt to in some way do more. Not with a baby there. Not if she had an infant bundled up, heavy in her arms.

So probably, then, the most likely explanation is that she didn't hitch. It would have been one of Tim Duke's friends who brought Lilly here. Some pal, a young criminal, juvenile delinquent, troublemaker, just out of jail, out on parole, out on bail, let go on his own recognizance. A kid with a raggy bit of mustache planted there on the sneer of his upper lip, a face with sharp, high cheeks, a bony forehead and a big jaw, his hair combed back stiff and hard, his ravaged skin tight on his face, drawing his eyes back so he looks vulnerable and mean at the same time, like somebody so stubborn he just keeps standing there, gritting his teeth, breathless in the face of that cold wind that can come gusting off the lake sometimes.

It gives him a look of slyness and resentment all at once, the kind of a face that coming your way right off makes you step down from the curb and cross over to the other side of the street, for your own safety and protection. A kid you would expect to be carrying a knife there where it might come in handy, down in the deep back pocket of his jeans. One who would have eyed Lilly, imagined her, been tempted maybe to reach for her, restrained only by the thought of Tim Duke's already proven rage, of what Tim would do if he ever heard that anyone had so much as thought about touching even one hair on the head of his beloved Lillyheart.

That's what he was calling her in the letters he wrote. Lillyheart. Dear Lillyheart. Lillyheart Duke.

"Take her away," Tim maybe said, his hands pressed flat on the cool surface of the Formica tabletop, his thumbs touching, his face a puzzle behind the metal mesh of the prison visiting-room screen. "Take her to Harmony. I got a little house there, down by the lake, at the end of a dead-end road, near the spillway, set back pretty in the trees."

A little house. A cottage. Well, to tell the truth, it was more like a cabin, a two-room shack that had belonged to Tim's grandmother, Mildred Merriweather Duke, who had died two years earlier—of old age and loneliness was what everyone, including Jewel, said.

My sister Jewel and her friends are our self-appointed chroniclers; they are the ones among us who can keep track of all the people who live here in Harmony. They join up all our personal histories with their words and their judgments and the stories that they tell. They know everybody's name and where they came from and where they'll most likely go. They understand who is related to who else and how. They can follow along the plots of our lives, and their talk about it keeps the parts and pieces of Harmony held together, like the squares and patches of some complicated quilt. They thread families and friends all together; their words are the stitches that link up one person's life with that of another. And my sister and her friends are quick to spot and recognize the repetitions and the patterns that they think they can see working themselves out.

"Well, isn't that just like a so-and-so, to go acting in that way?" one says, because she can remember that this person's grandfather did something of the same kind of thing to his wife's cousin not less than fifty or sixty years ago.

Jewel has said to me that sometimes it feels to her that she could just about almost get a glimpse of the beauty of the whole fabric here, as her gossip works to stitch it into stories.

"Wouldn't that be a sight?" she asks me.

Like looking down upon the blue blot of the lake, the square plowed fields and the scrub hills and the patchy woods, from an airplane window way up high above us, flying overhead across the broad expanse of our sky.

What Jewel told me was that this Mildred Duke had at one time been a Merriweather girl, one of the three daughters of Mehitabel and James Merriweather, two zealots who were convinced that the signs they were reading in the sky and the clouds and the trees around them meant that their Lord was coming soon, and — anyway, at least they had the courage of their convictions — they acted on their hunch by getting rid of every item of clothing but what they were wearing on their backs, every piece of furniture, each bowl and plate and bit of bread, every stitch and stick they owned in the world. Then one long night in December they huddled together in their empty shack, singing and praying, reading the Bible out loud, peering up at the sky, sniffing the air, listening to the wind, waiting and hoping, only to finally doze off at dawn and wake up again to the blinding morning sunlight, daylight full and bright and strong as ever.

There they were, and there was the rest of this wicked world, too — intact, unchanged, unjudged, unsaved, unended. There was nothing for it then but that they flee Harmony. There was not one thing left for them to stay here for, except maybe extreme embarrassment and profound shame. Of course, they knew how foolish they looked, how they would be held up for ridicule in town, how people would be whispering, shaking their heads, continuing on in their old evil ways. And besides, their disappointment must have been overwhelming, their disillusionment complete.

So they went away. Disappeared. Drifted off and never came back. They didn't have any possessions left to pack, so they just sneaked away, stole off under cover of darkness, in the middle of the night. Crept out of town and vanished, maybe made another end of the world for themselves someplace else. What they left behind was their three baby daughters, including Mildred, and some kindhearted aunt and uncle came forward to take them in and raise them like they were their own. Then, when the girls all came of age, each one of them found a husband, and all but Mildred moved away. She married Tim's grandfather, Elijah Duke, and they lived together in that same old shack that had once belonged to her parents, the place that had been her childhood home. Elijah got killed in the war not too long after Tim's father was born, and Tim's dad grew up alone by the lake with his mother until finally he moved away out of Iowa, to Nebraska where he made a living in construction and married Tim's mother and they had some children, including Tim.

What Jewel and the others didn't already have of this whole

tale came to them through the newspapers and the magazine stories later, when they were making the connection in the tabloids between Tim Duke, the murderer, and his great-grandparents' strange vigil, expecting the Rapture, pining for the Lord to come and take them both away.

It would have been that Tim had visited his grandma Mildred at Harmony Lake sometime when he was a child, though no one later was able to remember anything about him ever being here, or come up with anything special about it if he was. But it was true that after Mildred died, somebody kept on paying the water and electric bills on the place, and even though it was maybe run-down and shabby, dilapidated and worn, still it was a place that belonged to Tim Duke, a secret place, sort of, and when he and Lilly were on the run for those few days before Tim was caught, they stayed there for one night. Unbeknownst to anyone in Harmony, of course.

"She'll remember," Tim may have assured this kid who would be bringing Lilly here to us. "She should be able to point out where. And if you touch her, one hair on her head, so much as look crosswise at her, if you even think . . ." The rest of his threat was left unspoken, too terrible to describe, planted like a seed in the imagination of a boy who had just been detained in Juvenile Hall for the crime of tying his two-timing girlfriend's dog to the back of his car and setting its fur on fire.

⚬✕⚬

I leaned against Galen Wheeler and watched through the grimy windshield of our white pickup truck as Old Highway 30 rolled around its bumps and curves, winding out from under his headlights like maybe we could have been making the whole thing up right there as we went along. With the cover of the night, and the trees hovering high overhead, blotting out the flat bowl of the horizon all around and leaking down the moonless shadows of that inky sky, I could find a way to half believe that this was new, that I had never seen it before, that I had not been on this road what must have been a thousand million trillion times, back and forth, from Harmony to the lake and back and back and back again, so I was friends with every fencepost and signpost and mailbox and telephone pole there ever could have been or was or would be along that way.

We'd been out to dinner at the Lakeside Supper Club. It was Saturday night; we'd stayed there late.

The club was nothing more than an old mill building at one time, but then when drinking and dancing got outlawed here during Prohibition the place was bought by some of the more enterprising businessmen, and they had turned it into a private club, a speakeasy I guess you could say, but now it's a restaurant and dance hall where we all like to go, there at the edge of the Harmony Fairgrounds.

That's a broad, empty field, fenced in by chain link and barbed wire on three sides, which fills up at the end of every summer with rides and games and exhibition halls for the farmers and the families who come here to vacation at Harmony Lake. They string up twinkle lights around the eaves of the building and along the footpaths to the fairgrounds out back so the place looks so special and fantastic that maybe it could be a holiday every day.

In the daytime the place is dusty with families coming and going, trudging around between the games and the rides, stopping to look at the animals there waiting in the pens and cages to be judged or auctioned off.

My sister Jewel is the creative type, and over the years she's entered her own handicrafts in just about every category at the fair that they have, I think, from table settings to quilts, afghans and pies and canned tomatoes and pickles and jams. She's won a few along the way, too, and she has her red and blue and yellow ribbons pressed flat between the pages of that big two-volume dictionary that the Book Club sent her for free that time when she joined.

The midway is crowded with rides and games, basketball and

the nickel toss, balloons and darts, beer bottle pyramids and squirt gun races. There will be a funhouse with a mirror maze and a haunted mansion with tape-recorded screams and snarls and howls. Food booths dish out corn dogs and hamburgers, sausages and cotton candy and taffy apples and lemonade made fresh. Teenage boys stand outside the rides and beckon to the kids, urging them to let go their daddies' hands and clamber on up. The ticket booths sell roll after roll of red and green and purple scrip.

At night the sound of music will spill over from the dance hall part of the club and get blended in with the clamor of the carnival—the screams of the kids on the loop-the-loop, the rise and fall of the calliope outside the bumper cars, the reckless rattle of roller coaster wheels against their twisting metal track—all of it echoing hard against the sky and then fading off softly in the still air above the lake.

And inside, Lakeside is always crowded, smoke-filled, noisy, and hot, even when the season's late and the night outside is cold. They bring in different bands from all over the state, so people can dance. Women in skimpy summer dresses lean across the tables toward the boyfriends in their sweaty shirts. There are men behind the bar filling up mug after mug with cold, foaming beer and girls in bow ties and white shirts and tight black short-shorts taking orders and carrying trays out from the kitchen, loaded down with plates of corn and steak and pork chops and potatoes, homemade biscuits and gravy, fresh vegetables, ice cream and pie.

Galen and I had taken our usual table at the back of the room, near the door, with the hope that maybe it would be a little cooler there, but it wasn't. I liked to sit with my chair pushed up against the wall so I could keep together a view of the whole big room in my sight, watching the other couples dance, their hands flying up around their ears, their feet scuffing, shifting weight, in the sawdust on the floor. They'd throw their bodies up against each other and, hands outstretched, fingers touching, away.

Galen and I never did dance together very much, and he didn't have any taste for the flavor of beer. He had pushed back his plate and was cradling a glass of vodka in one hand, hanging on to a cigarette with the other. The smoke was curled up around his head like horns. The flesh of his face was smooth upon the fine ridges of his bones. Pink circles the size of quarters flushed against his cheeks. His eyes were a shocking, beautiful cold blue, and there was about him a carelessness that seemed exaggerated by the trim, expensive-looking, businesslike cut of the clothes he wore. His white dress shirt was wrinkled, its cuffs rolled up, its collar unbuttoned and hanging open, curled back against the darker hair on his chest. The jacket to his seersucker summer suit was thrown over the back of his chair, and his tie hung unknotted, ragged and sloppy around his neck.

I have been able now to keep in my mind a whole scrapbook of these kinds of pictures of Galen Wheeler. I have inside me so many different images of him. I see parts of him, bits and pieces of his body. His ankles and the long, thin tendons at the backs of his feet, standing in puddles of water on the bathroom floor just after he's stepped out of the shower, with the steam still billowing off his back. Sitting, one leg crossed over the other — the vulnerable look to his shin, exposed like bare bone between the roll of his sock and the cuffed edge of his pants. The back of his hand, the thin veins there, the fine hairs. His thumbnails, flat and white. The part in his hair; the soft curved edges of his ears.

The way he could look on a cloudy day, in a bottle-green sweater, his skin pale, his eyes gray blue. His cheeks chapped and pink in the winter. Standing with his back to me, one hand in his pocket, his jacket hitched up, one knee bent, the slanted balance of his hips. The pile of things from his pockets that he left every night on the table by the bed. A piece of gum. A torn receipt. A rock he had found out on the edge of the lake. A piece of wood. A butterfly's wing. The bright crimson heart-shaped petal of a rose. His wallet. A money clip. His watch.

When we were first married and living in our cottage down by the lake, I would go into the closet if he was gone during the day, and I'd bury my face in his pile of dirty laundry, drinking in the smell of him. Of the two of us together.

The lines around his mouth; the gaps between his teeth.

It was August. We were at Lakeside, finished with our dinners, Galen drinking vodka and me sipping on a beer, smoking cigarettes, listening to the band, watching the dancers, trying to stay cool, and still burning up anyway. And Jewel was there with us, too, telling Galen about this scheme she and her son Peter, who would have been about nine at that time, had dreamed up for taking a little motorboat out onto the lake and cutting down the dead trees there to use and sell for firewood in the winter.

This was a dumb idea; Galen thought so, too, I could tell. I imagined the treachery of the stumps that Jewel would have to leave behind. She was talking about trimming the branches of drowned trees, hacking them off and leaving their sodden trunks, half buried below the surface of the lake, lurking there, ready to snag an unwary boater, trip up a water skier, drag a fisherman down.

But Jewel was full of it, going on and on about how clever her boy was to think up something like this.

I guess that while Jewel was talking, on and on, I'd been looking just past Galen, over his shoulder, and maybe it was in a way that gave him the unsettling feeling that I was looking through him, as if he were see-through, insubstantial and invisible as thin glass to me. As if by ignoring him, I had somehow made him disappear.

There was a guy there who had caught my eye. My guess

was that he was one of those carnival jobbers who came to
Harmony for a few months every summer to work at the fair,
taking tickets or running the rides. He was lean and long-jawed,
with tattoos twining on his forearms, his shirt opened to the
waist, his sleeves rolled up high, tight greasy-looking blue jeans
clutching at his thighs, and thick-soled muddy work boots heavy
on his feet.

"You have to admit those trees aren't doing anybody any good
the way they are," Jewel was telling us. Sweat shimmered in
her hair. She leaned against the back of her chair, tilting up
her chin, smiling so sweetly at Galen that her mouth was like
a small red bow stuck there on the wrapped-up package of her
face. "All we have to do is take the boat, go out there, and cut
them down. Then we've got enough firewood to heat up all of
Harmony from now until next year and maybe even more."

It was a good job for a boy, she was saying. Something he
could do to contribute to the family, help pay his own way.

Galen twirled the glass of vodka in his hand, dandling it
between his thin fingers. He looked at me for a minute, and
then he turned back to her.

"You want me to be honest with you, Jewel?" he asked, his
eyes narrowed with an intensity and a keenness so sharp I could
see it startled her, made her shiver and pull back.

Sometimes Galen seemed to be so much out of his own
control; he could be a fool, bumbling, so stupid and so stoned,
and yet charming, too, so you could feel sorry for him and
think maybe you could do something to help him out, like he
was a little boy—you could straighten his collar or brush his
hair out of his face, stand by him, give him confidence, lend
him some support. But the truth was that he wasn't stupid, and
he wasn't a fool, either, and he could all of a sudden coil up
like a snake, tighten and strike, like that, full of venom, swift
and accurate and sure. Plenty of people didn't realize this about
Galen Wheeler, and Jewel, who had never been known to go
looking for any depth in anyone, let it take her by surprise.

She cleared her throat and started to pick at her fingernails, snapping them against her thumb.

"Well, of course I want the truth," she said, probably really believing that she did. "What else do you think?"

"I think if you're bound and determined to do a thing, then whether I tell you I think it's a good idea or not won't make one bit of difference. But if I were to come right out and be honest, if I were to let you in on what I really see in it, you'd get good and mad and tell me I don't know what I'm talking about, and then I'd have to wonder why it is you brought the whole thing up to begin with."

But it wasn't true that Jewel would get mad at Galen. At that time, she would not have known how.

Well, I was looking over at this guy at the next table. He was tapping the toe of his boot against the floor in time with the music that was being played on the stage. He rolled his fist up and down his leg, kneading the muscle with his knuckles.

He was probably one of those kids who slept out in the camp-grounds at the edge of the fair, curled up in the back seat of his car or, if he was lucky, in a tent that he had pitched near one of the barbecue pits there. Cooking his dinners in cans over a fire or buying plates piled up with potatoes and meat and gravy and green beans at Mrs. Olson's coffee shop in town, drinking beer at night until he'd killed off all his dreams, rolling out of his sleeping bag in the mornings, brushing his teeth in the camp bathrooms, smoothing his hair back with his fingers, splashing water on his face.

Grease would be so ground into his skin that it permanently blackened his hands, pressed into the backs of his knuckles, the whorls of his thumbs, the edges of his nails. He would have people that he was trying to run away from, a past that he was hoping to forget—a mother who had abandoned him, a father who took his rage out on his children, beating them bloody with his belt when they angered him, a sister who sat in her bathrobe all day weeping and watching her stories on TV, a brother he had seen murdered, a girlfriend who had been caught without her clothes on, in bed with his best friend.

"Ask me," Galen was saying, "a person ought to be happy with what she's already got."

He mashed his cigarette out in the shiny tin ashtray on the table. In the middle was stamped *Lakeside Supper Club* over the strutted circle of a Ferris wheel.

"Not always be wanting more and more and more," he said.

What he meant by that, of course, was me.

My legs were tight in their shiny stockings; my hips were snug in a straight black skirt. I'd been wearing my hair styled that summer, poufed back from my face and curled behind my ears. Rings twinkled, stacked up on my fingers, one above the other, silver bands and braids, cut stones and cabochons, platinum and gold. My fingernails were long and manicured, enameled pink to match the lipstick that I left like kisses on the edge of my glass.

Galen watched me smile and run my tongue across my teeth. When I reached up to fluff my hair with my fingertips, the bracelets chimed, the rings glistened, and the soft white skin under my upper arms flashed. I could feel my breasts lift up gently under the bright flowered fabric of my blouse.

The legs of Galen's chair screeched against the floor as he pushed himself away from the table. He stood, staggering, wobbly on his feet. He reached out and took me by the elbow and, squeezing hard, he pulled me up. I came to him with ease, surprisingly pliant in his arms, when he could have expected me to resist.

"Holding me . . . holding you . . . loving him . . . ," the singer on the stage was crooning now, his hair plastered to his head, his long throat thick with tendons and slick with sweat. Somehow he could ignore the rattle and clang of the glasses behind the bar, rise above the raucous laughter of a man near the stage, stay deaf to the call and holler of a full table at the back.

Galen had gathered me up close to him, and he pressed his long legs up against mine. Then together we were stepping, dancing, two forward, one back, side to side. My fingers were twined in his, and we moved through the crowd, along the back wall and out the door, into the night.

Cars and trucks were parked willy-nilly in the unmarked lot out front. No matter how hot it had been inside, outside there was still the chill of summer sneaking off, leaving the nighttimes cold and wet, with the promise of a winter freeze.

LAKESIDE—the neon sign crackled on and off, a sizzling arch of red and blue twiny letters strung out between two rugged stone pillars. Galen kept hold of my hand and led me along through the grass and then the crunchy gravel to our truck.

"Taking you home, Clodine," he said. "Now."

What it was is he was drunk.

He made me climb up into the cab of the truck by myself, and then he spun out of the lot before I even got the door closed all the way. I had to lean out and pull it shut with both my hands.

I could just make out the pale outline of my own face shining back at me, reflected in the glass of the side window. My eyes were black holes, my mouth a tight knot, my hair a woolly cloud that had gathered like a storm around my head. My earrings sparkled as if they could be lightning flashes somewhere out beyond the trees.

"I think Jewel's just stupid to be talking about taking down those trees," I said to Galen, staring at myself, watching the black hole of my mouth open up to hold the words. "She can be so completely crazy sometimes, Galen, don't you think?"

He snorted, and he pressed his foot down harder on the accelerator, and he let that truck fly. I could feel the strain and tension of his body under the starched fabric of his shirt as he leaned into a curve, steering nice and easy with the flat of his hand pressed up firm against the wheel, one arm flung back over the seat across my shoulders, that hand draped down over my breast and rubbing up against it as if by accident, like it was some kind of a mistake.

Even this most casual touch from Galen could make my breath come short. My legs in their sheer stockings were shining smooth in the dim green light from the dash; I could just make out how the long muscles in Galen's thighs tightened and let up again when he pumped the brakes or pressed down oh-so-gently on the gas.

"Down on me-e-e-e!" the radio was screaming.

And there had been the news report just then, too, about a boy named Tim Duke and how his trial was finally over, and he'd been sentenced in Nebraska to die.

Later we would be watching television, and we would see the screen filled by a black and white news photo taken from behind of a tall, handcuffed man held firm between a pair of burly policemen who stood against him like two walls, closing in. Baggy, colorless prison clothes hung loosely from his thin frame. His head was turned, and he was peering back over his shoulder, frowning fiercely at the camera with eyes that glowered beneath his heavy brows. His face was fine-boned and fair, his hair thinning and blond. Lilly kept that same photograph of Tim in the cabin, by her bed, on a table that she had fashioned out of some cardboard packing boxes she'd found.

Galen had turned to me, and he was frowning. He pulled his arm away.

Sweat had begun to glimmer on his forehead. I could see that his jaw was tight, his teeth clenched. The vein in his temple pulsed; he was breathing heavily through his nose. Still looking at me, he leaned forward and groped around under the steering

wheel until it seemed that the night had closed in around us
—everything disappeared, it all went black, deadly and dark,
and it was a moment before I knew that what had happened
was that Galen had found the knob he was looking for and
without slowing, maybe even speeding up a little, he had turned
off the headlights on the truck.

"I could be killing us both, Clodine!" Galen was screaming
at me then. "And I could be doing it right now!"

I sucked in my breath and held it, gritting my teeth and
squeezing my face up tight as a fist, reaching my hands out,
locking my elbows and bracing myself up hard against the dash
as we hurtled along blindly, diving into nothingness, it seemed,
sailing, flying, out of control.

Galen was counting backward, "Three, two, one—"

And he wrenched the wheel hard and sudden to the left.

The truck careened straight off the smooth flat surface of the
road, skidding out over the sandy shoulder and rocking down
into the drastic emptiness between the trees, bouncing wildly
in the ruts and potholes, bumpers dipping down and scraping
front and back, tires spraying dirt and gravel and weeds and
grass.

I could imagine my own death then. Soaring black skies,
sweeping light, emptiness, an abyss of endlessness, an oblivion
of forever and ever, going on and on, everything and nothing
at all, both at the same time.

"Oh no-o-o-o!" I opened my mouth, cried out in terror, as
the truck jolted into a pothole and my teeth closed down hard
on my tongue, biting through. Blood welled up warm salt and
copper in my mouth. "Mmmmph!" I pressed the back of my
wrist up to my lips, wincing with the ache of it as Galen braked
and, reaching forward again, flipped on his dim yellow parking
lights to reveal the little-used, half-forgotten side road that forked
off the main highway and wound down through the woods to
the overgrown grassy edge of the lake.

He wrapped his arm back over the seat again and squeezed

my body up so close to his own that I could feel his heartbeat pounding in his chest and think that maybe its heavy thud was somehow joined together in this world with mine. Swallowing blood, I leaned against him. Limp and breathless, I buried my face in his chest and snaked my arms up around his neck, my sudden fear and panic still a mean black hum, like wasps, angry, inside my head.

He let the truck glide along slowly then; its tires crunched in the gravel and ground to a stop just before the road dipped down and abruptly disappeared under the glassy black surface of Harmony Lake. The water stretched out before us, its inky breadth broken by a forest of drowned trees—their skeletal remains the casualties of the flooding from when the Harmony River was dammed with boulders and it backed up over its banks to roll out and bury the town and the fields beneath the lake.

These were the trees that Jewel and her son were scheming to have chopped down.

Galen cut the engine, killing the radio and the lights. The lake below us glistened, gently lapping at the mud along the week-choked shore. Between the trees the twinkle lights of the Ferris wheel at the fair were glittering in the sky, dropping down like stars always falling, for making wishes, over and over again.

Galen got out of the truck and came around the back to my side. He opened my door and graciously, like a servant, a gentleman, a valet, he took my hand as if I were a lady, and he helped me down. My legs were weak, and I clung to his arm.

He stood me up straight and took me by the shoulders and pushed me away from him, holding me out at arm's length, his thumbs pressed up against my collarbone.

Then the weight of his hand was off my shoulder. He spread his fingers and raised it, brought it up high back behind his head. I could hear it whistle then as it came smashing down, flat and hard, across my face, knocking me back, throwing me off balance, resounding in my ears.

Galen stumbled away from me and cracked his shoulder

against a tree. He straightened up and rolled his head hard from side to side, throwing off his drunkenness like a dog shakes water from its coat. He had the thick butt of a broken tree branch in his hand, and he was brandishing it like a cudgel, swinging it wildly over his head as he lurched across the grass toward me. He reached for me and caught me. His fingers closed around my arm and he pulled, dragging me over toward him. With his other hand he had raised the branch up over his head, hauling off with it as if he meant to bludgeon me, but already I had begun to jerk away from him and I wrenched out of his grasp even as he brought the branch down hard. When I ducked, it whooshed past me, and Galen was spun with the force of his own swing, checked only by the solid body of his truck as the club slammed into the headlight glass, shattering it with a ringing, shimmery, stunning crash.

And I was stumbling off ahead, leading Galen Wheeler down through the woods. He dropped his club and staggered after me, caroming across the path, bouncing off the trees from one side to the other.

"Clo-*dine!* Clo-*dine!*" he called after me as I rounded a corner, the bottoms of my feet flashing back at him, daring him, like the tail of a doe in the darkness, to follow me and bring me down.

Galen was trying his best to run. He lurched forward, throwing his weight along the path.

"Damn!"

He rounded the corner too fast, the smooth leather soles of his dress shoes slipping on the damp grass, and he hit me from behind, so I tottered and almost fell.

I pushed him off and stood stock-still. My tongue felt ragged and bloody where I had bitten it; the place on my cheek where he had slapped me throbbed.

"Hush," I was growling. "Galen, listen! Do you hear?"

He stood behind me, weaving. "I don't hear a" — he swayed, catching himself against me — "thing."

The water below us lapped the docks and rocked the paddle-boats tied to their moorings, so they clattered together softly, like solemn, gentle applause. And above it, an eerie wail that started out low, then rose up, swelling strong, full pitch, until it was carried off, echoing far out over the lake, distorted by the compact acoustics of the water and the trees.

I turned to Galen; his long, pale face was shining back at me.

"Oh, God," I was crying; goose bumps shivered up and down my arms. "What is that? Can't you hear it? I can't stand it."

For a minute there I was thinking that maybe it was only me. That he had done some damage. That he didn't hear what I was hearing; it was in my head, wailing, crazy, crying, ringing in my own mind there, resounding within my own skull.

I stepped forward and pressed myself up against Galen, molding my body to his, hands clapped hard over my ears, and I blotted out every sound—the chirp and squeak of crickets and frogs, the whine of the cicadas, an owl swooping overhead, bats flapping between the trees, a fish splashing up off the glassy surface of the water, the far-off rumble of a boat's small engine—with a wayward moaning of my own. Galen Wheeler hovered over me, burying me there in his embrace. I let myself go and melted into him, as soft and unformed in his arms as a handful of lake-bottom mud.

$\sim\!\!\times\!\!\sim$

Across the lake, through the skeletal trees, there used to be a narrow footpath that led up from the beach to the clearing where the old Duke shack stood crouched in shadow. Its white paint had peeled away to leave the bare wood shining soft and gray; the front porch drooped dangerously away from the main frame of the structure, the chimney was crumbling, the roof sagged, the door was hung lopsided on a single rusty hinge. One window at the back had been forced open, and the figure of a young woman could have been seen silhouetted there by the soft glow of a table lamp. The wailing that I had heard, which touched me and chilled me and frightened me all at one time, came keening up from here. It was an infant's nighttime cry.

Lilly Duke would be on her knees, bent down over the baby that flailed fitfully in the nest of clothing and blankets bundled up in one corner of the bare wood floor. She hoists the infant up into her arms and hobbles gracelessly off her haunches to her feet. The baby's neck is weak, and its big head falls forward and back, wobbled by Lilly's awkward movements as she slings her baby, still wailing, up onto the slender shelf of her hip and carries it over to the old mattress that is her own bed pushed up under the window against the far wall of the room. Leaning back, she lifts up her nightshirt, exposing one small breast, and holds the hungry baby up to nurse.

"Hush little baby, don't say a word . . . ," she is singing, softly trilling. The baby suckles greedily, milk dribbling from the corners of its mouth, its lips thick and wet against her skin. "And if that mockingbird don't sing . . ."

When the reporters asked, Lilly told them that she was only looking to be left alone, but hiding out was what some people around here, including Jewel, were more likely to call it, their gossip fueled by the fact that there she was, holding that tiny baby in her arms and there was Tim Duke, in jail, on death row in Nebraska, praying to have it over with at last, begging them to get on with the thing, drop the appeals, forget about him, leave him some dignity, allow him to die.

When the television people heard about Lilly, they came and parked their cars and vans there in her meager yard. They set up their lights and their cameras and their microphones, and they let their thick cables coil in the grass like snakes outside her door. But Lilly wouldn't do more than open it a crack and beg them, in a voice so quiet that it stopped everybody moving, to leave her alone. They were stilled, frozen by the softness of

Lilly. If she had shouted, if she had screamed or cursed or yelled, they wouldn't have been so afraid of her. They would have called out their questions. They would not have held back. Someone would have come up onto the porch. They would have dared to maybe force their way inside. But instead they only leaned forward some to hear her better and thrust out their microphones to pick up what it was she said.

"Please," she whispered, "not now. I can't. Go away." When they ran the footage for the news shows the next evening, she seemed stunned by the glare of the spotlights, like a deer in the middle of the highway, caught by fear against the deadly on-coming rush of rubber and steel and chrome.

We could hear the baby's cries in the background, wailing from inside the cabin behind her, and she added that it only needed to be fed, as if maybe she thought we might be suspecting something else.

I've seen those pictures they have in a magazine that my niece, Jewel's daughter, gets. They'll have two cartoon drawings printed side by side, exactly alike, you think, until you read the caption— WHAT'S WRONG? And then when you look a little closer, you can see that in one picture the woman is wearing a long dress and in the other she has on a coat. There is an extra branch in the tree. The stones in the walk are slightly smaller. The cat in the window is a dog.

And I wonder if maybe it's not these same kinds of details in Harmony that were somehow changed for me, and I begin to believe that if I really studied it, went over and over the places that I know so well, driving up and down the roads, walking the streets, riding a boat out onto the lake, looking closely, comparing what I see here now with what I remember, I could spot the subtle differences and see that they are in Harmony and not, like Jewel says, in me.

✳

The original town of Harmony had dwindled down and just about died off altogether before they built the dam and drowned the whole place in the river, leaving it to rot there at the bottom of the lake. They dug up the cemetery and moved it over onto the hill. The post office was hauled up to where the county road meets Old Highway 30, and a cluster of buildings grew around it, one by one, until the population of Harmony had risen — less like a phoenix from the ashes of its ruins than as tadpoles hatched upon the surface of a pond, or toads spawned in a puddle of mud — and climbed back again to above three thousand souls, not even counting the vacation people who come in over the summers to sleep out in their campers and tents or live in the rental cabins on Harmony Lake out to the far west of town.

Now Old Highway 30 runs right through the middle of Harmony, past the white clapboard houses with their screened verandas and sagging steps, the boxy brick storefronts with tattered awnings hanging out over the sidewalks, the high school and the elementary school, both new-looking, painted pink cinder block with big glass windows that reflect back the blinding glare of the morning sun.

An American flag hangs flat against its silver pole in the windless sky. The roof of the Presbyterian church is domed with greening copper; the Baptist marquee proclaims JESUS LOVES US ALL THE SAME in foot-high red plastic letters. The plate glass window of the hardware and feed store has been painted over, advertising a locksmith, a sewer-cleaning service, and a fix-it counter. There is one windowless bar, The Web, with a blue neon cobweb strung up above the door, and a coffee shop — Mrs. Olson's, it's called, although there never was anybody here by that name, only Red Forester and his daughter Elana, who together have run the place for as long as I've been aware that it was here. He serves meat loaf and fried fish, hamburgers and mashed potatoes on red-checked plastic tablecloths. The menu is written in chalk on a blackboard that hangs from a nail above the grill.

There is an insurance office, Pajek's grocery store, with the day's specials painted on butcher paper and taped to its outside walls, and a real estate office that offers lakefront property on a bulletin board display with blurred snapshots and white press-on letters.

Three thousand people. We had a billboard that some of the merchants had made and put up off to one side of the highway, just past where the WELCOME TO HARMONY sign was, and on it was painted what looked like a big thermometer, indicating the health and strength of Harmony—except it measured population growth instead of temperature. The red bar rose up between calibrated lines each time a new baby was born or another family came to live with us. Some people were writing letters to the paper, warning how it was possible, too, for that red line on the thermometer to go up too high, bringing on a fever of population that would be bound to pollute the lake and the woods and overcrowd the streets and the schools and the neighborhoods and the stores.

And now, out at the far end of town, along Edgewater Road, there have begun to sprout some bigger parking lots under the bright white lighting of the larger discount stores. There's a clustering of movie theaters, two new motels, one with a sunrise sign and the other a sleepwalking bear, a huge boat and auto dealership, a bowling alley, some drive-through fast-food restaurants, a gas station, and a quick-stop store.

Some of the older families here, like the Pajeks and the Foresters and the Ferrings and the Zurns, have lived in Harmony all along, even back before there was a lake, and they have a full row of stones in the Hillside Cemetery to prove it. And then there are others, latecomers who maybe vacationed at the lake one time or another and then just never left, folks who seemed to have no place better to go. They enrolled their kids in our schools and then the women took on jobs, waitressing at the bars and restaurants around the lake or clerking behind the counters of the stores in town. The men drive fifty miles north every day to work at the jobs they can get in the factories and mills and packing plants that are clustered on the river in one of the bigger cities upstream.

I used to believe that somehow because I had lived in Harmony for my whole life and I had seen it so many times, through all its seasons, from so many points of view—before a big storm, after a blizzard, when it was raining or snowing, sunny or cloudy, hot or cold, at sunrise or sunset or in the middle of the night—that I had come to know, finally, all there was to know about this place. I felt that I could begin to understand Harmony and how it got to be here, and how it was before I was here, and how the people who were here before me were very much like me, different only in their ages and in their fashions, their circumstances and their times.

But now I have instead this nagging feeling that there is more, as if I have somehow come upon another room, one that has until this moment gone unnoticed, taken for granted or hidden, its door concealed behind a heavy piece of furniture, plastered over, bricked up, painted in. I've read about houses with odd spaces that, thinking about them later, never really made any sense and now seem inappropriate—an odd corner, cut off too soon from the rest of the house; a wall too short for the dimensions of the adjoining halls and closets. And when that wall is moved during a renovation, it is found to be false, built to hide away some unsavory remnants of the past—manacles, whips, slave records, Confederate cash. A history the inheritors of the house were only vaguely aware of is revealed and made as real as those heavy pieces of iron, as immediate as the jingle of Confederate coin.

It was this feeling I began to have an inkling of when Lilly Duke came to the lake with that baby in her arms.

Until then I had looked at Harmony and thought that just because I had lived here all my life and had seen it so many times, I knew all there was to know about this town. And that knowledge, that familiarity made the place seem like a haven, somehow safe.

What bad could possibly ever happen to me here? What real danger could there be? I couldn't imagine myself, or my family — or, for that matter, Galen Wheeler — hurt, our bodies broken on these sidewalks, in this street, drowning in that water, floating face down between the trees on the edges of our lake.

2

I CAN'T HELP it, no matter how really terrible I guess it must sound, I still get the feeling there is some part of my sister that is secretly happy now that Galen is dead.

I know that wasn't what she intended. And that it must be wrong, ungrateful, paranoid, and mean of me to keep believing it, but I suspect that somewhere, deep down inside, there is a place within her that is glad. She would never in a million years admit to this. But the truth is, my loss has made her useful. The aloneness of me has given Jewel one more worthwhile thing to do.

Clayton denies it. He is sincerely shocked that I would even imagine such a thing, much less talk about it and believe it to be true. We sit together, our shoulders touching, on the front steps of the house, watching Emma pedal her tricycle back and forth along the sidewalk. I've had Jewel trim Emma's hair for summer, and every time her tires bounce over that bump by the driveway where the asphalt is cracked from the roots of the fir tree that have grown out and begun to buckle it, pushing it upward and outward like a fist flexing underground, her hair flops, the trike wobbles, and I prepare myself for her fall.

I'm tensing up the muscles in my legs and unlocking my elbows, ready to spring from the porch in a bound and pull my daughter up into my arms, disengage her from the awkward jumble of pedals and handlebars and spokes that is her over-turned trike, kiss her bruises and her scrapes, brush away her tears with the back of my hand.

Nevertheless, somehow she is always able to stay upright.

"But Jewel loves you, Clodine," my brother-in-law is telling me. He has put his hand on my shoulder, as if he thinks that in this way he will be able to hold me down, keep me in place, rooted here where he believes that I belong. His hand is huge and heavy, his fingers thick and slow. He is afraid that I might begin to drift away, and he means to anchor me here with the weight of his touch and the burden of how much he cares.

"Don't worry" is what he tries to tell me. Nothing else can happen now. No one else will be hurt. No more bruises, no more pain. Not if Clayton can help it, anyway.

Which, we both know, the truth is, he can't.

Side by side, our knees are flat and square, his covered in a fine down of curly blond hair, mine shiny and smooth.

"And you know how much she cared for Galen, too," he says.

It's true; Jewel did love Galen. Even when he was wrong, she stuck up for him, defended him, took his side against mine.

After Galen's accident, Clayton and Jewel were good enough to take me and Emma in to live with them. I had thought at first that I would rent a place of my own in town, the little apartment up above the grocery store, maybe, but then Jewel sent Clayton in with money to pay Agatha Pajek to lie and tell me that her son had changed his mind and needed that place for himself.

Clayton would do anything, just about, that Jewel asked him to. He likes to cooperate. He is happy to do whatever it might take to please.

And Jewel is pleased to have me to take care of. She enjoys the idea of nursing me back to health again, as if I'm a bird

with a broken wing that she has found out in the grass. As if she thought she could dip bits of her homemade bread in a mixture of milk and honey and poke it down my throat with tweezers, feed me and make me strong enough to learn to fly off again and find a new family on my own.

But it's been almost two years already. I can see that Jewel has begun to expect me to be moving on.

I don't have any idea where. I might leave Harmony altogether. Take Emma and a map and head west until we find a place we like, a spot where we think that we could stay.

Only I can't go back to live in our empty cottage down by the lake. Just the sight of it still can bring me to tears sometimes. I don't like the way it makes me feel. All jumpy and crawly; I have to cup my elbows in my palms to keep my hands from flailing out. I walk with my knees locked, shuffling my feet, just to keep myself from turning away and taking off. I still can find myself sitting perched on the edge of my chair, ready to jump up and run. My heart pounds in panic. My fingers grip the edge of the table so hard it makes my fingernails turn white.

When that happens, I feel just like I am a crazy woman. I feel then as if the best thing might be for me to give it up, tie a weight around my neck, walk into the lake, and drown.

But that isn't anywhere near all the time. I am getting better. In fact, I think I'm almost all the way over it by now.

❧✕❧

Clayton Jenkins is a large man, tall and thick, with heavy bones and broad, muscular limbs. When he's working he wears dark three-piece suits that look uncomfortable on him — shirts that pinch his neck, ties that are too wide, sleeves too short, shoulders too tight, pants too high in the waist. He wears brown wingtip shoes that are huge on his big feet, and they make a heavy noise like far-off thunder in the hallways of his house, even on the rugs, after he's drummed the kids up out of their beds and then come downstairs himself for breakfast in the mornings.

He has a drawer full of linen handkerchiefs, and Jewel has embroidered each of them with his initials—C Y J—in the corner. He carries them in his breast pocket, as much for emergencies, he says, as for the look. He uses these bits of folded white cloth to sop up runny noses and to wipe away the traces of other people's not always completely sincere tears.

Clayton's job is an insurance investigator. He travels all over the state and even the country sometimes, looking into the legitimacy of other people's claims. The home office of the company he works for is in Chicago, but he hardly ever visits there. He writes up his reports and fills out the forms that they need, and then he sends these off in the thick brown envelopes that are scattered like fallen leaves on the floor around the desk Jewel keeps set up for him in the little bedroom downstairs. Clayton carries a brown leather briefcase filled with his papers with him wherever he goes, and he drives a wide black car that he bought used several years ago. He has a wooden rod that fits between the windows in the back seat, and when he travels, he hangs his shirts and ties and suits on it to keep them from getting mussed. My daddy was a salesman, and he used to do the same thing.

When Clayton comes home, he puts his business clothes away and, dressed in shorts and tennis shoes, he goes down to the lake to fish. He is a man who could sit in a boat for a whole day long and never feel a need to move. He is as quiet as the water. As calm and deep and still as a pool.

Sitting here beside him, I see that my legs are almost exactly half as long as Clayton's. We both happen to be wearing shorts, baggy and brown. The sleeves of my sweater are pushed up past my elbows. The visor of his baseball cap shades his face and hides his eyes.

I don't for a minute doubt the truth of what Clayton has been trying to say to me. With his words, that is. That his wife, my sister, Jewel Jenkins, loves me, I mean. But I also know it in my heart that she is, in her own way, glad. I can see that she's

been taking a certain satisfaction from seeing that I have been somehow abandoned — left helpless, she would like to think — and, except for Emma now, alone.

And Clayton's gestures, well, I know how he would like to be the one to bring me reassurance. How it would please him if he saw that I had been convinced that the world is just as safe and secure as I was always led to believe it was. What he wants me to understand is that Galen's accident was just that, an accident. An unfortunate mistake. And there isn't anyone for me to blame, least of all myself.

What he means for me to know is that even if she does fall off her trike here in the driveway, Emma will not be hurt. Not so very badly, anyway. Nothing that a Band-Aid and a mother's kiss won't fix.

Jewel has said it before that the Lord never gives a person any more burdens than they are able in this life to bear.

My sister has always been an endlessly, tirelessly creative person. She is forever making things, or growing things, or putting things together in ways that would never have occurred to anybody else. She and Clayton have two children already and, though you wouldn't know to look at her yet, she says she's pregnant with their third.

The oldest, Peter, is twelve. Jewel has buzzed his fair hair so short on the knob of his head that his scalp shows, and his ears stick out, sunburned and peeling, tender-looking lobes that give him an expression of helplessness that if he understood it he would be sure to hate. Jewel says, not without some pride, that her Peter is a very independent little boy. What someone else might take for stupidity or stubbornness, she claims is singularity of mind. That boy has a will that's all his own, Jewel likes to exclaim.

Clayton has given him a boat this summer, a tin dinghy with a little engine that he uses for puttering around, back and forth across the lake. Peter dresses himself in camouflage cloth, green-

and black- and brown-splotched long pants and cuffed shirts, even on the hottest days, and dirty socks and boots with clumps of mud and grass caught in the notched grooves of their rubber soles. His laughter is a high, breathless squeal. He can whistle through the gaps between his front teeth loudly enough for his mother to hear him from as far off as the spillway when there isn't any wind. He makes sloppy farting noises with his lips until Clayton finally turns to him and tells him, firmly, to knock it off.

Mary Alice, his sister, is seven, a beautiful fairy princess with bright dabs of shiny polish peeling off her fingernails, plastic beads strung around her neck and bouncing against the level panel of her bony chest, satin ribbons strung through her hair — a curly ponytail or twin arched pigtails or a complicated French braid — shimmery painted barrettes, short pastel dresses, puffy sleeves, lacy socks, a purse, toy makeup, plastic shoes, and a faint, whispery voice.

My Emma is almost two years old now. Her skin is pale, and her hands and feet are so small that it's difficult to resist reaching for them, cupping one securely there in the palm of your hand. Mary Alice has said that Emma's thin, transparent fingernails look to her just like the white petals that fall onto the asphalt from the apple tree that grows on the rise alongside Jewel's house.

Jewel and Clayton and their children live here in this big brick house on Lake Boulevard across the street from the park. That park is a blessing, Jewel says, the best thing about this house, even better than the clothes chutes or the deep closets or the knotty pine paneling in the kitchen or the big glass window in the den.

That's because Jewel's children have such freedom — they can come and go all on their own there in the park. It's like having a giant front yard just made especially for play. There are baseball diamonds and bike trails, a field long enough for football, a clearing empty enough for flying kites. There is a playground with a slide and a merry-go-round and a sandbox, swings, monkey bars, an asphalt basketball court, and all of this within plain sight of Jewel's own front steps.

In a T-shirt with dancing ducks on it, brown plaid shorts, blue canvas tennis shoes, a chef's apron, sunglasses, and the baseball hat turned around backward on his head, Clayton stands frying eggs and bacon at the stove in Jewel's kitchen. His legs are as wide as tree trunks.

When Jewel comes in, her thick short hair is still damp from the shower; it sticks to her head. She is wearing a long, gauzy pink skirt and a white tank top, and her rubber thongs slap the bottoms of her feet as she walks.

Clayton turns and holds the spatula up like a swatter in his hand. Jewel stands on tiptoe to give him a little kiss, a peck on the cheek.

Peter isn't speaking to his mother this morning. His resentment rises into the air around him like it was a living thing, as ponderous as the sallow sky before a summer storm. He sits hunched over his bowl of cereal, wrapped in his sullenness, glowering over at me. What he's so angry about is that Jewel has enrolled him in some morning summer-school sessions to make up for the bad grades he made in his classes last spring. Peter would rather be playing baseball with his pals. He'd like to be out on the lake, catching tadpoles in a peanut butter jar, scooping minnows up with a net, chasing dragonflies through the tall weeds.

"Peter has difficulty concentrating," Jewel tells me, skimming her fingertips over the resistant stubble of his hair. "He finds it hard to focus."

He scrunches his head down between his shoulders, shrugging away his mother's touch.

"It's like a learning disability, is what they've been telling me. Otherwise, all his teachers agree, every one of them has said the same thing, that our Peter here is just as smart as a whip."

And it's true that Peter does have some trouble sitting still. At the breakfast table he squirms and wriggles, kicks his foot against the wall, scratches at the bug bites on his elbows until they bleed. He reaches for the cereal box and topples a glass, splattering orange juice across the table and onto the tile floor.

Peter has been telling his dad about a kid he heard of who went into the boys' bathroom at the park without his mother or a friend along to watch him and then some crazy man, a bum, came in and locked him up in the stall and pulled his overalls down and then cut his penis off with a butter knife.

"Peter!" His mother swats at him, snapping the towel she's used to sop up the spilled juice.

And I'm thinking, in spite of myself, A butter knife?

Well, it is true that there are bums, transients who sleep on the park benches, doze in the grass, roam the playing fields, stand like statues, silent and inert, under the shade of the trees. Harmony is not a big town, but because of the lake and the campgrounds, we've become used to the sight of a stranger here. We're accustomed to the crowds of summer people who come and go, and maybe it's this that makes us somehow different from other towns our size. If not exactly cosmopolitan, at least we're tolerant of other people's lives. We mind our own business, that way, and it pays us back by how the tourists get to feeling so comfortable here, just like it was their own home, too. They always like the idea of someday coming back.

One time last summer a bum came right into Jewel's front yard and up onto the porch and stood there waiting for I don't know what, until finally Peter ran out hollering and chased the guy off with a stick. Clayton was out of town then, off on one of his trips, and Peter was only doing what he thought was the manly thing, his job, protecting his mother and his sister, and Emma and me. The women of the house.

Still Jewel didn't agree that what he'd done was right. She tried to tell Peter that this poor man was only an old hungry hobo, not out to hurt anybody probably, just half starved and needing a bite of food, or maybe a bed that was warm where he could lay down his head.

"Well," Jewel asks, "what if that was the Lord himself came up to our house asking for food or water or only a place to stay. In disguise, say. What if it was a trick? What if he was testing us? Do unto others, he told us. What you do for them, you do for me. The least of these. Do you want to be the one who takes the chance of maybe turning him away? By mistake?"

So now she has made it her habit to leave plates of food out there by the gate sometimes. Leftovers wrapped up in plastic, sandwiches covered in foil.

Jewel raises vegetables in a small garden out back of her house, and she uses a basket that she made herself, out of ivy vines, to carry what she's grown into the kitchen where she'll can it or freeze it or cook it for dinner. She keeps chickens and rabbits in pens behind the garage. Peter has two green snakes and a turtle that eats live goldfish. There's a duck, three cats, any number of dogs that come and go as they please, a mouse, a rat, and a pair of hamsters that got out of their box and disappeared and never were found, although we all looked everywhere, we thought, and even Emma helped.

There was a rooster for a while once, too, but that thing made so much noise all night long that finally Jewel just had to get rid of it. She thought she could kill it, and she tried to wring its neck, but it seemed like that bird just would not die. She swung it around over her head until she thought for sure she'd heard its bones snap. It was limp in her hands then, and, she believed, dead, so she wrapped it up in a paper sack and stuffed it down into the trash can and pressed the lid closed down tight. But when the garbage men came three days later, and they took off the top of the can, what but that rooster came squawking up, in a furious flurry of feathers and flapping and claws. The men were pretty upset with Jewel about that, and they threatened to never come back to take away her trash again. It scared them half to death, they said.

She named that rooster Lazarus and drove him in the car out to a field near somebody's farm. She and Peter tossed him out the window and then they sped away home fast.

Jewel has a loom set up in the basement, where she weaves blankets and rugs, and a kiln in the garage where she bakes her bowls and pots, bright with warm glazes in colors that make them look welcoming and deep.

She sorts through the scraps of fabric that have accumulated in a cupboard. Looking at each piece, calico and plaid, cabbage roses, pin stripes, heavy wool, stiff cotton, slimy-feeling synthetics, Jewel tells me she can just about recall every single thing she's ever made. Pillows and dresses and quilts, curtains for the guest room, costumes at Halloween, slipcovers for the cushions on the wicker furniture out on the back screened porch.

On a sweltering hot summer Sunday, Jewel will close up all the windows and pull the curtains shut and turn on the air conditioning so the house is as cool and quiet and dark as a cave. She skips church to spend a whole day hovering over her stove, boiling dozens of glass jelly jars, putting up the fruit and berries, canning the tomatoes and the pickles and the beans from her garden, stowing them in the cupboards, preserved, sterilized and sealed.

The radio in the kitchen plays a selection of piano sonatas. Peter crawls around on the floor, constructing futuristic, sprawling cities out of colorful plastic blocks. Emma and Mary Alice are together at the kitchen table, painting pictures in some new coloring books that Jewel's given them. The paint is built into the paper already, so when Emma dips her brush into a glass of water and then dabs it on the picture she's doing, the colors come to life on the page, spreading out like magic in a brilliant blotty stain.

I guess it could be true there is a part of me that envies Jewel for the man that she has found in Clayton. He is so big and slow and simple, as if the size of him, the roundedness of his muscles and the weight of his bones prevented him from hiding anything, from seeming faceted and strange. Maybe that's why Jewel expects other people to be predictable and plain, because that's how Clayton is, and he's the best friend she has, the one person in the world she knows and understands the most completely.

She has always bragged about this friendship to the other women she knows, holding it up to them like an object for their admiration. She's proud of it, as if it's something she herself accomplished, some triumph, a trophy that makes her feel as if she's won some kind of game.

She met Clayton in Chicago, when she was working for our uncle Charlie at the insurance company there. They dated for a long time before finally she quit her job and married him and they both came back together here to live.

Jewel says she will never stop being surprised at how honest her husband is. How benevolent and kind. He's got nothing going on, she says. He never plays games. What he says is what he means, and what he means, he says. There is no more to him than simply that.

Not like Galen, who was thin and sharp, many-angled, a labyrinth of conflicting emotions and points of view. Galen could be something new every time you looked at him. What he said could have meant a million different things, and I might lie awake nights, turning his words over in my mind, trying to interpret and understand their sense.

Galen was always remaking himself, becoming something else all the time, so it was almost as if you could turn him in your hand and watch the pieces of his personality, like bits of colored glass in a child's kaleidoscope, shifting and settling, forming and reforming, fashioning and refashioning, in a steady cycle of pattern and movement and change.

"It was his family," says Jewel. "Anybody who had to grow up with a home life like that . . ."

Like what? Galen had been brought up by his grandmother in a nice big house on the bluff above a creek. The photographs show his front yard sloping down to the street, grassy, bordered by flower beds, shaded by large trees. A gravel driveway wound up from the roadway to the house and stopped under the shelter of a stone-pillared porte cochere. There was a tiered garden in the back, with rosebushes and limestone walls. And a wire fence all around the twenty acres of property, even along the edge of the bluff, with signs posted — NO TRESPASSING — to keep the hunters and the hikers and the drifters out.

Galen remembered afternoons in the autumn when he and his friends went out into the woods to shoot squirrels with their BB guns. He talked about the winter days when they poured water on the snowy lawn to make a sled run down the hill. They constructed an entire train system in the vacant lot next door, with main lines and sidings, junctions, trestles, and tunnels. The rails were made of laths that they stole from the construction sites nearby. The locomotives and cars they built from sections of two-by-four timbers with wooden buttons nailed to the bottom to keep them rolling on the rails.

They slapped together a sod dam in the summer and stopped up a portion of the creek to make a swimming hole. They hung a rope from a tree limb over the bluff and, screaming, holding on with both hands, knees bent, elbows locked, hair flying, they threw themselves away, off what must have seemed like the very edges of the earth.

"A home life like what?" I'm asking Jewel again, but she only sucks in her cheeks and raises her eyebrows. She lifts up her chin and looks down along the edge of her nose at me. What she means is, Well, Clodine, honey, if you don't know, then I am sure not going to be the one to tell you.

Except, of course, she does. She can't help it. She's not capable of holding herself back.

"You can imagine what it must have been like for him," she says. And before I've interrupted her, she's telling me again the story that Galen told us, about his parents.

"My father murdered my mother," Galen said to my sister and her husband and me.

It had begun with an argument that Mrs. Wheeler had with her husband. She'd ended it by locking him out of his own house. And he had come back later, in the night, and stormed upstairs and cut her throat and then gone down into the basement of the house and tied a scarf around his neck and hanged himself from the pipes in the ceiling of the furnace room.

Jewel is only repeating this same story that Galen told her, word for word just about. Her voice is breathless with the stupid brutality of it; her strong fingers, twisting and tearing, have ravished the dishtowel in her hands. His parents had fought — about some office girl who'd been overheard confessing to her friends that Mr. Wheeler had taken her out for a drive in his car more than one time, if they knew what she meant — and then the words had blossomed into accusations and denials and counteraccusations and counterdenials, until it had become a long and loud and bitter argument that would not end until finally Mr. Wheeler slapped Mrs. Wheeler across the face, and then she pushed him down the stairs and threatened him with an umbrella until she'd forced him out onto the porch and away from the house. She locked all the doors and went upstairs and emptied out his closet and his dresser drawers by dumping all of his clothes — pants and underwear, overalls and jackets and sweaters and socks and even shoes — out through the bedroom window and down into the yard.

"Can't you just picture it, Clo?" Jewel is asking me.

Poor betrayed Mrs. Wheeler, standing in the bedroom window, the curtains billowed by the wind, her hair wild, her dress torn. The boy, Galen, huddled behind her, pulling on her skirt, crying, begging her to stop. The snowy lawn is splashed with the dim colors of all that clothing scattered below. Mrs. Wheeler's screams rise with the whistling fury of the wind as Mr. Wheeler tears down the back door, rips it off its hinges with the strength of his bare hands. He rushes up the back stairs, the knife blade flashes, he grabs his wife, gathers her hair up in his fist, yanks back her head, and cuts her throat, straight across from ear to ear. He leaves her then to bleed to death on the crisp white cotton comforter while the boy cowers, hidden in the shadows underneath the bed.

Mr. Wheeler throws the knife away, out through the opened window. It soars, glinting in the moonlight, arcs and falls, skidding out across the hardened surface of the snow. Mr. Wheeler, drained of all his rage, hands hanging, head bowed, trudges downstairs to the basement and then, with one of his wife's lovely flowered silk scarves, he hangs himself from the pipes in the ceiling of the furnace room there.

Jewel's face is flushed with the thrill of telling me this story again. Her hands are fussing with her hair, and they flutter around her face now like birds.

During my pregnancy with Emma, there was a dream I had again and again, about some wonderful huge house full of lovely rooms with thick carpeting and gleaming hardwood floors, flowered wallpapers and heavy draperies, fireplaces and paintings and wing chairs with Queen Anne legs. I'd run my fingers out along the smooth wooden banisters, climb the staircases up and down, walk the hallways through this house, in and out of bedrooms and sitting rooms, a music room with a big black baby-grand piano and a library lined with books, a dining room with a marble-topped sideboard, a sunporch with violets growing in clay pots placed on glass shelves.

I was thrilled by how beautiful this was, amazed by its variations and its size, until I found the one narrow back stairway that I followed down and down into a corridor behind the walls where the pipes were clanking with hot water running through, and the furnace was roaring, blowing air so hot that it stung my eyes. The inside, the gut of the house, where all the real work was done. And at the end, a door that when I reached out to open it, unable to stop myself, unable to resist, even though I knew that what I would see there would be so awful that even before I'd begun to turn the crystal knob I was already screaming . . .

My sister told me then that it was not insignificant that I was pregnant when I had this dream. She figured it meant that in some way I was afraid, deep down within me somewhere, terrified to death of the baby I was carrying inside.

"There in the part of you where the real work is done," she said.

But I always suspected that the house was not my body, and the place behind that door was not my womb. It was the furnace room in the basement of the house. And what was in it was not my baby, but a vision of my father-in-law, hanging by his neck from a scarf tied to the pipes, swinging in the draft from the furnace, his toes just skimming the smooth-as-glass surface of the cold cement floor.

⌒✕⌒

Jewel is, in her way, more superstitious than me. We're sitting here, across from each other, in the wicker chairs on Jewel's sun porch after dinner, and Emma is with her cousins, chasing fireflies in the yard. She puts them into the jar that Peter holds. It glimmers like a lantern in his hand. He takes a bug and tears it into pieces, places the fluorescent bit of flesh on his sister's finger.

"A ring!" Mary Alice cries, waving her hand around her head. "A ring!"

Clayton's gone out of town on business again, on one of his trips where he ends up in some little place in the middle of nowhere and starts drinking with the locals in the bar on the corner—investigating, he calls it, looking into things, interviewing witnesses, going on hunches, following leads, gut feelings, all a part of the job—until he's had one too many; then he calls Jewel up in the middle of the night to tell her how much he misses her.

But I will hear the sound of the phone ringing through my sleep and start to dream that it's Galen who's calling, and then I'll hear his voice. He'll be telling me that this has all been a big mistake and nothing's happened, he's okay, really all right. He's phoned to say he's on his way home right now, if I'll have him, and in a few minutes more he will be here.

Jewel is describing for me the Harris brothers who live in that barn-shaped house near the spillway. They've sworn they saw a flying saucer swoop down over the lake one night last summer, and so now they sit out there in the yard with their cameras and binoculars, hoping to get a glimpse of it again. I try to picture the two of them plopped down side by side there on the grass, their faces as round and blank and white as paper plates, gazing wishfully upward into the starry sky. When I laugh at the stupidity of this, Jewel gives me one of her looks and frowns.

"Well, Clodine," she says, "you know a person just cannot ever be one hundred percent certain. Anything is possible. I wouldn't be so smug if I were you. I wouldn't be so quick to act so sure."

She waggles a finger in my face. She thinks that the things she feels in her heart will turn out in the long run to be in some way true.

This is what keeps her careful. She avoids walking under ladders. Throws salt over her shoulder. Picks up pennies and tucks them into the bottom of her shoe. She tries keeping track of things, writing them down, hoping to find a pattern in what has happened already and what might be about to come. She looks at her life as if it was some kind of a test. She thinks that the world ought to make sense, and probably does, if only we were smart enough to know what.

That's wisdom, Jewel tells me as she stirs a boiling caldron of fabric dye on the stove. Knowing what. The steam billows around her head; she is coloring clothespins that she will string together into necklaces to sell at the Ladies' Auxiliary Bazaar. The end of the wooden spoon that she waves in the air is stained a brilliant orange.

The way Jewel looks at the world, she believes that she can see some purpose in it. No such animal as an accident, she says. Like what happened to Galen, is what she means. She believes in reasons, cause and effect, the big picture, the grand scheme. One thing leads to another, she likes to tell me, looking over her shoulder, her chin tucked down, her brow furrowed, her gray eyes shining with meaning. She thinks that it might be possible to understand what is going on, to see the big picture, to get the master plan, if you could only figure out what the pattern is.

Like when they give you those arithmetic puzzles.

In the following series, the fifth number is omitted.

$$56 \ldots 35 \ldots 20 \ldots 10 \ldots \underline{\quad} \ldots 1$$
$$\text{Which is it?}$$
$$2? \quad 3? \quad 4? \quad 5? \quad 6? \quad \text{or } 7?$$

Jewel thinks that if she could understand the sequences in a problem like this one, then she would know what is going to happen next. What is to become of all of us tomorrow and then the day after that.

So far, though, she's only been able to work it out backward, after she already has the answer. She's like a person who cheats on the crossword puzzle in the Sunday paper, sneaking a look ahead at the solution and then nodding of course, of course, as if she'd known the right word all along, only had trouble taking hold of it in her mind.

"I knew that," she would like to say. "I was going to say that next. It was on the tip of my tongue, I swear."

And so later, after Lilly's baby died, I saw her nodding, her arms folded over her chest, her elbows cupped in her hands, and she was smiling, as if she understood, as if it all made some kind of sense to her somehow.

"Of course," was what she seemed to me to be saying. "What else?"

As if it should have been obvious to all of us that this was how that part of it had been meant to end up all along.

⌒✕⌒

The first time that I saw Lilly Duke, actually came face to face with her, close up enough to touch, it was through the murky haze of a hangover, past the spreading ache of a bruise the shape and size of Galen's flat hand, and she didn't even know that I was there. She didn't see me watching her. She thought that she was all alone, with only her baby nearby.

A large hawk was circling the bright blue disk of sky above the skeletal trees in Harmony Lake. It wheeled and turned, soaring, gliding, its eyes glued to the ground, searching the grasses for any kind of movement, the rustle of a mouse, the quick flicker of a snake. I was winding my way down a narrow dirt path through the tall grass near the edge of the lake. I was sweating and hot, my hair was stuck to the back of my neck, the grass brushed against my legs, tickling me behind my knees so now and then I had to stop and bend over and scratch. I felt the surge and pound of a headache hovering, ready to wash over me like a wave, brought on by the heat and the dryness and the traces of the beer and vodka I had drunk with Galen at Lakeside the night before. The side of my face where he had hit me still throbbed. It was red and sore — a bruise would bloom there later, flower out purple and blue, then fade away to gray, pale yellow, forgotten, gone.

I could hear the whiz and buzz of gnats and bees; grasshoppers bounded out of the way, startling me. The path tapered and died in the field near the top of the spillway.

Arms outspread for balance, I climbed down the dam, hopping along the heap of sun-bleached boulders. Clean, cold water from the lake cascaded over the edge at the center, down into the Harmony River below. I stopped, perched on a boulder, and pulled off my shoes and my socks. I closed my eyes and ducked in under the falls, where I sat hidden, huddled up against the wet rocks, peeking through a window of water at the riverbank rippling below.

This had been a favorite place of mine, here behind the spillway. There my headache seemed to dissipate, dissolved in the roar of the water, scattered in the fine white spray from the falls. It seemed like I could read my own reflection shining back at me through water that was as clear as a sheet of glass, as opaque as a mirror.

But I knew the face that I was watching couldn't really have been mine.

It was the unfamiliar figure of another woman that wavered there before me. And even though her appearance was only vaguely similar to mine, still it seemed just like I'd come upon my double. She seemed like she could be a part of me, facing me, looking past me, just beyond arm's reach. This woman, this other self, was an illusion, an apparition, a mirage, a double-goer, a doppelgänger, a looking-glass reflection of myself.

That was how I saw her that first time. Lilly Duke, Lillyheart. She was wading in the river, sloshing through the shallows near the rocks, and then she headed out until she was standing up to her waist in the gentle current at midstream. The skin on her arms was wet and slick, gleaming, so pale it seemed almost translucent, and I remember thinking, That girl will burn out here with skin like that. She'll fry.

She was dandling a baby between her hands, holding him under his arms while he kicked out his fat legs, splashing water in her eyes so she squinted, squeezing up her face, pulling in her chin. She bent backward, still lifting the baby up above the water, and she dipped her head down and came back up with her hair slicked back, as sleek as an otter. Her T-shirt clung to the slight form of her body. The baby flailed. Beyond the throb of my own pulse in my head and the roar of the falling water in my ears, I could just pick up his high, delighted squeals as they chimed and echoed above me, out over the lake behind me, into the sky and up, and away.

$\sim\!\!\times\!\!\sim$

Jewel has been hinting that maybe it would be a good idea now for me to go looking for some kind of a job. Be out on my own. Meet people. Even Clayton agrees that it would probably help me if I could find something useful to do. Get out, enjoy myself.

Stop watching over Emma, is what he means. Stop worrying all the time.

Jewel is pregnant again, after all. And the new baby will be needing to use my room.

I've considered going back to school. And I've thought about what it might be like to start my life all over again, from scratch. To reinvent myself. Start a new story. Become somebody else. Move away from Harmony to some other town, where nobody's met me before, a place where my face is new and doesn't carry with it any stories that people who already know me might love to get the opportunity to tell.

But when I reach for the want ads in the paper that Jewel has left out on the kitchen table, what I'm seeing is a picture of Timothy Duke there in black and white on the front page.

He has his hands cupped around his face. He is glaring at the camera. His hair is cut close. A stubble of beard shadows his gaunt cheeks. His nose is thin and sharp. His mouth is tight. Circles of fatigue ring the wide hollows of his eyes.

. . . will be electrocuted here at the Nebraska State Prison next Tuesday at dawn . . . convicted of first degree murder . . . sentenced to die. Duke waits in an isolated cell . . . final meal of steak and eggs, orange juice, hash browns, and coffee. Breakfast is served at 5 A.M. Half an hour later Duke's head will be shaved, as well as a small patch of skin on his right calf. Daubs of conductant will be applied to speed the electricity.

Then he will be dressed in a white shirt and the trousers of a blue suit.

The jacket will be withheld until later, draped over his shoulders for the funeral.

. . . has shown no signs of remorse.

3

I wake up in the middle of the night, and I can't fall back asleep again, because my head is full of an image that I have such trouble shaking—the moving picture of a body floating face down among the dead trees on Harmony Lake.

Fabric billows out around the gray, bloated limbs, scraps of color spread against the dusky surface of the water, snagged on a jutting bit of branch. The body bobs and circles, comes undone and continues to drift along, bumping against a fallen log, caroming off a broken stump. The tangled tree boughs are outstretched overhead, twig ends like fingers reaching, and I have the feeling that when I turn away they will be bending over, creaking, and they will lift the body, gather it up into a careless rough embrace of crumbling bark and sodden wood.

I lie awake, shivering, in the dark beneath my pile of blankets in the sewing room of Jewel's house. She's given me the daybed here, in this small, yellow room upstairs. It has a slanted ceiling, a dormer window, sheer flowered curtains, and an orange rug. Her sewing machine, an old black Singer with a wrought-iron foot pedal and an oak stand, is set up under the window. Her chair is small, chintz-covered, with a pleated dust ruffle that reminds me of a child's pinafore, church clothes, a party skirt on a little girl.

A gray dress form lurks in the shadowy corner—armless and legless, headless, wide-hipped, with cone-shaped breasts. Jewel has tied a sofa cushion to its waist because she's been working on patterns for the maternity clothes that she'll be needing again soon. Jewel says that she is fed up—"to here," she says, pressing the back of her hand flat against the fleshy underneath part of her chin, so her head jerks back and she's looking down at me along the short, spirited slope of her nose—she's had it up to there with those childish-looking flowered blouses, ruffled sleeves, and Peter Pan collars that the maternity shops sell. Baggy pants, pocketless, with stretchy waistbands and wide legs that flap and rub. Shapeless jumpers in heavy fabrics that Jewel says make a woman look like a davenport walking down the street.

She blows her hair out of her face and places her hands flat on the table, thumbs touching, fingers fanned. Jewel's hands are small and useful-looking. Her fingernails are short, broken from prying off lids and picking at paint chips and handling tools—pliers and scrapers, hammers and wrenches and screwdrivers and saws. She can't keep polish on them, and she doesn't try.

Clayton travels so much, and is gone so often, that it's usually up to Jewel to see to it that things around the house are kept running and in good repair. She fixes the leaky faucet in the kitchen sink. She lights the pilot on the furnace when a winter wind has snuffed it out. She wires lamps and puts up storm windows, shovels snow and mows the grass.

I've noticed the large calluses that have built up on the palms of her hands. The tip of her index finger is roughened from pushing a needle through fabric. A flesh-colored plastic Band-Aid is wound around the place on her thumb where she tore the skin trying to replace the spring latch on the front gate. There is a half-moon scar on the back of her wrist—a burn. Her only jewelry is the plain gold band that Clayton slipped on her finger fourteen years ago. Inside, it is engraved in looping script *Forever*.

"A pregnant woman wants to look dignified," Jewel tells me. "She feels absurd and ridiculous enough, in her condition, without adding insult to injury, ribbons and bows and ruffles and lace on top of all that flesh. She wants clothes that will flatter her fullness and at the same time keep her from feeling what she is, which is, to tell the whole truth, fat. Nobody wants to go around looking laughable and foolish, like one of those ballerina hippos in a tutu and tights."

According to Jewel, a pregnant woman doesn't want her femininity to seem stupid and dull, all soft and milky, round edges and rosy cheeks. She's not drawn to flowers and teddy bears. She doesn't care for pastels. She wants serious colors and serious prints. Checks and plaids. Thin, vertical stripes. Blacks and grays and deep, meaningful blues and purples and greens.

I am remembering how it was for me with Emma. How Galen would watch me then. How he wanted to touch me, place his palm against the mound of my belly, skim his fingers across the spongy pouches of my thickened hips. I can recall the first quickening flutter of Emma's life, how it startled me, like the brush and rustle of a winged insect trapped. The intimate gut thunk of her flailing fetal foot. The sudden, heavy gush of warm water down the insides of my legs. The clenched slamming fist of each contraction. The prickly warm gathering of milk into my breasts.

How Galen turned his face away from us then, and looked the other way.

"A pregnant woman should not be allowed out of her house dressed in anything that's pink," Jewel says. "Or powder blue. Just because I'm going to have a baby, that does not make me a gift. I am not a package wrapped in pretty paper. I am not Clayton's porcelain doll."

*

I lie in the bed here, contemplating Jewel's gravid dress form, waiting for my pounding heart to quiet, my racing pulse to slow, the sweat that's beaded at my temples to cool and dry. I hold myself very still, on my back with my arms at my sides and my legs out straight, feet poked up under the covers, and I listen to the night sounds of the others who are sleeping and breathing and dreaming in their own beds here in Jewel's house.

A cough from Emma in the room with Mary Alice down the hall. Peter cries out. Clayton turns heavily, the bedsprings creaking; he groans in his sleep, and snores. Jewel tiptoes to the bathroom, there is a rush of water running, she shuffles in her slippers, and falls back into her bed. She drifts off into sleep again with a sigh.

Jewel's dogs are deep breathers, sprawled in the hallway on the braided rugs she's made from scraps and then set out for them. The shepherd's bowels grumble like a far-off storm; the puppy whimpers, and his feet scrabble against the rug as he races through the grassy fields of some wild canine dream. The cat's tongue scratches on her fur as she cleans herself, compulsively licking her body, arranging and rearranging her hair. The mouse wheel squeaks and turns and turns in the cage on the dresser in Peter's room.

These sounds calm me; they soothe my nerves. Their independence works to hearten me, reassuringly constant and routine. The air of Jewel's house, in the dark, in the middle of the night, is filled with such a symphony of peaceful, unexceptional sleep, untorn by ugly images, unscarred by gruesome pictures, untouched by my intolerable visions, the unbearable repetitions of my own dreams.

Still, I'm getting up out of my bed and, shivering, I'm creeping like a ghost, running my fingers outstretched along the walls, down the hall to Emma. She is completely buried under her covers, her body a small mound at the bottom of the bed. I wonder how in the world she finds enough air to breathe.

I pull the blankets back gently, and stand gazing at the sight of her. Her face is round and full—she still has her rosy, baby cheeks—her eyes are wide, her lashes thick and long. She is sucking her thumb.

Her knees are up against her chest. The bottoms of her feet are flat, her toes curled. Her short hair falls away from her face, damp with sweat. Her eyes are slightly open, but she is sound asleep.

I slip my fingers in under her back and pull her up toward me. I've gathered her dead weight in my arms and hugged her up warm against me, draped her hands back over my shoulders, wrapped her legs around my waist.

She is growing so fast, Jewel says. She is getting to be too heavy for me to carry like this anymore. Her head lolls against my shoulder. Her breath is hot on my face. She moans. I carry her back to my bed. I nestle her in there with me, curl her up against the curve of my body. I fold my arms around her and press my face into the back of her neck. I close my eyes and listen to the quick, birdlike flutter of her pulse, comforted by the reliable staccato rhythm of her shallow breath.

If I would wake up next to Galen in the middle of the night, some times during those first years after we were married, before Emma was born, what I listened to then was not a silence exactly, but what seemed like an emptiness, an enclosed quiet, where the only sounds were disconnected, trivial and remote. An owl flapping through the trees beyond the walls of our house. A mouse gnawing in the rafters. Branches scratching at the window, brushing up against the eaves. Leaves rustling in the gutters. An airplane passing overhead, so high and faraway, its roar diminished to an insubstantial, distant whine. A car on the road, tires humming, its headlights crossing the ceiling, turning the corners, angling the walls.

I would try to match my breathing to Galen's, until I was breathless, dizzy from its length and depth and steady rhythm.

I would curl up against him, lulled by the dim shuddering hammer of his pulse.

⌒⨯⌒

People who don't know us already might have a hard time making the guess that Jewel Jenkins and I are sisters. I myself can't see that we are anything at all alike.

Although Jewel is older than I am, she is also smaller and rounder, but it wouldn't be exactly true to describe her as compact. There is no solid sort of neatness to her as with some women who are petite. No, even as little as she is, Jewel still seems fluid and loose, graceful and soft. Her clothes — too large, old, in dull colors, faded, their fabric softened by many washings and much wear — hang on her, billow out behind her, bunch up against her, flowing and full. Her hair, wavy and short, flowers out around her face, bouncing on her head as she bustles through her house, upstairs and downstairs, carrying loads of laundry, spraying furniture polish and air freshener, snapping dust rags, attacking the dirt on the baseboards and the cobwebs in the ceiling corners with a long-handled mop.

The dogs jump up into her lap and lick her face. The cat rubs itself against her leg, buries its nose in her neck, purrs, works its claws against the clumpy pushed-up wool of her sweater sleeve. Her children hang from her hands, crawl through her legs, wind their arms around her waist. Even Emma feels welcome in Jewel's lap. She will climb up and snuggle there, settle in against the soft curve of Jewel's breasts, wrap herself in the warm, protective hug of Jewel's arms.

Clayton, next to her, is huge. He towers over her, splays his hand across her back, engulfs her in the utter size of his embrace.

I met Clayton's father one time, when he came to Harmony for a visit after his wife had died. He was staying for a few days with Jewel and Clayton, and Galen and I were invited to come over for dinner to visit with him.

I remember him as larger even than Clayton, and slow, because, like a giant, his movements needed to be only half as long to take up twice as much space. He didn't hurry, but following Jewel, made it from the dining room to the kitchen in only three steps, compared to her ten. His hands on the curved handle of his cane seemed meaty, his fingers fleshy, hairless, speckled like a wren's egg. He smoked cigars, blowing out billowing yellowy clouds of smoke that wafted up and hung, gauzy against the ceiling, and he left their soggy butts, like drowned rodents, floating in the pool of ashes at the bottom of Jewel's glass ashtray. After dessert, in the middle of a conversation with Clayton about the soaring cost of insurance premiums, he fell asleep, snoring, in the wicker chair on the sun porch.

His wife, Clayton's mother, had died some years before, of cancer. She was ill, with a tumor growing in her belly, for two years before her husband noticed, finally allowed as how something might be wrong, and took her to the doctor. He hadn't listened to her complaints or regarded them as a sign of anything that might be remotely serious — her belly was full of fluid that they drained off with tubes slipped in under the surface of the skin. The tumor was the size of a basketball by the time they took it out. Mr. Jenkins told Clayton that it had been a woman's thing — and father and son both thought of it as something slightly shameful, mysterious and feminine, having to do with babies and eggs and monthly blood. Clayton hadn't taken it seriously either, until his father called and told him that his mother was dead.

Mr. Jenkins used a cane because his knees were bad. The man had been a professional football player once. The coaches and the teams had loved him for his stamina and the sheer, immovable strength and stubbornness of his size. They had nicknamed him The Wall.

Jewel told me later that Clayton had been a terrible disappointment to his dad because he had no competitive spirit.

Clayton had the size but not the heart, was how Mr. Jenkins described his son to Jewel. Clayton told her how his father would lash out in anger with his cane, brandishing it like a sword, whipping it through the air so it whistled, catching Clayton across the back of his calf, his hip, the broad flat side of his thigh.

And it is true, Clayton is not a team player. He is a very private person. He prefers to work alone, traveling the country by himself, interviewing people, taking statements, investigating their claims.

A woman swears that her husband's death was an accident. He was not depressed, she tells Clayton. He left no note. He did not kill himself. His death was not a suicide. She says that her husband was blown off the roof of their eight-story apartment building by an untimely gust of wind. She has his insurance policy. She would like to collect.

But Clayton visits her and looks the building over. He obtains a weather report that proves a wind velocity of only five miles an hour, not enough even to disturb the two inches of wet snow on the roof. He has police photographs of the man's footprints in the snow, and they are pointed outward, they lead up to the very edge of the sheer, empty space, and then they stop.

Another man tries to claim a disability by contending that he suffers from head and shoulder tremors that make it impossible for him to keep a job. And yet Clayton has a box of super-8 movies that show this same man sneaking out the back door of his house and going to work every morning at a manufacturing company where they know him by another name.

Clayton says he learns a lot about people this way. He maintains that he will never lose his fascination with what he describes as an infinite variation on the single theme of greed. This is not a cynicism, exactly. Clayton tries to find what is best in everyone; he looks for a reason to like just about anybody, including even the people that might be out to hurt him most.

"People are basically greedy, Clodine," Clayton tells me. "And they'll do just about anything it takes to get whatever it is they think they need."

And then he adds, "But usually what they do turns out not to be their fault."

Clayton Jenkins just does not know how to be critical. The same thing that made him such a disappointment to his dad and kept him from being competitive on the football field also precludes his being judgmental in his life. He seems to be almost bottomless in his understanding and appreciation of other people and their peculiar situations, their particular needs. Clayton could always find some way to explain why people do the things they do, even when what they've done is illegal, even when it's hurtful and selfish and wrong.

It only troubles him sometimes that other people won't give him half the chance that he is willing to give them.

"It's because they're selfish," Galen would say.

Clayton could only shake his big head. His fleshy earlobes would wobble comically.

"Uh-uh," he'd answer Galen, mumbling, frowning, scratching his head. "Seems to me like people always think they have some better reason for what they've done," he'd say. "Something that turns them into an exception, that excuses them, and makes their motives higher than the rules that would keep them from getting what they need. They could always come up with a way to explain to you the what for and the why of it."

Galen thought that Clayton was gullible and naive about other people. Clayton, who traveled and met families of all classes and races and backgrounds and intentions and dreams, thought that Galen didn't know one thing about the real world, the world that was populated beyond the borders of Harmony, out past the horizon of the lake.

This made Galen raise his eyebrows and curl his lip and laugh.

He would rattle the ice cubes in his glass and cross his legs, lift his chin and close his eyes. Put out his hand and reach for me.

The cottage that Galen and I lived in was on the lake. It wasn't much to look at, really, nothing like what Galen had been used to, in his grandmother's house with three stories and seven bedrooms and a maid who had a room near the kitchen and served the family meals. We only had two little bedrooms upstairs and one bathroom. A living room with a stone fireplace on one wall. A breakfast nook separated from the narrow kitchen by cupboards with glass doors. A garage with counters and shelves and a washer and dryer at the back. And all around us trees and woods. There was a narrow path that led down through the trees to the lake. Galen built steps there, out of railroad ties. And I planted tulip bulbs along the brick walk.

I changed our sheets every morning, so that at night, when Galen and I slipped into them, they would be cold and crisp and clean. I spent hours ironing his shirts. I made dinners that it took me days to prepare. I gathered wildflowers from the woods and arranged them in a cut glass vase or a pewter pitcher. Their fragrance filled our house. I collected acorns and pinecones. I made a Christmas wreath out of dried grape vines. I picked mushrooms and wild berries. Galen caught fish in the lake.

Jewel's house is nothing like ours was. Hers is bigger, of course, but it's also messy and chaotic, arbitrary and strictly functional. She doesn't bring home things she can't use, although she does keep everything she's ever had, even when its use is no longer obvious. She throws things together, buying her furniture secondhand sometimes, just because she likes a piece all by itself, not because it goes with what she may already have. The things in Jewel's house have been picked up, chosen and bought singly, one by one, and when they are put together they become an expression of Jewel herself, a reflection of her mood, an extension of her personality, an embodiment, somehow, of her self.

But I selected what I owned with a picture in my mind of how one thing fit in together with the rest. So that the furniture and the linens, the pictures and the decorations, the throw pillows and the drapes, the wallpaper and the paint in my house were chosen not for their individual appeal, but for their value in relation to each other.

One thing, then, would lead to another, and I am always limited in my present choices by what I've chosen in the past.

Lately I've been spending some time in the Harmony town library, looking in the medical encyclopedias and books and journals at articles and essays on the subject of drowning. I have this idea that if I could somehow understand the biology of the thing, I might be able to put away my bad dreams. The librarian, Mr. Curry, won't allow me to check the books out, because they're in the reference section and have been stamped along their edges in red ink: DO NOT REMOVE. Otherwise I would tuck them into my bag and lug them home, sneak them into the house past Jewel, throw the latch on the sewing room door and sit, propped up by pillows, on my bed, with the dress form looming, and read through them in private. As it is, however, I feel compelled to follow the rules — I can't imagine how I would smuggle volumes of this size out of the library, even though Mr. Curry is old and hunched over and half blind and most likely wouldn't notice or might not even care.

I've seen him leafing through some of the more lurid paperbacks that people donate by dumping them into a box in the far corner of the reading room. I've watched him burrow his beaky nose into the pages of a dirty men's magazine. He squints hopelessly through the heavy lenses of his glasses, runs one twiggy finger down along the blurred outline of a model's perfectly photographed breast.

"Drownings?" he echoes my question, throws it back at me like an accusation.

He is leaning closer toward me, rubbing the sandpapery grizzle of his chin. He smiles.

"Well," he says, "now isn't it just funny that you should ask?"

Flakes of dandruff are drifting on the collar of his shirt like snow.

The textbook that Mr. Curry has brought me is big and square, with a burgundy leather cover and print so small that in order to read it I have to lean close, poke my own nose in, follow along the lines with my finger, frown at the words, and squint. It's a technical text, and I have had to use a dictionary to decipher some of the medical jargon here.

But basically, what I've been able to learn is this: drowning is not an especially unusual way for a person to die. In fact, it is the third most common cause of accidental death in the United States. And just about seven thousand people are dead from drowning every single year.

A person falls into water, can't swim, struggles, sinks, loses consciousness, passes out, begins to fade away. His heart is beating, he breathes in water, his lungs fill. How bad this is for him may depend on how much water he brings into his respiratory tract and what solutes and solids the water that he's aspirated contains.

Or death might not even be caused by the water at all, but by "asphyxia secondary to reflex laryngospasm and glottic closure."

Asphyxia: a lack of oxygen in the body that is caused by an interruption of breathing and that causes unconsciousness and, ultimately, death. Glottic: in the empty space between the vocal cords.

The victim's throat closes, and he is suffocated by his own paralyzing reflexes, drowned in the mud of his own fear.

If the victim's arms are reaching upward, stretched out over the head, groping toward the sky, his body will sink down deeper under water, wish denied. But if his hands are hanging, if he's given up, stopped struggling, if his arms are held down at his sides, then it is more likely that his body will rise to the surface, and float.

"A severe pulmonary injury often occurs, resulting in persistent arterial hypoxia and metabolic acidosis."

The very difficulty of this is what makes it somehow reasonable and real for me, serious and meaningful and grave. These complicated words and sentences in their nondescriptive explanations remove me from my visions of bloated limbs, of dangling hands, sodden, wrinkled white fingertips, exposed buttocks, floating like water lilies through the scum surface of algae on edges of the lake.

Peter does a dead man's float. It is a trick I've watched him use plenty of times, for showing off. It always scares the girls on the beach; they put their hands up to their faces, gasp and squeal, squirm on their towels. Mothers will jump to their feet and shade their eyes against the sun. The lifeguard springs from his perch, drawn down with self-important, serious purpose into the water.

Peter will take in a deep breath, and then fall forward. He floats, relaxed, his arms stretched out from his body, his elbows bent, his hands dangling, his legs sprawled. He wears baggy cotton swim trunks with flowers printed on the fabric, and his legs grow out of them like thin white stems. His body turns with the current, so limp and lifeless that for a moment I begin to fear, a lightning flash of panic sparks through me, my heart jerks and skips, contradicting what my mind knows for sure is really true: "This is a trick, Clodine. Peter's teasing you; he's only using this to have some fun."

And then I can see him twitch, I can watch the water stir and feel him begin to collect himself, drawing energy, pulling in his muscles, gathering his arms and legs and springing out of the lake, surging upward, gasping for air, sputtering and splashing and grinning crazily from ear to ear. And searching our faces, too, his mother's and mine, looking into our eyes to see whether we weren't just a slight bit frightened, trying to find a hint of doubt, to see whether it hasn't crossed our minds that maybe what he'd done was not a trick, not a joke, that this time it was real.

And then satisfied when he can see that yes, as a matter of fact, it has.

I have to worry that someone I know will come up behind me where I sit taking notes at my carrel in the library. That they might look over my shoulder and see what it is I've been reading about. This would be taken as a very bad sign. Well-meaning and kind, a friend would worry and deliberate and finally decide that it would be best to approach Jewel and tell her that my behavior has begun to seem morbid and strange.

But the truth is, drowning yourself is no mean feat. The instinct for survival is so strong that even the most determined suicide will find himself, in spite of himself, struggling to stay afloat and swim. A desperate man hangs bricks from his belt loops and, sinking, still musters the strength somehow to pull off his pants and come up. A distraught woman tries throwing herself into the river and then can't keep from treading water and dog-paddling back to the shore. She straggles home, soaking wet, and explains to her drunken husband that she had an accident, she fell. Having learned her lesson, determined to succeed, she goes back the next morning to do it again, this time with rocks from the riverbank wedged into the pockets of her coat, or dangling like a locket from a rope around her neck, enough weight to bring her down and keep her there.

I've tried holding my head down in the bathtub at Jewel's house. Lying back, letting my knees bend up, islands on the soap scum surface of the water, I slide down so the water rises, laps against my neck, over my ears, around my cheeks, my eyes, my mouth, and finally my nose.

Jewel's bathroom is old-fashioned, no nonsense, black and white. A rust stain blooms around the drain of the cast-iron tub. Its claw feet are clenched against the penny tiles laid out in zigzag patterns on the floor. Kids' toys — sponge animals and tugboats, foam dinosaurs and plastic submarines — molder in a wicker basket behind the door. Jewel's stockings and underpants and lacy brassieres hang from the towel bars. The window on the street is opened to the sounds of the children calling to each other in the park. A horn honks. There is a sudden screech of someone's car brakes.

But me, I'm drowning. I'm going deaf. I hold my breath and count. My chest aches with it, like a hunger, and I'm not strong enough. I can't resist. I have to quit and come up, moaning, sucking in air.

I've read that all the experts, policemen and coroners, doctors and detectives, they all of them agree, they all of them have said the same thing, that the ugliest corpse of all is a floater. It comes to them, bloated and blackened, sodden and slick. The eyes will be swollen over into blinded slits, the cheeks distended, tongue hanging, lips torn. Sausage fingers, tumid hands and feet. Hair like seaweed slapped against the skull.

⌁✕⌁

I got up early in the morning and used the last of the milk on my cereal, toasted the heel from the bottom of the bag of bread, scraped up the end of the butter, so Galen and I had to drive our truck into town for supplies. I was sitting in my pajamas at the kitchen table with the sunlight streaming in, sipping coffee, reading the paper, doing the crossword puzzle at the back. I was thinking I would do some laundry. Strip the bed and wash our dirty linens. Hang them out to dry on the clothesline out back. I liked the idea of the sound of wide white sheets flapping like flags, snapping in the wind. Clothespins in my teeth. A large laundry basket cradled in my arms.

I would cook an early supper. Roast beef and rosemary. Potatoes and parsley. Asparagus and dill.

There had been Lilly's picture on the inside front page of the newspaper, next to a terse item about how she had taken up residence here in Harmony with Tim Duke's baby, and how her husband was in jail. The photo was of a thin, waiflike woman standing on the sagging front porch of a summer cottage by the lake. Her face was a pale blur; her hand was small and white against the heavier frame of the screen door. She had a diaper thrown over one shoulder, and a satin ribbon tied in her hair. Her eyes were wide and dark, blank-looking, stunned. I wanted to see her better, to examine her features up close, but when I brought the paper near the picture became less clear rather than more, it disintegrated into a meaningless cluster of black and white disconnected, minuscule dots.

This was a Saturday, in the summertime. One of those stifling hot mornings, when the air is heavy and thick, sodden with moisture and heat, and not even noon yet. Galen had been outside tramping around the yard with his camera, taking close-up photographs of weeds. He wore faded jeans and his torn plaid shirt was damp with sweat under the arms and around the neck, in a wobbly line down the middle of his back. His tennis shoes were old and rounded, grayed leather, scuffed at the toe, with worn heels and smooth soles. The jointed steel band of his wristwatch flashed in the sunlight.

Lilly had been in town before us, and when we got there people were still telling each other about how she came in with that baby on her hip, shopped up and down the aisles, filled a basket full with milk and cheese and bologna and crackers and bread and then laid a crisp new twenty-dollar bill down on the counter to pay for it all. Agatha Pajek, who, with her son, owned the store, had stood there behind the cash register, snapping the twenty between her fingers, turning it over and over in her hands, holding it up to the light to be sure that it was genuine. Her son James had bagged Lilly's groceries for her, in a plastic sack with a handle so she could slip it over her arm and still have two hands free for the baby. They were all of them wondering where Lilly got money like that, and they assumed that it must have been in some criminal way.

We passed Lilly on the road on our way back home. She was walking on the shoulder, her feet slipping in the bone-white gravel. The billowing dust from passing cars would have been like grit against her teeth. Her hair was limp and plastered to her neck with sweat. The sack of groceries dangled from one arm, the bread smashed under the weight of the carton of milk. The baby was so big in Lilly's arms that she kept having to heft it over from one hip to the other. We passed her, and I looked out the back window to see the fierce frown of resolve that was making a fist of her face.

I put my hand on Galen's arm and told him to stop for her.

"For God's sake, Galen, we ought to offer her a ride," I said. "It's the least thing we can do."

Part of me just wanted to get another look at this girl. I wanted to see her for myself, up close. I wanted to hear her voice.

"She must be just dying in this awful heat. I know I am."

I could feel sweat trickling down my own neck, gathering in the crevice between my breasts.

Galen looked at me, a smile wavering in the corners of his mouth. He was curious, too, you could tell. He stopped the truck there in the middle of the road and threw the gearshift into reverse. He fishtailed backward until we were right there next to her, alongside Lilly Duke.

The groceries in the bed of our truck jostled and rattled. There was a beef roast for dinner. A pork loin. Potatoes. Spaghetti sauce and noodles. Honey and bananas and coffee and bread. A big box of laundry detergent and even a small set of dish towels that had caught my eye so I just had to have a set.

They had a picture of a girl printed on them, in a bonnet and a smock, bent over in a field of tall grass, gathering a bouquet of blue flowers up into the small embrace of her arms.

Lilly kept on walking. She didn't even turn her head to look at us.

"Hey, you," Galen called past me, through the open window, guiding the truck alongside her, slow. His hand was relaxed on the steering wheel. He glanced forward at the road and then over again at Lilly Duke. He sucked on his teeth and winked at me.

Her face was reddening with the effort of walking and the embarrassment of not knowing what in the world to answer to me and Galen.

Galen laughed, a hard, single "Ha!" that sounded like a cough.

The baby regarded us solemnly over Lilly's shoulder. Drool glistened on its chin. Her shirt was damp from where the baby had been gumming it. The grocery sack rustled and slapped against Lilly's bare thigh.

She was wearing worn gray canvas shoes with a hole torn in the toe. A pair of cutoff jeans. Her legs were thin and white, her ankles bony, the tendons at the back of her heels long and narrow and taut. Her T-shirt was yellow with a black happy face printed on the back. It looked something like the baby's head, round and inane, wobbling and bouncing in Lilly's arms.

But she would not get into our truck. Lilly could not be persuaded to accept our offer of a ride. She just kept walking, her face burning red with effort and swelter and shame.

Finally she did look at us. She didn't have much other choice. She stopped and turned. She chewed on her lip and eyed the shattered headlight on the front of our truck, as if searching the orb of its busted glass for the right kind of answer to our unasked-for approach. Finally she sighed and raised her face toward me, her chin tucked down, her eyes level.

"No, thank you," she said, her voice cracking and hoarse. "I believe I'd rather just walk."

Galen shrugged at the rejection. He pulled away fast, kicking up a billowy cloud of gravel dust, and he left her there. He turned to me and, sneering, he smiled, cocking his head to one side.

"I believe I'd rather just walk," he said, wiggling his shoulders and wrinkling his nose, a mimicry of her prissiness.

Later I went and borrowed an old bike out of Jewel's garage, and I left it in the yard outside the cabin for Lilly Duke to find. Jewel's garage is so full of junk, she didn't even know it when the bike was gone. And when they saw Lilly riding it, even Peter didn't recognize that the bike had at one time been theirs.

Well, a person can't walk around everywhere she has to go, was what I told Galen.

"She needs to be able to get into town, doesn't she? She's got to have groceries and things. She can't do it all, everything by herself," I said.

Galen mocked me. He laughed at me for getting involved.

"She's going to bite your hand, Clodine," he warned me. "She's no better than a wild animal. Watch and see."

He told me that my reaching out to Lilly was like trying to chum up to a squirrel. They look so cute and fluffy, but any one of them that's brave enough to come down to the ground and let you pet it is sick, rabid, diseased, and it would just as soon kill you with the bubonic plague as become your best friend. The others, the smart ones, the well ones, stay up high in the branches and can't be bothered with you, no matter how hard you try to simper and coax.

"Let her be, Clo," Galen told me. "Mind your own business. Better for everybody if you make the choice now to keep yourself safe and stay the hell away."

But Lilly Duke did get around town on that old rusty bicycle of Jewel's that I left out for her. It had a white basket on the front that she used for carrying the baby in. She bundled him up in blankets and nestled him down there safe and snug. Other women, including Jewel, said that this was a terrible thing, a disgrace. They pursed their lips and clucked to each other, well, I'll be, did you ever, what in the world, and so on like that. They thought that it was dangerous and irresponsible of Lilly to be carrying her baby, that precious creature, around in the straw basket of a bike. What if some fool like Galen Wheeler was to have one too many martinis one night and drive out along Edgewater Road and lose control of his truck on a curve and swerve off onto the shoulder, plowing into Lilly Duke on that bicycle and running her right down into the ditch. What about the baby then?

Except Lilly didn't ever ride the bike at night, of course. Only in the daytime, in the lazy afternoons, into town and back. She would prop the bike outside against a tree and carry her baby into Pajek's little market where she bought all her supplies. Bread and milk and cheese and fruit. Cans of soup. She paid for everything with crisp new twenty-dollar bills.

⌒⨯⌒

And so probably it would have been about then that I first began to get the desire, like an itch, a craving hunger, an urgent need, running in my blood, hammering inward and outward through my heart. I caught it like a disease. It was as persistent as a winter cold.

I wanted a baby. I needed to be pregnant. I had to have a child of my own.

This was something that had never crossed my mind before. Or Galen's either, I don't believe. But after I saw Lilly and her baby, then it seemed like it was just the one thing I had always wanted in the world, the only thing that was important, the easiest thing for me to do that would make my life with Galen meaningful, that would somehow turn it real.

I was half expecting to be able to feel it when it happened. Jewel had told me that some women can tell, they just know the moment of conception when it comes. I would lie completely still on my back after Galen had rolled away from me, and I would listen to my body, to see if anything was different, if somehow there was more. Weeks might go by, and I'd begin to think I was a day late, or two, one time even three, and just when my hopes were up and I started to believe it that this time . . . well, then I'd feel it, that warm, slow seep between my legs, tickling the insides of my thighs, damp in the lining of my underpants, and when I looked down to see, the stain was like an ink blot, full of meaning, telling me no, or anyway not just yet.

Around the time when I turned ten and Jewel was twelve, our mother got very sick. The doctors weren't sure what exactly was the matter with her, except they said it was something about her kidneys, an infection of some kind. Her whole body began to swell. Her feet got too fat for her shoes, her ankles puffed up, her wrists were bloated, her fingers thickened around her wedding ring so she couldn't slide it off, not even with dish soap, not even with lard. Her cheeks were blown out, the skin stretched taut over the full, rounded features of her face. Her lids bulged and sagged, loose and flabby around the sockets of her eyes.

Dad took her into Harlan where the doctors gave her every test and finally pinpointed the kidneys as the cause. They put her on some drug to fight the infection and sent her home to recover, but then her kidney threw off a blood clot that went into her lung, and that was what almost killed her.

Her face, so swollen, was moonish and pale, squeezed up into a grimace against the knife stab of pain in her chest. When she brought her handkerchief away from her lips, it was spotted with a pinkish slime. She pressed her hand up flat against her breast, gasping for breath. Tears rolled down her cheeks. She was dizzy. She swooned.

Dad gathered her up into his arms and carried her out to the car. Her head lolled against his shoulder. Her hands hung, her eyelids fluttered, her lips were slack, her breathing was labored and short. Her white chenille bathrobe had fallen open. It billowed out, draped down, was dragged along behind her through the mud. I opened the car door, and Dad laid her down in the back seat. He rushed around to the driver's side, keys jangling in his hand.

"Jewel, you watch Clodine now," he shouted over the top of the car. "I'll be back, girls. Don't worry, she's gonna be just fine."

He looked up at the sky for a moment and shook his head, as if tossing off any clinging remnants of doubt, and then he ducked down behind the wheel of his car. Our mother was a white ghost slumped against the window in the back seat. The long tie to her robe had got caught in the door, and it flapped madly against the fender as the car sped away. It seemed to be wildly waving to us. "Goodbye, girls! Goodbye!"

"Oh, jeez, I think she's going to die, Clodine," Jewel told me. "I have this feeling. I can't help it. We're never going to see our mother again."

Jewel's eyes were wide and teary with fright. She pressed her fist against her lips.

And I reached out and pushed her away from me with both my hands. I shoved hard against her shoulders, so her head wobbled, snapped sharply, forward and back. She stood on the steps in the circle of light from the porch lamp, and blinked at me.

"Shut up! Shut up! Shut up!" I was yelling at Jewel.

I could have thrown myself on her, knocked her down, ripped out her hair, clawed her face, pummeled her head and her chest and her stomach and her legs with my fists.

Because I knew that my mother couldn't really die. That was impossible. Not my mother. Not in my life. And no matter how ugly and grotesque she might have become with this, still there was nothing really that was changed. My mother was still my mother. Maybe Jewel saw a face that belonged to someone else, a woman unfamiliar to us, with only the vaguest resemblance to the person we had known. She had turned into a stranger, and Jewel seemed to think that this was enough, and a person could die just from the consequence of that change.

But Jewel was wrong. Our mother recovered, of course. Strangeness can't kill you. Even a serious disease has a hard time conquering a person's will to go on, to live, to survive. The doctors fed my mother the medicine to thin her coagulated blood, the clot was dissolved, and she got better. The pain went away, and she was able to get her breath back again. Even her kidneys were healed, and after a while she lost all the water that had accumulated and filled up under her skin. She regained her regular shape and size. She shrank back down into the thin grace of her body, the gentler contour of her face, her slender ankles, her delicate fingers, the dainty bones and tendons of her hands.

But what the whole incident did was it brought each of us to somehow value her more. It was as if we all, and especially Dad, had been made by this to realize then how much she really meant to us. How we depended on her, how we wanted her, how we treasured her, every minute, every day, all the time. We would not ever let her go.

And there was a way that I can see how this was very much the same as it came to be between Galen and me. He loved me and who was ever strong enough to turn her back on that? No matter how he may have hurt me? No matter what he did?

The strength of Galen's feelings had captured me, and he used his passion to hold me fast. I was pinned like a butterfly, drugged and trapped with the knowledge of how I had come to be required in his life. I couldn't resist the power of how much he loved me. He held me to him with the strength of his desperation. He caught me in the emptiest, most hollow places of his heart; he bound me to the enormity of his need.

I went after Galen. I wrapped myself around him, clung to his back, tackled him to the floor. I tore at his clothes, grappled with his arms, wrestled against his legs. I could have smothered him with my caresses, blinded him with my kisses, strangled him with my love.

Because I wanted to make a baby. For that, I would have lain with him for as long as it took, every hour of every single day.

Outside our bedroom window, there is a furtive rustle in the leaves. A listless waving of the higher branches of the trees, like sleepers stretching, waking in the beginning whispers of the springtime storm. The air is so heavy and still, the silence so deep that I feel like I've lost all hearing, I've gone deaf. The smaller trees are whipped, the fir in the front yard bends over backward, the flowers in the garden are bowed down. The clothes that I've hung out on the line are waving their empty arms. I'm watching their wild gestures, their hopeless struggle against the crazy forces of the wind.

And then Galen has come after me, and he's grabbed me from behind. One arm is circled around my waist, he is squeezing my breath away. His other fist moves back and forth over my head, across my shoulders, above my face. There is a quick snicker of metal blades. And a flash like lightning, the mean, sharp glint of steel. Lace curtains surge and billow in the opened window as the rain begins. Drops splatter, heavy in the film of dust against the sill.

And huge, ragged clumps of my hair are falling, they drop to the floor at my feet, as sodden and lifeless and pointless there as the dark drowned bodies of dead birds.

4

THREE YEARS AGO Mom and Dad gave away just about everything they owned, they sold the house and the car, and they moved south to Florida, abandoning me here.

Galen and I got the walnut bed and Mom's pine blanket chest. Jewel took the breakfront and the sideboard, the china and the silverware and the collection of Christmas plates that Mom had been buying for herself one by one every year since before Jewel was born.

So now my parents live in Florida, on a tiny island in the Gulf of Mexico, connected to the mainland by a long thin bridge that is strung out across the water, as fragile and ethereal as spun glass. This island is famous for its seashells, which wash ashore by the handful and lie glimmering in the sun at low tide, waiting to be found, like Easter eggs, buried treasures, small gifts left out for the lucky on the sand.

My parents own a condominium they bought with the money they made when they sold their house here. Dad had invested in stocks and bonds over the years and has enough of an income now from that to live on comfortably for the rest of his life.

"Well, we don't need much," he tells me, smiling. "Our life is simple here. And cheap."

Their condo has thin plaster walls, sharp corners, aluminum

windows, sprayed plaster ceilings, white and lumpy, the color and consistency of cottage cheese. The view from their sun porch is of the gulf, a huge warm sea, where the water is salt instead of fresh, the waves high, sometimes treacherously so, driven by hurricane winds, the bottom far away and dotted with strange fish, creatures that ooze and crawl, coral reefs, sandbars, the shattered hulls of ancient sunken ships.

Mom says the water makes her feel at home, but the gulf is nothing at all like the lake that shimmers here, under an unbearable hot summer sun, its far shore a glimmer on the horizon, dead trees poking up like armless dress forms wading; or spreads out, flat and dull, opaque, frozen over in winter, hard as rock, under a gauzy white blanket of snow. Harmony Lake has turtles and frogs, dragonflies and water bugs, green algae that grow like moss on its surface, cattails that sway in the shallows, minnows and perch, and the ruined buildings of the first Harmony, buried like Atlantis in its mud.

Their island is even smaller than our town. My parents don't own a car anymore, because wherever they need to go now, they can walk. They send us postcards instead of letters, scrawled with messages like "Wish you were here!" and "The weather's been heaven!" as if they were away on a permanent vacation, which is exactly what Dad says retirement ought to be.

After Galen died, they tried to get me to move in with them, but the most I was able to muster was a short visit. Ten days, two weeks. Emma and I flew down to stay with them last winter. I slept on a futon, close to the floor, curled up against the bright white walls of their guest room. I ate breakfast and dinner at the Formica-topped table in their kitchen.

"No need for formal dining here," Mom said. She used to be the kind of woman who would insist her family be there for dinner, on time, that we all sit together at a table fully set with a knife and a fork and a spoon, whether we needed every utensil or not, that we say a blessing of some kind together — "God is great, God is good . . . ," "Oh the Lord is good to me . . . ,"

"Some have meat and cannot eat . . ." — and that we carry on some sort of an intelligent and friendly conversation, and be sure to keep our elbows off the table and our napkins in our laps. Even on special occasions now my parents sit beside each other on the couch, and they eat off metal trays in front of the TV.

Their living room has sliding doors that open out onto a patio that is crowded with flowers in terra cotta pots. Mom loves it that these plants can stay outside all winter long. She never has to bring them in. There is no frost. And that seems just like some kind of a miracle to her.

There are long, thin cotton drapes with huge, colorful flowers and leaves printed on them. Dad keeps two parakeets in a cage in the kitchen. The carpet on the living room floor is green, like grass. All the furniture is white wicker — the chairs are padded with bright, soft cushions and the tabletops are protected by thick sheets of beveled glass.

Mom's kitchen sparkles with a newness that blinded me, enthralls her. The utensils are shiny and cheap. The refrigerator door has a dispenser for ice and cold water. The stove and the dishwasher are polished chrome. It's all such a luxury for her; she still thinks of the whole thing as some kind of a dream come true.

Because our house in Harmony was old, crumbling at the edges, like a soggy cake, with leaky plumbing and quirky electrical, peeling paint, creaky hinges. Mom's furniture was shabby — a sagging sofa, scratched tables, hobbled chairs. But in Florida now, everything she owns is new.

It's as if she is thinking that she and Daddy can somehow be new there, too. I suspect that she believes it might in some way serve to make them young again.

She will walk around all day in nothing more than a bathing suit — modestly high cut, with flat straps that press against her shoulders, a thick waist, wired breast cups, and a skirt gathered along in a line around her belly, above her hips. It flounces discreetly down across the tops of her thighs. Her legs are tanned brown and leathery, her skin hangs, sagging into delicately curved creases over her knees. There are times when she won't even bother to put on shoes. The bottoms of her feet are white and callused. She paints her toenails a pale sunrise orange.

When she does get dressed, my mother wears thin, flowered dresses — housecoats with wide collars and big plastic buttons down the front. Her shoes are flat, scuffs with rubber soles. When it's cold, which is hardly ever, she will throw a blanket over her shoulders, or put on one of Dad's big bulky cardigan sweaters with patches on the elbows and leather buttons on the front. She doesn't even own an overcoat, she tells me with some pride, as if she thought she could take credit herself for the consistently warm weather. Like it was her own doing in some way.

Dad wears shorts and tennis shoes and knit shirts with tangled emblems embroidered on the pockets. His bare legs are knobby and bowed. His shins look bruised. His socks are thin, and they creep down into the heels of his shoes. He only owns one suit now, a few good white shirts, and a single striped tie. He wears these to church on holidays like Easter and Christmas, when Mom gets dressed up, too, and forces him to go.

Some of the men who are Dad's friends have already left their jobs, quit their work, retired, been let go, sent off with everybody's best wishes, a goodbye party, a cake, a pension, and a gold wristwatch. But not many of them have been able to make a total commitment to the island the way Dad did. Like me, they don't seem to be able to tear themselves away and leave Harmony behind.

So instead they can be seen sitting in the chairs outside Pajek's store, and heard talking to each other about their roots and their families, even though most of their children have moved off to work and live in other cities, even other states. These older men spend their days together fishing, or alone puttering around the house, planting flowers around the edges of their yards, repairing loosened hinges, fitting new washers onto a drippy faucet, fixing a broken window with another pane of glass. The wives complain to each other about their husbands, and how since they're not working anymore, they're all the time getting in the way.

But then, in the middle of the winter, after Christmas, when the holidays are over and the kids have gone back to their schools or their jobs or their families again, when winter has settled down with bitter seriousness over the lake, these people drive out of Harmony, south to the island, and they join my parents there. Then the snow here is no longer a wonder, but has become an unwelcome nuisance. The wind has turned spiteful; the sky looks bruised as black clouds hover low above the lake, churning the freezing water, spitting ice, sleeting, dropping chunks of hail big and hard enough to shatter a window, or crack a man's skull.

Mom says winter can be harder to live through every year; the older a person is, the more difficult the cold will be to bear. People in a cold climate don't live as long. They die younger here, she says. Pneumonia takes them. Or flu. They slip on the ice, break a hip, go into the hospital and never come out. Drive a car off the road in a blizzard. Suffocate in an odorless cloud of carbon monoxide fumes that seep out through the cracks in the pipes of a broken furnace. Burn up in a fire that blazes out from the red hot coils of a space heater that's been left on too high, too close beside the bed. Fall asleep and freeze to death under a pile of blankets in the kitchen of an unheated house.

The people from Harmony come to the island and time-share condos there. They rent apartments above the water in the marina. They walk back and forth along the beach, stooping to collect seashells, waving to each other, nodding, murmuring greetings. They meet at the produce counter in the grocery store, and together they marvel over the fruits and vegetables — mangoes and kumquats, kiwi and papaya and baby artichokes. These are natural wonders that were surely never to be seen at Pajek's store in Harmony.

These people, my parents and their friends, feel secure there on their island; with so many familiar faces around, it's as if they've never left home. They have found a way to take Harmony with them even when they've gone so many hundreds of miles away.

Our parents have been together for such a long time now that Jewel says they've even begun to look a little alike, the way a dog will start to resemble his master in some uncanny, subconscious way. They talk at the same time, relating the same stories, simultaneously, using the same words to describe what they've seen or heard, to tell about what's happened. Jewel says it sounds to her sometimes as if they've rehearsed it, practicing at night, in bed. Or they've talked to each other, and said the same things again and again in the same way, until they have it memorized.

They will turn an idea or an event over and over in their minds, examining it between them, studying it, worrying it like a rosary until their analysis has become a litany, their understanding like a prayer. Their finest time is when they have two people to listen to them. Then they don't have to take turns or fill in each other's blanks. They can talk at the same time, one to one person and the other to the other. And then their words overlap and seem to echo, reverberating back and forth between them like a melody, polyphonic and contrapuntal, a harmony, a symphony of their lifetime together, of their friendship and of their love.

"Pete and Repeat," Galen called them, mocking. "Tweedledum and Tweedledumber."

My dad worked for years as a salesman before he finally gave up and retired. He was successful enough at what he did, at least for as long as he believed in the worth of what it was he had been given to sell.

Jewel says it's how he can talk to people that was what made our father so good. He does have a way of listening, of looking you in the eye, of smiling and nodding, that leaves you feeling that whatever you've been saying to him must be something he has never heard before, something meaningful and worthwhile and new. He knows how to tell a good story right back, besides. He can come up with just the joke to get a person to smile and feel at ease. But best of all, for him and for the companies that hired him, he has a knack of passing on his own passion for a thing, an enthusiasm so contagious that you begin to believe that you are just as much in love with whatever it is as he is. And that you simply must have one just like it for yourself.

He could sell a person just about anything, I think, and, at one time or another, I guess he probably did. He sold cars, both new and used, aluminum siding, the kind of foam insulation that they shoot into the walls of a house with a hose. He sold furniture and cleaning supplies, gardening tools, farm equipment, boats, fishing tackle. Whatever there was for a person to buy, he sold it. He had plaques and awards hanging up all around our family room walls — High Achiever, Biggest Turnover, Salesman of the Month, Seller of the Year.

"Your father," my mother says, smiling with a sort of wistful pride and touching her fingertips lightly to his arm, "could sell a glass of water to a drowning man."

She nods; he shakes his head. She insists.

"He could."

She turns to him, scolding now, angry with his modesty and with the way that he is denying what she swears is true.

"You know you could."

She imagines that she means this literally.

But the truth is, my father was out of work more often than not. He moved on from one job to another, like a big bull grazing through a field, because he never could be satisfied with what he was doing at any given time. He was always thinking maybe there would be something else that could bring more money or be more important or seem more interesting for him to do. No matter how enthusiastically he went into one plan, it never did seem to work out. A job never led to more. My dad didn't climb any ladders. He was all the time starting over again, from scratch.

There might be months go by when he was completely out of work. Then he spent his whole long days fishing off the end of the dock. He hung around with the older men, drinking beer with them, watching football games, ogling all the tourists that came and went around the lake. They might go hunting in groups together in the fall.

Or else he was there at home, his hands hanging uselessly, his back stooped over, his shoulders hunched down in defeat. He was waiting for me and Jewel when we came in after school. Then he might fix us something to eat. He might offer to give Jewel a ride somewhere. Or he'd be standing there outside my bedroom, his fists jammed down into his pockets, his body leaned up against the door frame, a toothpick rolled around and around on his tongue.

"So, what's the good word, Clodine?" he'd ask me.

I'd have to stare at him. Because I never did have an answer to that question of his. I never could think of what it was he expected me to say.

"Well, I love you, Daddy," I would whisper hopefully. And that seemed to be all he needed to hear.

Then something would come up, he'd get an offer for a new job of some kind or he'd have heard his pals talking about somebody who was looking for a man like him, and my dad would dive in with such enthusiasm, so much energy my mother said it wore her out just to have to look at him. He'd be working every single day, even Sundays. You couldn't get him to stop.

He'd start out early in the morning, before sunrise. I would straggle downstairs for breakfast, yawning, my hair still damp from the shower and hanging in my eyes, my shoestrings untied and dragging, blouse untucked, dress unzipped, jacket draped across my shoulders, and Dad would already be up and drinking coffee, chewing on a sweet roll or a piece of toast. His face was rosy and clean, scrubbed and shaven, his hair combed back hard away from his brow. I'd find him sitting there at the kitchen table, surrounded by a fragrant cloud of soap-smell and cologne, dressed in just his undershorts, his white shirt, and his tie. His dress shoes, so stiff and straight and formal, were set out and waiting for him, like patient dogs, on the floor nearby. His feet were tucked away snug into the dark wool socks he wore held up by elastic garters that encircled the bunchy breadth of his calves with an almost feminine grace. He'd be going over catalogs, shuffling through piles of papers, reading pamphlets, filling out order forms.

"Good morning, Clodine." Grinning, cheery, so his white teeth sparkled and the shiny tip of his nose glowed. "What's the good word?"

It seemed then like he hardly ever took the time to even sleep. He'd come home long after dark, sling his briefcase up onto the counter, pour a glass of scotch, loosen his tie, unbutton his shirt, roll up his sleeves, bury his face in a book or the evening papers until long after the middle of the night had passed. He'd prowl through the house, test the locks on the windows and the doors, turn off the lights, sneak upstairs where we were all already asleep, creep along the hallway, whisper to each of us, to me and to Jewel and to Mom, "Good night, kiddo, peaches, darling. Good night."

But it never did last. In the end, my father always wound up quitting whatever job it was. He'd just get so disillusioned. People didn't live up to his expectations. He stopped believing in the honesty of his own pitches. He lost faith in the value of the item. He came to know it too well, he said, and then began to doubt the truth of its worth. That kind of skepticism can be the ruin of a good salesman, my father said. The minute you stop trusting in your product, that's when you can stop expecting anybody else to trust in it, too.

So he ended up arguing against himself. He would explain to the people that he called on why they didn't really want whatever it was that he had at the moment to sell. He would look at their situation and shake his head and pack up his samples, turn on his heel and, head bowed, walk away.

One winter when he was out of work, Dad brought out an electric train set and put it together for us to play with. He built a miniature landscape on the broad expanse of plywood between two sawhorses in our garage and put together a track that ran between some hills, along a painted river, through a mountain tunnel, beside a clustered town of tiny houses laid out upon a maze of well-kept, stringy streets. He had black locomotives and streamlined silver engines whose windows seemed to squint with speed. A rusty red caboose. Coal cars, passenger cars, freight cars. Trestles and bridges and grain elevators and mail drops. A water tower, a freight yard, a business district, fields and farms. A lake.

Dad controlled the switches. I listened to the deep, satisfying hum of the transmitter beneath his hand and it seemed like I could almost feel its vibrations running through the centers of my very bones. The electricity that powered the trains flashed sparks and buzzed with a life of its own along the metal tracks.

It was a whole world in miniature. A universe so much smaller than my own that I could stand next to the table, watching the trains as they lumbered around and around in circles, curves, ellipses, and eights, never straying away too far, always returning back home again, their route predictable and repetitive and plain.

I was a giant looming over this small, compact place. I let my huge shadow fall like some monstrous cloud cast across the surface of the land.

I could lay my hand down upon the gentle sloping rise of a hillside. I could caress the thick creases in the plaster of paris landscape. Like Galen's palm pressed up against the sharp curving angle of my hip. Like his fist rolling over the muscles at the small of my back. I could caress the landscape. Run a finger down along the canyons that cut between the mountains. Trace the path of the river. Dip my thumb down into the darkest painted water, into the very deepest center of the lake.

❧✕❧

Now, from that giant's point of view, from that distance and height, picture Lilly Duke on her bicycle, riding along the dusty back roads, from her cabin by the lake, through the trees, into Harmony and then back home again every day. Her baby is in the basket, bundled in his blankets. He waves his small fists; he squalls. His face is squinched up red with anger; his cries are torn and carried off like rags flapping after him in the wind. Lilly's teeth are bared. She pedals furiously and fast. Her elbows are bent and pointed out, her body is hunched, her hair flies, her eyes are filled with tears.

Lilly Duke kept on coming into town on the bicycle that I left for her, and she kept laying down those bright new twenty-dollar bills until finally people began to talk and wonder out loud where in the world she was getting them. She bought a pillow and a box of diapers. A sleeping bag. Some pots and pans. A lamp.

Some people were speculating that she had a whole stash of stolen money out there, buried in a glass jar in the woods or hidden under the floorboards of the cabin, behind a brick in the fireplace, in a bag in the back of the toilet, in a box at the bottom of the well. Someone was still making the payments on the utilities, writing checks to keep the water and the electricity in her cabin turned on.

Lilly Duke had taken up with a convicted criminal, an admitted murderer, a condemned man waiting to be electrocuted, in a cage on death row at the Nebraska State Penitentiary in Lincoln. And besides that, she was the mother of his baby, conceived on a prison visit during the trial when she wore a full skirt and sat on his lap by the window, gazing out through the wire mesh and iron bars at the barren trees and the browning yard, pressing her fingers down hard on the windowsill, swaying and singing to herself while he strained, sweating, moaning, biting her shoulder to keep from crying out and attracting unwanted attention from the guard who stood enveloped in cigarette smoke, leaning in the doorway, looking the other way.

Now here she was living alone in the woods, in an abandoned cabin, with no one to watch out for her, nobody in all of Harmony who cared a fig about what happened to her.

Except for maybe me.

She was loose in the world. Disconnected. What people thought was, it made her fair game. She was an easy mark.

Jewel Jenkins could be heard proclaiming her belief in the fact that a woman like Lilly Duke shouldn't expect to be treated the same as anybody else. She had already crossed the lines of decency by getting mixed up with that Tim Duke in the first place. Jewel and the other women who stood around in Pajek's, fingering the bolts of fabric there, sipping coffee together, munching on the packaged doughnuts and the fresh sweet rolls that Agatha Pajek sold for fifty cents apiece, they all thought that Lilly Duke was a disgrace. Not a one of them had sympathy enough to stand up for her, though they all would have loved the opportunity to steal away her baby and take it for themselves, care for it in a way that they were convinced Lilly Duke could not possibly maintain.

And so what happened was one night some boys who had been listening to their mothers' gossip and taken seriously the disdain that these women held for Lilly Duke — boys with nothing much to do, boys who believed in their own superiority, who couldn't stand not knowing where that money came from—they took the dare and they broke into the cabin, terrorizing Lilly there. They didn't hurt her, anyway not physically. No one touched her. Not one of them laid a hand on Lilly. Not a finger. It was only a schoolboy prank, the sheriff said. Unfortunate, of course, but, after all, no real harm done.

These boys—and maybe Peter Jenkins was among them; maybe that was how Jewel knew—began the thing by shining their flashlights in through the windows. They howled and whistled, just to scare her, they said, each one egging the others on. They hurled stones at the cabin. They pounded on the outside walls with their fists. Finally they came all the way up onto the porch, and then one of them tore down the front door, ripped it right off its hinges and threw it back over his shoulder, skimmed it over the grass and left it lying there flat in the yard.

Lilly was huddled up in her bed with her baby cradled in her arms. She stared back at them, with speechless defiance, refusing to answer their questions, turning a terrified, deaf ear to the obscenity of their insults and the cruelty of their taunts.

They must have been surprised by how small she was and how helpless she looked. How young, as young almost as some of them.

One of the bigger boys swaggered around the room with a broomstick perched on his shoulder like a gun. He was braver than the others. He poked through the cupboards in her kitchen, lifted the lid on the back of the toilet, turned over the boxes that she had piled up on the floor beside her bed. The rest of them all held back, cowed by Lilly's helplessness.

I believe that if she had stood up to them, or tried to fight back, it would have been worse. If she had asked them to leave, or challenged them in any way, then they would have felt at liberty to do whatever they wanted to with her. As it was, they only jostled each other in the doorway, afraid to step all the way into the room, but still curious enough to be craning past the others for a better look.

Finally, their energy dwindled, oddly unsatisfied, because

they hadn't found any money, hadn't been able to bring themselves to touch her, or to do any real harm or damage, the boys gave it up and left, straggling off in pairs or threes, looking back over their shoulders as they went, kicking at the door that lay in the middle of the yard, picking up one stone and flinging it high up into the air. It thumped and rattled against the shingles of the cabin roof and rolled down off the eaves onto the porch.

One of the boys was later taunted mercilessly for having actually excused himself. He took off his hat and held it in front of him, and, looking at the toes of his shoes, he apologized right then and there to Lilly Duke.

"I'm s-sorry, m-miss," he said, stammering. "I d-don't know what musta got into us. I s-swear it, I don't."

The baby stared at him without expression, and only after everyone was gone did it begin to cry.

Those boys didn't find what they were looking for because they didn't know where to look. Although there really was a hidden stash of money—a secret stack of loot, some awkward bundles of crisp new twenty-dollar bills—it was not where any boy would think to hide it. Lilly had concealed her cash in her baby's blankets, rolled it up into the folds of his diapers, sewn it into the backs of his jumpers, buried it in the bottom of the sleeping bag, stuffed it down into the bundles of his clothes.

The next day Lilly pedaled her bicycle into town and bought a shiny rubber-handled hammer and a box of nails and hardware at the store. She tore some of the siding off the dilapidated shed beyond her cabin, and she used the planks to cover all her windows, nailing them up and down like bars across the openings. She fixed the hinges on the front door and installed a lock, a deadbolt, and a chain.

And then, before I knew it, what had happened was I ended up in over my head, obsessed with that girl, Lilly Duke. When I closed my eyes, I could see the white smudge of her face. She haunted all my thoughts; she roamed through the ruined buildings of my dreams.

I wanted her for my friend.

I began to steal things from my sister to give to Lilly Duke. I presented them to her like they were some kind of religious offerings. I left them for her there on the altar of her sagging front porch. The bicycle was the first thing. Then the dog.

After those boys came by and terrorized Lilly that night, then it seemed obvious that she was in need of some protection. Living all alone like that, without anybody, not a soul, who would look after her. No friends, no husband, no one who cared enough to see that she was safe. What she needed, I decided, was a dog. Some kind that was fierce and loyal, one that would guard her, bark and bare its teeth, and also be her friend, curl up at her feet, sit beside her, follow her wherever she might take it in her head to want to go.

I couldn't have given her a gun, could I? I mean, she was a criminal, after all, or as good as one anyway, just by virtue of the fact that she was associated with a convicted felon, a killer, a murderer, Tim. There was no telling what she might decide to do with a gun. Maybe more than just brandish it to scare away some curious boys. I couldn't imagine her pulling off a stunt like that with any kind of believability anyway. Holding a gun up over her head. Pointing it at someone. She would have had to hold it with both hands, outstretched, elbows locked, its weight bringing an ache into her wrists, her shoulders hunched up against her ears, her face turned away, eyes squeezed shut against her anticipation of the noise and the smoke and the kick if she did pull the trigger and the gun did go off.

Or she might decide to use it for more than just self-defense.

What about when all those crisp new twenties ran out? What then? What if she took the gun that I gave her and she went into Pajek's store and tried to hold up the place? What if Agatha Pajek or her son didn't take Lilly as seriously as they should and they refused to hand over the money in the register? Everybody knew that the Pajeks kept lots of cash around. We had all seen the roll of bills that Agatha carried in her pocket, held together with a big blue rubber band from off a bundle of broccoli. Sometimes a grocery store has about as much money on hand as a bank. Especially in summer, when the tourist trade is heaviest.

So, what if Lilly Duke went into Pajek's with a gun, and Agatha, who loves the smell, the feel, the weight of that wad of rolled-up bills in her sweater pocket — what if Agatha said, flat out, "No"? And maybe reached for a gun of her own, under the counter. If she had one there, which I wouldn't have been at all surprised to find out she did, or her son did — they'd be fools not to is what Clayton says to me when I ask him what he thinks, Does Agatha Pajek have a gun or doesn't she?

So, Agatha would bend down and reach under the counter and Lilly could tell she was going for a gun of her own, so Lilly, who was nervous enough already anyway, would have to shoot her! Dead! Or wounded so badly . . .

I just read in the paper about a man who is fighting to have the victim of his crime — armed robbery, shooting — kept on a life-support system, even though the guy is as good as all the way gone, brain dead, because if they take away the feeding tubes and the guy dies, then what our friend faces now is no longer robbery, or assault with a deadly weapon, but murder. In the first degree.

So, what if Agatha got shot by Lilly in the course of an armed robbery, blood all over the store, spattered on the window behind the counter there, on the fabrics and the canned goods, a terrible big mess?

And when they got to asking questions, the detectives came in, the sheriff, tall men with big belt buckles and sunglasses and shiny badges, khaki uniforms, hard-rimmed hats, guns on their hips, notepads, and when they got to the part about where did Lilly get a gun in the first place, then all eyes would turn to me, and they would all find out she got it from me.

"Clodine Wheeler," someone would say.

I gave it to her. For her own protection. After what those boys did that night.

But, anyway, I wouldn't have known where to get a gun, even if I had wanted one. Even if I had decided to give a gun to Lilly, I wouldn't have had any idea what kind. I don't know one thing in the world about guns.

But dogs. Well, Jewel had at that time five or six of these strays that she takes in after they've been abandoned by the summer visitors, campers who have decided they'd be better off, more footloose, freer, less entangled without their pets along to hold them down. There are always dogs in the woods, animals left behind on the fairgrounds after the carnival jobbers have all moved on.

Jewel feels that a big part of her purpose in life is to take care of the things in this world that need taking care of. Like Emma and me. She thinks that as a woman it is her responsibility to nurture and maintain the goodwill of the world. Her humane generosity in this respect is reserved for helpless animals and family members, however, and does not reach far beyond the boundaries of Harmony or the lake. She had no such compassion for criminals, little sympathy for lawbreakers like Lilly Duke.

I had spirited away one of the more recent arrivals so that when Jewel missed him she would only think that he had run away again, and it would not occur to her that I had stolen him.

"Once a stray always a stray," I said, when I heard that Peter had asked. I shrugged my shoulders and squinted knowingly off into the woods. "You know what they say, Jewel, about teaching old dogs new tricks."

I chose the big mongrel that Clayton had named Hero. He was a ferocious barker, protective of his property, and that was what I wanted him for. I put a leash on him and drove him in Galen's truck to Lilly's cabin early in the morning, while Jewel was busy feeding breakfast to her children and before Galen had even started his complex morning ritual of getting up out of bed. I led the dog up with me onto Lilly's front porch. I peered through the cracks in her boarded-up window, but it was dark as night inside. I pounded with my fist on the hard wood of her newly hung, triple-locked door.

There was a faint creaking in the floorboards, and so I knew she had to be standing there on the other side. I heard her hush the baby, cooing to him, whistling softly through her teeth.

"It's only me, Lilly," I called. "A friend. Clodine Wheeler."

Not that she had any reason in the world for knowing my name. She wouldn't be able to associate the name Clodine Wheeler with anything at all. The only people in town that she had ever spoken to were the Pajeks and the other folks who worked behind the counters of the stores, and she may not have even known their names, much less mine. All she ever said to them was "This, please," pushing whatever it was that she had chosen to buy across the counter toward them. Or "I thank you kindly," after she had passed over her twenty-dollar bill and accepted back the change, counting it out carefully in her palm and then tucking it away safe down into the pocket of her jeans.

Except when Galen and I had offered her a lift home. That time she had told us she would rather walk.

"I saw you the other day," I said to her now, prodding, urging, coaxing her with the softness, the gentle honey of my voice. "On the road. I was the one in the truck, remember? We wanted to give you a ride?"

I didn't mention the bike. I wasn't sure whether she knew

where it had come from, dropped from the sky like the answer to a prayer, or brought by those boys to tempt her, to offer her a sense of security that they had proven later was quite false.

She stopped cooing, and there was such a silence that I thought I could just feel the strain of her breath held there on the other side of the door.

"And I saw you on the television, too. We all did." I laughed, a friendly chuckle, meant to hearten and to reassure. "You're famous, Lilly. I guess you must know that by now."

Though, of course, there wasn't any way she would have known it. The last thing she would have had in her cabin was a TV, although I resolved right then and there to do my best to try and find a way to get her one. Or anyway a radio, at least.

"I have this present for you," I said.

The baby had begun to whimper. The floorboards were creaking in a frantic kind of rhythm that I took to mean she was rocking him back and forth there in her arms.

"I don't want to hurt you, Lilly. I just want to be friends, okay?"

I stood there a moment longer, listening, but Lilly had stopped moving. I imagined her slipping her small white knuckle in between the baby's lips to hush him. It was very quiet, but I could still feel that she was standing there. She hadn't gone away. She was waiting, and I was waiting. I could feel her breathing. I could sense the sparrowy scutter of her heart, panicked, not knowing what in the world she should do.

And then the baby sneezed.

I whispered, "I know you're right there, Lilly. And I understand you're afraid. Why, I'd be afraid, too, all alone out here in the woods like this. A little thing like yourself, and with a baby, too. No one looking after you. No one watching out. I only want to be your friend, Lilly. I only want to help."

And I kept on babbling like that, trying just to calm Lilly, and the baby, too, with the warm spill and tumble of my voice.

Finally, the door moved. Just the faintest crack. I took two steps away and folded my hands behind my back. The dog was sitting next to me, obedient, panting. My smile was as open and friendly as I knew how to make it be, to show her that I meant well and intended no harm.

"Hi," I said. I could feel the sudden heat of blood rushing to my face.

Lilly stared back at me through the crack in the door, un-blinking. Her eyes were round dark holes in the pale mask of her pinched face. I can imagine now how I must have looked after what Galen had done to my hair—chopped and careless and wild.

I brought the leash forward and put out my hand to give it to her.

"For your protection," I said.

She stared at the leash, and then the dog, and then at me again, her eyebrows brought up into a small, questioning frown.

"His name is Hero," I said. "He'll protect you." I smiled. "Really he will."

I waggled the leash and, at last, she reached out and took it. Her thumb brushed my palm. I glimpsed the scars on the inside of her wrist, half-moon tears that seemed to shine and glow, whiter even than her skin. The backs of her hands were splat-tered with freckles. Her wrists were bony, fragile as fine china, and thin. She pulled on the leash and opened the door wider, and the dog stood up, wagged his tail, shook his heavy head, and allowed her to lead him inside. Lilly still stood looking at me through the crack in the door.

"Well, I thought you should have it is all," I said.

Finally she said, "Thank you," in a voice that was high and hoarse, breathless-sounding, like a person who's been socked in the stomach and had all the wind knocked out.

Her hair was messy; strands of it fell into her face, and I was tempted to reach out and brush it from her eyes, pick it up and tuck it back behind an ear, sweep it away like cobwebs. But I knew that if I touched her, if I made a move that was too sudden, then she would panic, slam the door, dart away, pull herself back in like some wild thing startled in the woods.

"You're welcome, Lilly," I said. I smiled and turned away and walked back to the truck and left.

Another time I took her a chicken. Jewel had hens that she kept in a coop behind her garage. They laid eggs all over the yard sometimes, so collecting could be like hunting them at Easter. You might come upon one that had sat there hidden in the high weeds along the edges of the yard for too long, cracked, and gone bad. Then if you stepped on it the smell would fill the air, rotten and sulfurous — wrinkling up her nose and shaking out her hands, Jewel called it the smell of death itself.

She used the good eggs for making cakes and eggnog. She fried them for breakfast. Poached them. Scrambled them. She made omelets with bacon and onions and cheese for dinner on Sundays. Soufflés and French toast and mayonnaise and hollandaise. She kept some of the shells intact, blowing the white and the yolk out through a pinhole that she punched into each end, and these she decorated, painting intricate designs on the smooth white surfaces with model airplane paints, arranging them in straw baskets or hanging them in the window — tied by nearly invisible fishing line, they looked like gems suspended in the air.

I nabbed one of the chickens, flapping and screaming, its legs scrabbling against my arm, birdy claws scratching me and drawing blood, and I stuffed it into a pillowcase, and I left it on Lilly Duke's porch. I thought that she could use the eggs for herself and for the baby, too, who must have begun to eat some solid foods by then. Jewel said that she had seen Lilly buying jars of baby food at Pajek's market. She must have begun to wean.

I pinched a blanket from Jewel. A frying pan. A set of towels. An old radio. A black and white TV.

*

I told Lilly Duke that I only wanted us to be friends. That was all. I showed her the palms of my hands as an indication of my innocence, a sign of my good intentions. But I guess I know now that what I was looking for was not exactly friendship. In fact, it was something else altogether. The truth was I was hoping to find a person I could use to wedge between myself and Galen. Someone who I could hold up against me like a buffer, to shield me from Galen's temper, and somehow soften his blows.

⌒✕⌒

My mother sends me postcards with pictures of sailboats and sunsets, the spidery bridge, seashells in sea foam. She prints the names of the young people that she's met on the island. Young people is what she calls them, even though they must all be in their thirties and forties. There is a man named Whitman who teaches math at the elementary school. A woman named Annis who runs the quaint little stationery shop in town. Mom wants me to bring Emma and come down to the island to live. She suggests what kinds of things I might be able to do there. I could make shell necklaces to sell. I could get a job in one of the shops—she's sure that Annis would hire me. I could teach school. I could do nothing. Lie in the sun, play in the surf, sleep on the futon in their guest room, eat dinner from a tray in front of their TV.

But I tell her what she already knows, which is that I can't leave here. I belong in Harmony. I belong to Harmony. This is my home. And for whatever the reason, I don't think that I could ever go. The truth of it is, I like it here. And, for now, I just have no other choice but to stay.

5

I WAS SITTING on the front porch steps, outside our cottage by the lake, in the late afternoon, and I was shelling peas.

The full pods were heaped in a woven brown basket on one side of me. I had gathered them from our garden where they grew in a row along the fence, their slender stems twined up and curled along the strings that Galen had tied for them to climb. It was late in the season. Early in the fall. The peas were very ripe; the pods were stringy and tough. They bulged, swollen and full. Each center seam was long and taut, restrained, held back. Open, emptied shells were scattered on a newspaper that I'd folded out behind me. My bare feet were flat on the second step. My knees were pressed together, tight. A silver bowl was cradled in my lap.

A song was circling through my mind — it rolled around and around with the green peas in the silver bowl.

". . . and if that diamond ring turns brass . . ."

I listened to the high whine of the motorboats out on the lake. Crickets in the trees. Frogs. Squirrels. Birds. The shouts of children playing at the beach. The wind hummed and whistled in the dried, browning leaves on the branches of the trees above my head.

The sun was low on the horizon. It had broken through the

broad white wall of clouds at the edge of the lake, and it beamed
through the porch balusters and rails, alternating warm bright
light and cool gray shade over me in a regular pattern of stripes.
The worn wood beneath the soles of my feet held its own heat,
paint baking, buckled and peeling back.

I ran a thumbnail along the edge of a pea pod, splitting it
open, and with my fingers, I pried its firm sides apart. I let the
round peas drop into the silver bowl in my lap and tossed the
empty shell away, over my shoulder, onto the newspaper behind
my back.

". . . if that looking-glass gets broke . . ."

"Clo-o-o-o-*diiiine!*"

And what I was hearing then was Galen. He was singing out
my name, dragging on the vowels, calling to me from the
bedroom upstairs, inside the cottage, far away. His voice was
muted, muffled, made faint by the empty space that filled the
rooms and walls that lay between us.

"Clo . . . Clo . . . Clo . . . Clo," he sang to me, over and
over and over again.

I hummed, "And if that billy goat won't pull . . ."

And I shucked the peas. I was shucking and humming and
humming and shucking; and Galen was crying out for me, "Clo-
diine! Clo-*diine!*"

The syllables dropped and climbed, rose and fell, two notes,
two tones, ululating, up and down. "Clo-*diine!* Clo-*diine!*"

Humming and splitting and prying and dropping and tossing.
My throat was tight; my fingers ached. I began rocking back
and forth then, caught in the repeated rhythm, the singsong
chorus of my own name. I made my body be a pod; I hunched
down farther and deeper; I closed in on myself, intent upon the
task at hand. My fingers worked furiously; peas rolled; shells
flew. I could hear the heavy thud of Galen's steps as he strode
the floors, up and down the hallways, in and out of the door-
ways, through our rooms. Doors were flung open; doors were
slammed shut.

He was looking for me. He searched the dark corners of our closets, peeked behind the solid shadows of our furniture, threw back the heavy folds of our drapes. Even though I was not hiding, he had set out to find me, and surely he would do that. Like a hunter, he would track me down.

"Clo? Clo?" His call had become a question. A wail. A cry.

Then I heard him moving, a scrape and shuffle at the screen behind me. The rusty hinges screamed, the door swung open so fast that it kicked up a quick breeze, and it crashed around against the side of the house. Bouncing back, it shuddered.

I could hear his footsteps, quiet now, measured, satisfied, and slow. I felt the hard, unforgiving toes of Galen's shoes pressed up against the edge of my leg. He was standing so close now that I could smell him. I could feel the heat of his anger as it surged up. It emanated from the pores of his skin; it rose to the surface like sweat; it rippled in waves off his body, formed an aura around him, a halo, the mirage of a puddle on a hot tar road.

And then his hands were lifted up like wings. They were swinging back. They were flapping up. They were bearing down.

Clap! Slam! Over my temples, against my ears, both sides.

I dropped the peas. I jerked and kicked; I threw up my hands, and I flailed my feet. The silver bowl spilled over and tumbled down the steps, clattering, bouncing; the sound was hollow, and it rang out against the wood — it dinged and chimed, and the shelled peas were rolling, scattering, strewn like bright green marbles on the steps, jewels on the bricks and in the grass.

The ache in my ears was hard and deep. It throbbed. It roared. My head felt swollen, my brain bloated; my thoughts were thick and turgid, slow-moving and blurred.

When I looked up into Galen's face then, I could see the fury moving there. It twisted and writhed, it bloomed and spread. Like clouds, roiling. Like water, seeping. Like a storm gathering, out over our lake, magnificent, breathtaking, terrible and powerful and murderous and strong.

Galen's blue eyes were the same as the lake. They dragged me in. They pulled me under; they brought me steadily, forcefully down.

I slipped in, submerged, and I let his weight carry me.

I drowned.

⌒✕⌒

By the time we'd gone too deep into that autumn, Lilly's baby was already six months old, and he had started to be able to crawl. She told me he'd been christened Chance—Chance Timothy Duke. Tim's idea, she said.

If he'd been a girl, she added, she'd had it all planned out that she would have named her Clementine, just so she could sing to her that song.

"Oh my darling, oh my darling . . ."

Lilly threw back her head and lifted her chin, drawling on the words, dragging out the vowels, strangling on the *r*'s and the *l*'s.

But he was a boy, and she called him C.T. She had shortened his name to those two initials, as if already she could imagine him as a man in a baseball cap, straddling a barstool in a tavern somewhere, his hands callused from whatever the kind of work he did, his shirtsleeves rolled up, a tattoo drawn in black ink across the hard bones of his wrist. A young man with a day's growth of beard, guzzling a beer while some thin-legged girl pressed her body up behind him, whispered, sighed, "Oh my darling, C.T."

Lilly set him down to play on the floor of the cabin's kitchen, on the bare linoleum that was warped and stained, torn, cracked and bent, and the baby pulled himself forward by his elbows, his hands curled into fists, his stomach sliding along on the floor, his feet dragging out behind him. He crawled the same way a soldier is taught to slink through the cover of a grassy field, sneaking into enemy territory under the barrier of a barbed wire fence.

Oh, but he was fast, too. He could scuttle, be gone in a minute, disappear in the blink of an eye, before you could even decide to say his name. Lilly and I would find him sitting up behind the bed, examining the soft fluff of a dust mouse, or on his knees in the closet, poking at a shoe, or on his stomach in the kitchen, rolling crumbs between his fingers and his thumb.

"Just don't turn your back on that baby C.T.," Lilly said, with some pride. "Don't look away. Oooh! Don't dare give that boy Chance one chance!"

She picked him up and waggled him in the air above her head, her chin lifted, her thin arms outstretched, her elbows locked. He squirmed and chortled happily there, smiling, drooling; one small white tooth winked out from under the heavy pink flesh of his tongue.

"You are a naughty one, you. Takes after his daddy," Lilly said to me. "There is just no telling what that boy might take it in his head to do."

She laughed then. She put her hand over her mouth to cover her teeth, and she laughed.

And, as always, I was struck by how childlike she was, flimsy and small, a waif, so young. Her legs were thin, and she could fold them up under her body, sit curled in a chair just like a kid. The tops of her shoulders were freckled and sunburned outside the slender straps of her tank top. Her fingernails were chewed. She wore her hair drawn back from her face by plastic barrettes that had been molded into the shape of dogs' heads or ruffled bows, baby pink and sky blue, grass green, bruise purple, lily white.

When we were little girls, Jewel and I played with our dolls in the front yard, on a blanket that Mom had spread out for us under a shady tree. Dad was outside in the back, pushing the mower around on the bit of grass that grew up against the fence separating our yard from the alley that ran behind our house.

Mom knelt in the sunlight near us, digging up the dandelions with a fork.

Hold a flower up under your chin and look for the yellow that just might be shown reflected back.

"Clo loves butter!" Jewel would scream, thrilled with the wonderful clairvoyance of a weed.

Tie the stems together for a necklace. Serve the greens in a salad, with tomatoes and peppers and dill.

"Everything is useful, girls," Mother said, sitting back on her haunches, the weeds in a pile next to her, looking worthless and pitiful and limp, I thought. She spread her hands out on her thighs. The fork glinted in the sunlight. Her face was shaded by the brim of a broad straw hat. "Everything has a purpose. Each smallest little bit of the world has its reason and its place."

Jewel and I held our dollies in our arms. We pressed their rubber faces up to our shoulders and rocked, humming lullabies. We patted their plastic backs. We brushed their nylon hair, braided it, tied it back with ribbons, washed it with real shampoo. We dressed them and undressed them, fingered the dimples in their elbows and their knees, bent back their wrinkly thumbs, kissed the smooth, cool, flat soles of their wedgy feet. We kept cardboard suitcases filled with tiny cotton socks, baby T-shirts, shorts, leather shoes. We cradled our babies in our arms, pushed empty spoons in between their lips, rolled their heads so their eyelids snapped open, fell closed. We held up clear bottles with hard, sharp, pink plastic nipples. These were filled with a milky white liquid that seemed consumed — it disappeared like magic, gone where? — when we tipped the bottles over, upside down.

One time Jewel lifted up her blouse and held her dolly up to her own flat, pink nipple. She pressed its nose against the smooth white skin of her chest.

"Suckling," she told me, whispering, as if it were a dirty

word. She tossed her hair back out of her eyes and informed me, "This, Clo, is how a real mommy feeds her baby."

Jewel said that she had seen Mrs. Fisher in the real estate office do it many times.

But hadn't cats been known to sneak into a nursery, to bound silently over the edge of a cradle, curl up around a slumbering baby and steal his breath away? Hadn't I heard of monsters that materialized in the darkest shadows of the night, bent down over the pillows and, with the most deadly kiss, sucked out a person's very soul? Weren't there bats that flapped in through an opened window and landed in your hair, sank their teeth into your neck and drank up every last ounce of your blood? Leeches, ticks, mosquitoes. All of them wanted nothing less than to be left alone so they could eat you up alive.

"Mine's not hungry," I told Jewel. I didn't want anybody sucking on me, not ever, not for any reason, even a baby, even for food. The thought of it made me dizzy and sick.

"My baby's sleepy," I said. I settled it down into the nest of towels that I had bundled up beside me in the grass.

"What do you want to be when you grow up, Jewel?" I asked her. "What do you think we'll do?"

Get married. Fall in love with someone who was handsome. Somebody who was rich. Someone who could take care of me.

"I'll have lots and lots of babies," Jewel said. She peered up into the tree, envisioning in the sky between the leaves the life that one day would be hers. "We'll have a whole house full of them. Children like us, who play outside all day and then come in and hug me, put their arms around my legs, hold my hand, play with my hair, sit in my lap. I'll bake cookies every day and let them eat as many as they want. I'll have luncheons where I'll serve little sandwiches cut into hearts and clubs and triangles, without any crust. I'll learn how to arrange flowers in a glass vase, and I'll play cards on Friday afternoons with my friends, while my children are in school. My husband will have a good job, in an office, with a secretary who adores him and a boss who admires the work that he does. He'll wear white shirts and dark ties, he'll drive a nice car, and he'll come home to me every night after work at five. He'll read the newspaper and drink scotch on the rocks. He'll listen to the news on the radio while I'm in the kitchen cooking our dinner. Our children will be upstairs in their rooms, reading books, doing homework. They'll kiss him on the cheek when he comes home. He'll pick them up and squeeze them till they squeak."

The truth is, Jewel fell in love, and she married Clayton Jenkins. He doesn't work a nine-to-five job. He doesn't have an office that he goes to in the mornings and comes home from at night. He isn't particularly handsome. He's certainly not rich.

But he does love her. Clayton loves Jewel. You could carve it on the trunk of a tree. You could spray-paint it on a boulder, plant it in a row of flowers on the side of a grassy hill. You could draw it in the wet cement, scratch it into the sidewalk, write it out behind an airplane with puffs of smoke across the sky.

My sister Jewel calls herself the luckiest girl in the world.

～✕～

Dad took me and Jewel along with him on a business trip one time. He drove us across Iowa and over the Mississippi into the state of Illinois, to Chicago, where he had a sales convention he was expected to attend. This was at a time when he was in the business of selling farm equipment and yard tools. The next year there was a drought and not much in the way of rain or snow—so bad that people were even asked to try and conserve by not watering their lawns. The result for us was that my dad had an especially difficult time talking any farmers into buying his lawn mowers or his snow blowers, much less any of the heavier stuff he had to sell. When he drove out to the fields and visited the families there, he saw that the soybeans were withered, the corn stunted and parched on the dusty hills, and he turned right back around and drove away.

Once again, he quit.

He had a whole briefcase crammed full of the catalogs with color photographs and raving paragraphs that described the pieces of equipment, but he told my mother he just couldn't bring himself to talk those poor people into signing up for things that would only bury them even deeper in what was already beginning to look like an overwhelming drift of debt. He didn't want anybody obligated to some fancy combine or newfangled picker without the promise of a huge harvest to pay it off with in the fall. He had seen too many of the old homesteads go under, he said. Too many family treasures, too many legacies, too many heirlooms sold off at auction to strangers who could not have cared any less.

He went back into the car business for a while then. He peddled luxury automobiles, with wide bodies, solid doors, white-wall tires, plush interiors, velvet seats, and engines that hardly made any noise at all. And he sold these to the bankers with their full pocketbooks instead.

My grandmother Mimi and my dad's brother Charlie and my cousin Naomi shared a big apartment in the middle of downtown Chicago, which to Jewel and me then was the very biggest of cities, a true metropolis, complete with tall buildings, milling crowds of all kinds of people, taxicabs, a subway, an elevated train, suburbs and ghettos, high-rise apartments and low-rent housing projects — the works. They lived together there because Naomi's mother had died, and our grandmother Mimi was bringing her up.

Charlie had a job as an insurance agent, and was truly a successful man, Dad told us — not without some pride, as if his brother's accomplishments in business said something by way of relation about him, too. Charlie even had his own office, with his name engraved on a sign outside the door. At Christmastime every year he sent out a calendar—a small cardboard thing with the name *Charlie Ferring* written in red letters across the top and a black and white picture of his face, chin in hand, glasses gleaming, in the upper corner. My mother took one look at that calendar, shook her head, sighed, and tossed it away into the trash.

"Well, it's too small to be useful," she told my father later, watching with her arms folded over her chest and her elbows cupped in her hands as he fished Charlie's picture back out of the garbage and shook off the carrot peels and coffee grounds that had stuck to it. "You can't write your appointments on it, you know. Why, the print's so small that you can barely even see any difference between the days. And anyway, who would want to look at your brother's face grinning back at them every day of every week of every month of the whole, long year?"

Mom didn't like Uncle Charlie, and she didn't like our grandmother either. She thought that they were both of them just too persnickety, was how she put it. She said that they were snobs and added that the truth was that Dad was lucky to have somehow managed to avoid the worst of his own family's faults. She told us that the irony of it was that instead of those two seeing themselves for what they were—which was, in her opinion, selfish and unstable and spoiled—they were always thinking that those very weaknesses were what made them better than the rest of us, or anyway superior to the likes of her.

She said that because they lived in an apartment in the city that meant they put on airs. Mimi wore lots of jewelry and surrounded herself with pretty things, just because she didn't know any better and believed that all of that somehow made her a better person just for the fact of having it there within her reach.

And it was true that when we sent a Christmas or a birthday present to Naomi, we hardly ever got any kind of a word of thank you back. No phone call. No little note. Mom thought that this betrayed the worst sort of bad manners, even conceding the fact that poor Naomi was a motherless child being brought up by her grandmother and so might have been forgiven for a lapse like that. Mom bought Naomi nicer and nicer presents every year, just to prove her point. And Mimi, in her turn, mailed me and Jewel money—checks written out to our own names in the loop and tangle of her stringy script—and we always sent back a letter of thanks, even though Mom said that cash was not a thoughtful gift, but then what else could you expect from people like that?

Mimi and Charlie and Naomi didn't come to visit us ever, either, which Mom thought on the one hand was an insult and on the other hand was a blessing. They had their own lake, Michigan, many times bigger and more important than ours.

"He thinks he's something else," my mother said to my father. "City slickers. I know your mother looks at me to be a bumpkin. Hayseed. Rube. Because I do my own dishes and iron my own shirts. You know I just can't stand the way she smiles at me, so condescending, that's all."

Mimi had been heard to comment at one time that our mother couldn't be expected to know any better than she did about some things, like china patterns or silverware, coming from the family that she did—her father had been a meat inspector for the state—and not having graduated from a college either.

"She's just not educated," Mimi had said to Dad, "and it isn't fair that anyone should expect her to act as if she were."

Of course, although Mimi thought that she was only being generous and forgiving, my mother never was able to forget how that sentence had sounded to her poor, ignorant country ears. In fact, she began to use it then herself—she took up the phrase as if it had been her own invention. She said it about herself so many times that it seemed like it began to take on a shape of its own, as if the words had been embossed there at the beginning of how people looked at her, both a condemnation and, at the same time, an apology and an excuse.

"Well, of course, everybody knows I'm not an educated woman," Mom would say, "but . . ." — and it never did stop her from telling Daddy and anybody else who was within hearing just what her opinion was about a thing anyway.

Still, she never did forgive Mimi for that. She said it only went to show, and nothing Daddy could think of to say could talk my mother into joining him in going to Chicago to visit Mimi or Charlie, so he took just the two of us, Jewel and me, along instead.

"Leave Mom at home to get some rest," he said, winking. "Give her a little vacation. She deserves some peace and quiet to herself, don't you think?"

I imagined she would spend the time working in her garden, because that was what she loved. Or maybe she would just stay in bed all morning. Go out for lunch by herself. Stop in at the library. Shop for hours in town. Take walks along the shore of the lake, collecting cattails and grand strands of white winter wheat. Steam a plate of the vegetables that the rest of us refused to eat. Watch the TV by herself, alone and undisturbed, in a house that was unnaturally quiet, uninterrupted by children slamming in and out the door, or by Daddy asking her to make him lunch, bring him coffee, sew on a button, iron his shirt.

We took the back roads, because that was how my father preferred to drive. It meant that he could do a little meandering if he liked, take his time and not be rushed by the four lanes of Interstate traffic that hurtled carelessly along across the fields with nothing much for us to look at except each other and an occasional billboard advertising cigarettes or feed.

Dad liked taking in the scenery. He drove with all the windows down so that the passing wind whirled through the car and stirred the shirts and suits that hung like Clayton's do, from hangers on a rail between the back windows.

My father was very much at ease behind the wheel of a car. He was comfortable to lean back in his seat, one elbow resting on the door, hanging out the opened window, burning in the bright sunlight. It gave him a lopsided sort of farmer's tan, one-armed, from the elbow down. His skin was milky white around his wrist when he removed his watch at night. Or he would throw the other arm out across the back of the seat, steer with his left hand, pump the brakes or press down on the gas with his big feet in their brown dress shoes. When he drove, he kept himself company by singing along with the radio or talking out loud, shouting over the rush and whoosh of the wind and the churn and roar of the engine.

If you sat in the back seat of my father's car, you got all that wind blowing in your face, so you had to squint your eyes shut against it. My hair would be blown back, tangled and wild, so knotted that I could hardly get a comb through when I went into a service station bathroom to freshen up. Sometimes you might feel a bug nick you on the cheek, or the dust from the gravel road would get in your mouth and coat your teeth with its grit.

No wonder Jewel and I both liked it better to ride in the front seat. There you could see out to the road and know what might be coming your way up ahead. There you could feel like you were all alone with Daddy, like you had him all to yourself for a while, like he was all yours. Whoever was sitting in the back got to feeling like she was only a hanger-on, a passenger, along for the ride, but not essential to it. Dad's shirts smelled like starch and dust and detergent and crisp cotton. Jewel and I took our turns sitting in the back, but because neither of us liked it much there, we fought for our rightful place in the front seat with great seriousness and determination.

"My turn!" "No, mine!" we cried, pushing and pulling on

each other—Jewel shoved me hard; I grabbed her by the elbow and swung her furiously so she pivoted around in the dirt on one sneakered toe—until my father had to yank us apart and stand us up straight beside the car in order to begin to sort out whose turn it really was.

He stood before us in judgment, his legs apart, his broad face frowning at us. He shook his head. He scratched his temple. He rubbed his chin.

"What I oughta do," he said finally, "is just go off and leave the both of you two brats behind. Just dump you off forever, once and for all, right here."

We looked around at the dilapidated filling station, the thin dog asleep with his chin on his paws under the porch, the grizzled mechanic in his baggy, torn overalls, his torso white and hairless and pouchy, pale flesh swinging off his upper arms, one thumb missing, his smile toothless and wide. Three dirty children were playing a game of marbles in the dirt under a tree. And Jewel and I both shuddered to think of joining them there, of becoming a part of what we imagined must be their squalid, miserable mean life.

"I suppose your mother'd be mad if I did that, though," Dad went on thoughtfully, as if he really had been considering with some seriousness the idea of abandoning us there, and only the thought of what our mother might say to him prevented him from actually carrying out his whim.

I usually came up the winner in this fight for the front seat, because whoever rode beside my father there also got to be the navigator and had to be able to read the map. I was, to put it simply, better at map reading than Jewel.

My own sense of direction has always been reliable and safe. But Jewel couldn't keep from getting turned around and confused about which way was up and which way was down. She never did figure out that you were supposed to turn the map around to fit whichever direction you were headed in. She didn't like it when you had to read the letters in the names of the towns and rivers and counties and states sideways or upside down.

And she did manage to get us lost more than only one time. "Turn left here," she'd call out. "No, I mean right. I think. That way. Or no, wait, go there."

She would point and turn her head from side to side so her hair flew in her face. She wrinkled up her nose and chewed on her lip and snapped the map between her hands so hard that she tore it down the middle, and then Daddy slammed on the brakes and almost skidded right off the side of the road and down into the ditch.

"Let Clodine do it, then, Jewel, if you can't get this right."

And I would hurdle from the back seat into the front, settling comfortably down next to my dad, taking the map up into my hands with some authority, flattening it on my lap, smoothing it out against my knees, and turning it so that the road ahead matched the direction of the red line in my hands. Jewel would have to get out of the car and go to the back. She huddled, pouting, in the back seat, with her arms hugging her body and tears glistening in her eyes as she sat there, staring forlornly and ashamed at her feet.

The truth was, I really did love to look at and study and read those maps. Dad had a whole packet of them in a leather pouch with a fold-over top and a big metal snap. There was a map there for every state in the Union, though it was not likely that he would ever need more than the few that covered the center of the country—his business probably wouldn't take him any place really far away, like Hawaii or Alaska or even New York. The maps were folded perfectly, fanned inward and creased along their edges, and I loved the puzzle of trying to figure out where we were, where we'd been, where we might be going to be. I read the symbols as if they were ciphers in another language, full of meaning and possibility and promise. I followed with my fingertip the double lines and single lines, the dotted lines, the yellow lines, blue for rivers that widened into sudden lakes, meandering railroads, sprawling spaces for the cities, concentric dots for the larger towns, single specks for the smaller ones — Dunbar and Gilman, Zook Spur, Kalo, Gravity, and Howe — the names of places that to me sounded like a list that would have been happy to accommodate a name like Harmony, too. A grouping that made me believe my own home town was really only one of the hundreds of friendly and safe spots in the world, settlements that dotted the countryside, places where the daily drama of the lives of people like me could be played out in the security of their own houses and side streets and alleys and back yards.

Even after the Interstate was built, my father still would rather travel his routes along the slower roads, like Old Highway 30. He liked touring through the towns, he said. He loved the sight of the bridges and the cattle crossings, the barns and silos and squatty outbuildings clustered together under a benign gathering of trees at the end of a narrow drive.

We could look past the fences into people's yards and imagine their lives spread out there for anyone in the world to see. There were whole wardrobes of clothes hanging out to dry on lines strung up between the trees. Swing sets and tree houses and wading pools and bikes. Children squirting each other with hoses, digging together in dirt piles, playing tag in fields of tall grass. Trucks rusted in browned yards, an old washing machine was on its side in the ditch, a sofa rested upside down just off the shoulder of the road.

All kinds of walls and fences rose up to separate one house from another, to mark the fields, to enclose the parking lots and business grounds. Pickets and barbed wire, chain link, stone, brick, rail and slat.

Dogs slept on front porches. Cats perched on windowsills. There was a gray pony tied up in the shade of a tree. Horses stood grazing in the rolling fields. Cows clustered around thin streams.

You could smell the hog farms coming and going. They filled the air and the car with a thick, meaty smell that lingered like a cloud. We held our noses and squealed, Jewel and I, while Dad leaned back and laughed, calling "Soo-eee!" in a voice so thin and high it sounded as if it must belong to someone else.

He stopped often along the way, pulling into a gas station in a small town to fill up and maybe engage in some conversation with whoever was there to listen. They mostly discussed the weather in talk that consisted of not much more than two- or three-word sentences.

"Nice day."

"Pretty hot."

"Darned dry."

"Might rain."

All this punctuated by replies like "Yep," and "Nope," and "Sure, you bet."

Dad might dig down into his pocket and pull out for me and Jewel each a quarter to go get a pop out of the machine by the side of the station.

After the sun went down, when it was dark, before we found some place to pull over and stop to spend the night, we might see a car coming toward us with only one headlight on, and then Daddy would always reach over to whoever was next to him there in the front seat and pull her up close and kiss her big on the face.

"Padiddle!" he cried. "Kiss your girlfriend!"

That was the tradition, he told us. People had been doing it for as long as there'd been highways to drive on, for as long as there'd been cars. He used to take our mother out, cruise along the back roads, waiting for a one-eyed car to come at him, then he'd stop, pull over, bring her up into his arms.

So then we did it sometimes, too. Fooled by a motorcycle,

we'd both of us, Jewel and me, get caught screaming "Padiddle!" and we'd throw our arms around his neck so hard he'd have to hold on to the wheel with both hands just to keep control.

When the radio was on, we sang along with it. Jewel and I tried playing a game of crazy eights on the back seat, but the cards kept slipping off and we would scream at each other — "You cheated!" "Did not!" "Did too!" — until Daddy's hand came flying back and smacked my sister's face hard enough to leave a red mark sprawled there across the whole side of her cheek.

Then Jewel turned herself all the way around backward on the seat. She pushed the hanging shirts and jackets aside, sat up on her knees and, with her chin on her folded arms, she watched the road wind out behind us, something finished, she said, land already been traveled, sights already been seen.

The little side vent on my side of the car was cracked open, and it whistled a mindless and high-pitched tune.

～✕～

What I can remember most clearly of Chicago then was the neck-craning height and breadth of the buildings there. So many windows, so much glass, and yet the lives of the people we saw seemed remote, hidden, concealed from us. Men and women stood together in crowds on the street corners, waiting for the lights to change, but no one seemed to know the name or recognize the face of anybody else. No one stopped to say hello, or to discuss the weather or the state of the economy. Taxis sped past, swerving, horns honking, brakes squealing, in and out around the lanes of slower-moving traffic. Buses heaved forward, tottering, groaning with the weight of passengers. The sun was blocked from view, its heat and light weakened by a gray filter of smog, so that it seemed to me it was always early evening, even in the morning, even when I knew for sure that really it was only noon.

We stayed over one night there with Mimi and Uncle Charlie

and our cousin Naomi in a black building with rounded walls, shaped overall like a clover leaf, and rising up into the sky above Lake Michigan. The apartment was on the sixty-first floor, and Mimi had decorated all the rooms in white—the carpeting, the furniture, the walls, even the tiles in the kitchen were white.

What I can remember best of Mimi now was how her hands looked, the skin as delicate and pale as if it were made of the finest porcelain, graced with the gold and diamond and emerald and amethyst rings on her fingers and the rosy sheen of polish on her nails. Her thin wrists were clasped by a circle of bracelets, and a string of real pearls was looped twice around her neck and then knotted there against the solid smooth sag of her breasts. She wore her hair drawn up and wrapped around into a thick bun at the back of her head, held in place by a scattering of crinkled copper hairpins. Naomi told us that Mimi's hair had not been cut since she was only a little girl, and that when she took the pins out at night, the gray waves of it flowed out around her face like smoke and hung so long down her back, it fell even farther than her waist.

Mom said that Mimi had been an only child, the daughter of a wealthy man, and that she still had lots of money that she kept all to herself and would not give away to anybody even if they needed it, which Daddy argued back that he never did, which she countered with that Charlie seemed to always be needing some and getting it too except my father was too proud to ever ask that was all and it just wasn't fair, is what my mother thought, folding her arms around her body and turning away.

"But you won't hear me complaining, Jack," she said. "It's good you've got your pride, is what I think. And besides, don't we have all that we'll ever need? At least the girls are taken care of, and that's what is really important."

Mimi had set up trust funds for me and Jewel, to be spent on our education, she said, which my mother considered only another insult to herself, of course. The truth was, though, that we would come into it when we were eighteen, and could do whatever we wanted to with it, go to school or not, which it turned out that Jewel did and I did not.

Naomi had in her room a canopy bed and a huge collection of stuffed animals, all of them soft and plush and furry and so clean that they looked untouched and brand new. Her closet was packed with dresses and blouses and skirts. She had a white fur coat, too, which she showed off proudly to me and Jewel, who stood gaping, feeling dusty and shabby in our own dirty shorts and gray blouses and smudgy tennis shoes.

The air conditioning in the apartment created a false climate, chilly and unnatural feeling, so we shivered. Naomi said the windows didn't open because if they did people might be tempted to jump, but when Jewel and I looked down, the ground seemed so far away that we couldn't understand why.

"You'd die if you jumped," Jewel said, matter-of-factly.

"Well, that's the point," said Naomi.

Naomi had dolls, too, but they weren't anything like what Jewel and I played with at home. Hers were not the kind that you could think of as toys. They were show dolls, Naomi explained, Ginnys and Madame Alexanders dressed in the colorful native costumes of exotic foreign lands.

"You can't touch them," Naomi told us, frowning, as serious and protective as a shop owner. "Mimi says they're to look at, and not to touch."

They stood frozen on shelves behind glass doors. This was what my mother meant by persnickety. No wonder, then, that Naomi had never bothered to thank us for our gifts.

The view from Naomi's bedroom window was of Lake Shore Drive where it comes together to cross over the Chicago River and begin its way back out of the city to the south. The road, divided down the center by a high cement wall, curved sharply at that spot, and it switched back against itself several times, so that drivers were forced to slow and take the corners so close behind one another that, from the distance of Naomi's sixty-first-floor bedroom window, they almost looked connected, threaded together like beads on a long string.

Naomi herself likened their movement to marbles through a wooden chute, rolling down in a zigzag, back and forth and back again. Sometimes, she went on, her eyes sparkling with the excitement of it, they would forget to slow, they would be going so fast that they couldn't stop in time, and then they wound around the corners with too much speed and lost control and went crashing through the barrier wall, over the edge, and down into the river. There they sank, in silence, in slow motion, so far away that even if you were there to see it happen there was nothing in the world that you could do to save anybody's life.

"It happens all the time," Naomi said, with conviction and even a hint of pride. "But mostly it happens at night."

Jewel and I stood with our elbows on the windowsill and our foreheads pressed up against the glass, watching, hoping an accident would happen, wishing for catastrophe, praying for the wild commotion of a crash.

Naomi was three years older than Jewel, five years older than me. But she seemed more fledgling, underdeveloped somehow, less substantial than either of us. My mother said that was because she spent her life inside, in an apartment, closed up away from the fresh air, with no mother to love her, only a woman like Mimi to bring her up.

Naomi's mother had died when Naomi was still just a little baby. So long ago, Naomi told us, that she had no memory of her whatsoever, not the vaguest impression of a face or a feeling or a touch, and she said this as if she thought of it as some kind of an accomplishment, an achievement, that she had managed so thoroughly to forget.

Naomi was slender and pale. She wore a soft flowered dress and a white cardigan sweater thrown over her shoulders and buttoned at the neck, its arms swinging loose behind her like a cape. She had wire-rimmed glasses that slid down the straight slope of her nose with lenses so thick that they magnified her eyes and made them seem even bigger and bluer than they were. Her mouth was small and thin and full of dainty white teeth. Her hair was blond, her skin so white it was almost iridescent, and you could see the veins and arteries that coursed through her arms and her legs.

Jewel said later that Naomi was just like that plastic biology model we had at school, of a woman's body, with clear, see-through skin, all her inner workings — bones and muscles, arteries and organs — wholly visible and exposed. The model had a hinged torso that you could swing open, and you could reach in and pull out the tangled clump of her intestines, cup the bitty purplish pea of her heart, her stomach, her kidneys, her liver, her lungs. If you held the pocket of her womb up to the light, you could see the outline of the fetus within, asleep and curled up against itself like a tiny shrimp.

Later Jewel nicknamed our cousin the Visible Girl.

We had dinner that night in the dining room, with the big crystal chandelier twinkling overhead, and soft music playing in the other room. I remember the gleaming silver, how heavy the handles of the knives, how delicate the pattern of flowers that was painted on the china plates.

Jewel and I sat there with our hands in our laps, hardly daring to eat anything at all for fear that we might do something stupid and rude and prove to Mimi once and for all that she was right, we were our mother's daughters after all and no more sophisticated than she. Naomi, completely at her ease and probably enchanted just with the fact of having any company at all, chattered and laughed, clattering her fork against her plate, happily passing along the platters and bowls, helping herself to butter, a roll, the pepper and salt, begging her daddy please to pour some of his red wine into her water for a special treat, her eyes shining, her voice rising and shrill.

When we had finished, Naomi asked to be excused, and Mimi wanted her to be an angel and begin to clear the table by carrying our dishes off into the kitchen. And after Naomi had taken the last plate, then she came dancing back into the dining room and, standing there in the kitchen doorway, she all of a sudden, and without any word, no introduction, no warning, no excuse, lifted up her skirt to reveal that she wasn't wearing any kind of underpants at all.

My father began to choke, coughing so hard into the curl of his fist that his neck turned red above his collar and his eyes were filled with tears. Uncle Charlie slammed his napkin down on the table and made the water glasses totter.

Naomi's bare thighs were bony and chalk white, marked by blue veins that ran beneath the surface of her skin like the rivers on a map. The cleft between her legs was thick and fleshy, pink, and as fuzzy and soft-looking as a ripened peach.

Jewel and I both were horrified. Of course, Mimi was furious. Her pale face was so flushed even her ears turned red. She pushed her chair away from the table with such force that it flew out behind her and fell backward with a crash against the floor. She crossed the room in what seemed like a single long, purposeful stride, and in one smooth motion she had swooped Naomi off her feet and had her tucked up under one arm and was carrying her away, removing her from our presence, getting her out of the room. Naomi was crying and screaming, and she kicked out her feet so her skirt stayed hiked up still, and her bare bottom shone like a moon as she disappeared down the dark length of the hall.

My uncle and my dad looked at each other. Dad cleared his throat, embarrassed. Uncle Charlie shrugged and shook his head.

"Women," he said.

He folded his napkin. He leaned back in his chair and lit a cigar, reached forward to pour some more wine.

Jewel and I sat frozen, like statues, side by side, our feet dangling down over the edges of our chairs, our hands in our laps, each of us overcome with a burning bright feeling of guilt and shame for Naomi, as if we had been a part of her mischief, as if we secretly shared in her embarrassment, just by virtue of the fact that we, too, were girls.

On our way back home to Harmony again, just after we had crossed the big bridge over the Mississippi, we came upon a camper that had crashed—gone off through the iron railing of a narrow bridge, over an embankment, and then rolled up to the edge of a dried-up creekbed and burst into oily flames.

Dad pulled over and stopped, just behind the line of emergency vehicles and trucks.

"You girls wait for me right here. Don't leave this car. Stay put," he growled at us.

Jewel scrambled up into the front seat, and we both leaned forward, peering through the grimy windshield to get a better look. Dad stepped out of the car and started to walk away. Then he turned and came back and at first I feared that he had changed his mind and decided not to stay here after all, to keep moving on, past this accident, out of the way of this calamity. But he only reached into the back seat without looking—his face still serious and intent upon the smoke and flames and people huddled together around the edges of the bridge—and he pulled out one of his suit jackets and shrugged it on. As if in a disaster he would like to be at least well dressed. Definitely not a victim. Merely a passing businessman who had stopped out of curiosity, for kicks, pulled over to have a look.

He shoved his hands down into his pockets and walked stiffly over to where the crowd had gathered. The wind pressed against his pant legs and whipped his tie back over his shoulder. It flapped behind him, waving back at us as gaily as a banner, as reassuring as a flag.

His body was a tall, shadowy, familiar form, outlined in silhouette against the bright light of the flames. He held a white handkerchief up to his face, covering his nose and his mouth against the smoke and fiery heat. And I was aware of the danger that he might be in just because he'd pulled over, because he'd stopped driving, had left his car and moved in closer so he could see better.

Dad stood with the clustered group of restless onlookers. He toed the gravel on the shoulder of the road and squinted up thoughtfully into the sun.

I imagined the heavy shudder of an explosion. The huge thunder of it. An angry, roiling fireball of heat and smoke that billowed out, spewing shards of glass. Shattered steel singing through the air like bullets, hurled outward with the force of shrapnel, tearing into the trees, blowing the form of my father down.

The family in the camper had somehow scrambled or been pulled free of the wreck before the fire caught. A mother and daughter stood hugging each other at the side of the road, their faces white and blank, their hair windblown, bodies swaying as if engaged in some kind of a dance, rocking for the simple comfort of it, rhythmically forward and back. Someone had thrown a brown plaid blanket around them, over their shoulders. The father sat alone in the grass with his knees drawn up to his chest, his shocked face buried in the bowl of his arms. Other children stood here and there, open-mouthed, gaping. One boy held what looked like a small white puppy, limp and unmoving in the tender cradle of his arms.

The lights of the emergency vehicles spun, blue and red and yellow strobes that flashed against the shredded iron railing of the bridge.

This was my first trip away from Harmony. My first time away from home. I wasn't overcome by any sort of lonesome homesickness, like what the kids who went away to camp for the summers had described. I had my father and my sister with me, and I was never really alone.

But I was engulfed in an overwhelming wave of this terrible realization of just how dangerous the world can be. Death and craziness might be lurking, waiting for you everywhere. Embarrassment and shame. Accidents and painful circumstances. Smoke and fire and unexpected grief. I thought that I could pretty much understand why my mother had chosen to stay behind at home, by herself, all alone.

And I couldn't wait to get back to our house to be there with her. My whole body seemed to thrum with this sudden sense of urgency. My blood pounded with it. My breath was full of it. My stomach clenched so hard around it that my insides ached. I watched the road roll out like string before us, drawing me toward her, reeling me in, like a fish, pulling me home.

All I wanted, all I needed in the world was to return to Harmony. If only I could make it back where it was safe, I promised myself, I swore, that I would never ever go away from here again.

And when I asked my mother, "Were you lonesome? Did you miss us?" then she pulled me close and hugged me tight and told me that yes, indeed, she surely was, she truly did.

❯❮❮❯

Picture a battered old white pickup truck, tearing down along the thin winding filament of an unpaved county road, between the trees, along a high bluff above the broad and empty sweep of a lake. The chassis sways, it rocks against the sudden swing of the road's unpredictable, meandering bends. The tires kick up a plume of dust that flies out like a spring storm at its tail.

And now it has skidded straight across a curve; it's kept on going straight with an initiative other than the simple winding will of the road. It's bounced up over the soft shoulder, and it's crashed through the guardrail.

It's flown over the sheer-dropoff rim of the bluff. For a few silent seconds it floats and soars, then it plummets, nose tipped slightly downward as it falls. It belly-flops, slapping the surface of the water with a huge hard whack. It drifts and turns, its tires momentarily buoyant, until, with a long deep slurping gurgle, the white truck begins inexorably to sink.

Lake water licks the fenders. It laps at the windshield; it pools in the truck bed. The tensile skin of water tightens, and it closes up across the rounded roof of the cab.

Faces are pressed against the windows. Hands grope across the seats, reach out for the handles in the doors.

But the truck is going down. Almost languidly, it glides and drops through the murk. It slips, and then it settles; it is nestled in the ample lap of lake-bottom slime and sludge.

A few telltale bubbles are flung upward. They break against the surface, as simple and soft, as airy and breezy, as satisfied and relieved as a deep-breathed sigh.

6

IF MY FAMILY had a secret, if there was anything unusual, different, or strange about us, maybe it would have to be the fact that my parents liked to fight.

They loved it. They enjoyed the fever of an argument; they felt good about letting themselves get worked up. They took something from their struggle to have the last word, from their shouting and their slamming doors. They threw things at each other — pillows or cushions or shoes — but nothing that was heavy, nothing that would break, nothing that could in any way be made to hurt. Dad shook a curled fist, pounded the kitchen table with enough force to make it hop. Mom folded her arms across her chest, pointed a finger in his face, stomped her foot against the floor.

Dad paced the bedroom, shirtless, in shorts with a seat that hung baggy in the back, making him look neglected and ineffectual, even pitiful, from behind — a belt loop missed, his knees scarred, his shins and ankles hairy and pale, his bare feet firmly slapping, back and forth and back and forth, across the hardwood floor. His appendicitis scar was a ragged and lumpy territory, a contour map laid out upon the furry hemisphere of his gut.

Mom stood her ground, she held it fast, unmoved, stolid and

unyielding, a rock, granite, iron in her white satin slip. The flabby flesh of her upper arms quivered. Her long legs had been shaved; they were smooth and shiny with sweat. Her armpits were slick, her shoulders rounded and lightly freckled, soft. A chain necklace with a pendant silver heart nestled in the hills and ridges of her collarbone; plastic earrings dangled, swinging heavily from the fragile lobes of her ears.

"You're wrong, Maggie. I never said that. Or anyway if I did, I sure didn't mean it to come out the way you're trying to make it sound."

"So does that mean you take it back?"

"No, I don't take it back. I don't take anything back."

"Just say you're sorry, then."

"Okay, I'm sorry. But I'm not wrong."

"You really hate it when you lose."

"I didn't lose."

"It drives you crazy, doesn't it?"

"Listen, if that's what this is about, winning and losing, then go ahead, be my guest. There you go. You win."

"Don't you patronize me, Jack."

"I'm not patronizing you."

"You get a great satisfaction out of feeling superior, don't you? It makes you feel big and strong, I can tell."

"Oh, it does not."

"Go ahead, hit me, then. Slap me around. See how it feels."

"Don't be stupid."

"Come on. Try it. I dare you."

"Come here."

"No."

"Get over here."

"No."

"I'm not kidding."

"Neither am I."

Thus the two of them argued. They quarreled and they

fought, squabbling and bickering, sparring in a way that seemed to me like it excited them. They shouted at each other and berated each other, took a side, made a point and tried to drive it home, came back with a counterargument, a rebuttal, thesis and antithesis, and yet, somehow, with all of that, there was no animosity, no hatred spawned between them, and their abuse seemed only to endear them to each other more. If you interrupted them in the middle and asked them what was the matter, what was it that made them so unhappy, why were they dissatisfied, they would stop and look back at you with great surprise, genuinely astonished to hear that you were thinking there might be something wrong.

Because the truth of it was, they were having fun. This was a recreation for them. A way that they had found to relax.

My mother blushed and smiled, the back of her hand pressed up against her mouth. Suddenly demure, she shook her head and tucked her hair back behind her ear, fiddled with an earring, fingered the silver locket at her throat. Dad laid an arm across her shoulders, jostled her, pulled her in close to him, pressed his lips against the part in her hair at the top of her head.

It was none of my business, he told me.

"Oh, sweetie, don't worry," my mother purred, snuggled there in the strong, protective circle of my father's arms. "It isn't one bit of what you might think."

They turned me around and pushed me away, shooed me off—"Now scat, Clodine. Never mind. Go play."—closed their door, locked it. I heard them laughing for a minute, and then it would begin, the yelling, the pacing, the pounding and the stomping, all over again.

～✕～

Summertime here, in Harmony, in late July or early August, it can get so hot sometimes, and no place to go, you can't escape it, not even in the shade, not even at night. The sun burns down all day long, early in the morning all the way up until nine P.M. sometimes, not one cloud in the sky, nothing but blue, forever and ever, at least until you come to the trees. And when the nighttime finally does decide to fall, then it settles in dusky, as heavy as ever and even deader for being so dark, thick with moisture and heat; not a breeze, the leaves are still, nothing moves, nothing stirs.

Our house was not equipped with air conditioning. All we had to cool us off was a fan that we put in the window in the living room, trying to bring up a breeze, hoping to stir some wind. At the end of the springtime, when the weather started to turn hot, Daddy would haul the fan out of the garage, set it on the sill, bring the window down against it, pushing hard to hold it there secure, and then Mom would shoulder him aside and flip the switch at the top to turn it on. She'd take some time to stand there in her bare feet, her toenails shiny with polish, the white slip shimmery against her belly, one thin, lacy strap sliding down off a shoulder, her hands pulling her damp hair up away from the back of her neck. She'd close her eyes and put her face right up into that hot wind and think of it as a relief.

The fan was a big round contraption, one of many that Daddy must have been trying to sell at one time, or maybe it was given to him as a gift, a bonus from one of the companies that was still pretty happy with his work. It had broad flat wings that spun, around and around, shiny, flashing, squeaking behind a protective metal mesh with rows of holes just wide enough to fit a child's small finger in.

And if you put your face up in front of those turning blades, if you shouted or you whistled or just sang a simple little song down into them, you could hear your own voice thrown right back to you all rippled and curled, wavy and distorted, so maybe you sounded just like somebody who was under water, calling out. You could think about the tip of your nose poking in too close and getting nicked, chopped clean off.

I might take my mother's place, after she'd wandered away,

gone off with Daddy, into their room, and I might stand there, just like her. I might lean forward, my chin up, my eyes squeezed shut, my hands clasped behind my back—"Watch your fingers, Clo," she'd warned me. "Keep your hands away."—my face in front of that fan, hair blown back, hot air gusting, the sweat on my neck and my temples tickling as it dried.

There was some music playing on the radio on the table by the couch. I was dancing, flapping fingers, clapping hands. I dreamed maybe I could be a ballerina when I grew up, dance on the stage with a man who could lift me and throw me, swing me back over his head and gently down, the sheer fabric of my skirt ballooning out behind me, full and fluffy as a cloud. I raised my arms, wrists loose, hands hanging, fingers spread, knees lifted, toes pointed, head straight, face forward, shoulders high, back arched.

All the doors in the house had been thrown open, held back with something heavy, a brick or a book or a stone, and the windows were all raised, it was that hot. Jewel reached out and turned the dial, cranked the volume on the radio up louder so it seemed like it filled up the room, pushed against the walls, rose up to the ceiling and bounced back down again, as tangible as the heat. Jewel was crouched on the lumpy cushion in Daddy's chair, her chin on her knees, arms wrapped around her legs, watching me, eyes wide, mouth solemn. The music was booming, as loud as thunder, as thick as rain. A white curtain billowed in the doorway like it could have been alive, a ghost.

Mom and Dad were at the back of the house in their own room, with the door left open still. Probably it was just too hot, too stifling, to have it shut. Jewel had her hand on the radio dial, and she kept making the music come out louder, even louder. She turned it up and up to drown out the shouting, Mom and Dad scrapping with each other in their room.

"Don't get too close to the fan," my mother had warned us. "Be careful. Sharp blades. Just like a cleaver. Like a hatchet. Like a knife."

And Jewel had moved closer. She had gazed into the fan, held by the blur, the turning, the menacing quick flash. She imagined the keenness; she could picture the whack and the hack and the chop.

I was dancing, whirling, twirling, dizzy with my heart pounding, the blood rushing in my ears, the music and the heat. The fan turning around and around. Me spinning around and around. Circle and bow, duck and weave, loop and pirouette.

"Keep your fingers away from that fan, Clodine," my mother had said.

The metal blades winking, flashing.

Otherwise, I don't believe I would have even thought of it. I wouldn't have dreamed of it. I wouldn't have known it was something a person, a child, reckless and wanton and wild, just might decide to do.

But my mother had warned me, and so there I was, and there it was, and I didn't know what I was doing. I was reaching out. I had stopped dancing. I had slowed and turned. I walked, toe heel toe heel, over to the window, closer to the fan. Breathless, panting, my thin chest heaving. The music pounding in my head. My hair blown back, my eyes shut tight, chin up, sweat drying, tickling on my neck, my temples, between my budding breasts.

And I raised my hand. I lifted it up oh so gracefully, the way that a dancer is taught to do, leading with the wrist, spreading the fingers, just so, allowing the thumb to hang, relaxed. One finger pointing, stretching forward, reaching out, elbow locked, through the mesh, into a rolling cruel blur and bite of blades.

There was a thunk and a squeak, a whir; the hum of the motor stopped, caught, skipped, whined, and Jewel was on her feet, and she had bounded up out of the chair, and she was springing like a cat.

She was wailing, "Clo-o-o-o! No-o-o-o!"

Well, I yanked my hand back. I pulled it up close to my body and cradled it there. Looking at it then it seemed like it belonged to some other person, someone else, not me. It was numb. It didn't hurt. Or anyway not yet.

My mother had heard Jewel's scream, even above the din of the radio, even over the clamor of her own raised voice, and she came running. Her one arm was lifted up to shield her face. My father was shouting, barking commands. He had his fist brought back above his head, as if he might be good and ready to pummel whatever it was that had hurt his baby girl.

Blood welled up, spurted, ran in streams and rivers down the back of my hand, sopped into my T-shirt, dripped off my wrist, coursed down along my arm.

Daddy lifted me, he picked me up, he whisked me off my feet and, running awkwardly, his knees bumping against my back, he carried me up the stairs and down the hall to the bathroom. The tiles were white; I spattered them red with blood. The porcelain sink, the smudgy mirror, my own pale face reflected back, eyes empty and black. My mother behind me, her opened mouth, her bared teeth, the look on her face, of disgust and revulsion and shock.

"You know I can't bear the sight of blood, Clodine," she said. She swooned in the doorway, staggered back, pale and faint.

Daddy had one arm wrapped around my waist to hold me up. His other hand gripped my wrist and held my finger under the cold water that ran steady and soft from the tap. The skin below my knuckle was torn, thick and white. It flopped back like the gills on a fish that I've seen circling through the darkest waters of the lake. The pain was a deepening, hard, frozen ache.

Mom came from behind and pressed herself up to me; her breasts wobbled against my back. Daddy was barechested, barefoot, barelegged in his shorts.

Slipping, skidding, his toes smeared in my blood that had splashed and splattered on the white tile floor.

"Better never decide to try and tell my sister Clodine not to do something," Jewel says. "That's just a certified guarantee for sure that she'll have to go and do it, no matter how bad for her it might look like it could be."

She skewers a tomato on a fork and holds it down in a pan of boiling water, loosening its thin shiny skin.

We both can remember the times when it was after dinner and I'd have crawled up to sit on Daddy's lap.

"Don't touch my nose," he'd tell me, smiling, so the fleshy pink gums around his teeth showed.

His knees were bony, they dug into the backs of my legs. The curly soft hair on his arms tickled the skin at the side of my neck. I liked to put my hand up to his face, to feel the breadth of his cheek against my palm, the strength of his jaw, the sharp stubble of his beard under my fingers.

"Don't you touch my nose, Clodine."

A smile playing there in the muscles of his face.

And Mom would turn from the sink, her hands held under the soapy water, as if they had been caught there, and she would peer over her shoulder at us, smile and raise her eyebrows, wink an eye, shake her head.

I'd be lifting up my hand and running my thumb over the high arch of his eyebrow. I'd flip a finger on his eyelashes, brush my knuckles against the solid cartilage of his ear.

"Don't you touch my nose!" he'd say again, louder, his voice deeper, and Mom's shoulders would shake. She was laughing.

Jewel would bury her face in her hands, knowing I was going to do it, that I wouldn't have the strength or the willpower not to, that I was going to have to give in. And when I did, when I let my hand go where it wanted to, when I allowed my fingers to do what I had been told not to do, when I touched the fleshy bulb of his nose, then my daddy would throw back his head and howl as if he'd been burned. He would clasp my body under my arms, his hands so big they seemed like they could circle me all the way around, and he would wriggle his fingers, dig into my rib cage with his thumbs, tickle and tickle until it seemed that I didn't have a breath left in me and I was going to drown in my own laughter, suffocate on my own hilarity. I gasped for air; tears streamed down my cheeks. And then when he finally quit, I collapsed against him, limp, drained, exhausted, spent.

But what Jewel means when she says don't tell me don't is not "Don't put your finger in the fan, Clodine." And it's not "Don't touch my nose." Daddy was fair-minded, and he played the same game with my sister a few times, too, but she wasn't good at it like me.

Jewel never once gave in. She thought he meant it when he said it; she believed that she should do as she was told and that her stoicism, her self-control, her restraint was proper, what he wanted, what he hoped for, what was right. She expected to be rewarded for being obedient and true, but Daddy always only turned away from her, let her slide down off his lap. He picked up his newspaper, turned on the TV, went in to help Mom with the dishes, preoccupied and bored.

No, when Jewel says don't say don't to Clo, what she is talking about is Galen Wheeler.

～✕～

Daddy had always hoped that Jewel and I would go on past high school to pick up a further education of some kind. He was ambitious for us that way. He wanted us to have a skill that we could use, something we could draw upon to support ourselves if we ever had to, like typing and shorthand, telephone manners, memo-taking, how to dress for success. Mimi had set up trusts for us to use whatever way we liked, but the understanding that Dad had was that the money was for paying our way through school and toward the start of some kind of a career.

"You're both smart girls," he liked to say to us. "Don't sell yourselves short. You could go some places, you know. You could do some things."

He expected that we would take degrees, find jobs, in offices, in the city—Chicago or Minneapolis, even Des Moines. He thought that we would ride to work every day in taxicabs, wear tailored jackets and straight skirts, silk blouses and pearl necklaces. Go in for manicures on Saturday mornings, have our hair done once a week. Call him on Sundays to tell him all the things we'd done.

My mother'd had to quit high school before she'd finished so she could have the time to be a wife to our dad. And she didn't much care for how it seemed like now he was implying that a choice such as the one she had made would be in some way not good enough for us.

"What's wrong with how we've found to live?" she demanded to be told.

She'd dog his footsteps down the hallway, insisting that he give her some kind of an answer back to that. He would lead her into their bedroom and pull the door closed and begin the argument there, at the point where he had to find a way to explain to her how what she had chosen was right in one way and yet wrong in another, both at the same time.

Mom's life was just fine for Mom. There wasn't one thing wrong with it that he could see. Nothing to make it better. No part that anyone would change. But it also was just not the sort of clear future that our daddy had been keeping like a secret in his heart for us.

"Every generation has got to do better," Dad explained. "The girls, they have to be able to do more."

"Well," said Mom, "I'm not an educated woman, as everybody knows, but . . ."

Mom had left school not, like some of the other girls that everybody could have pointed out by name, because she had to. She wasn't pregnant; she wasn't desperate. She was only a woman who'd fallen in love. And she had been bound and determined that my father would marry her before he set out on one of his sales trips and got hooked by somebody else, before he went off down the road and maybe didn't come back, before he had a chance to stop and think and even find a reason for a painful change of heart. Mom made sure that she was onto him nice and tight; she had rendered herself completely necessary to him, made herself into someone he would think that he could never bear to do without.

She had wanted to live in his house and sleep in his bed, cook his meals, wash his clothes, iron his shirts, sew up the holes in his socks. Be a mother to his kids. That was all.

"And, you tell me now, what do you see is the matter with that?" she shouted, heaving one of his shoes that missed his body by a mile and sank instead into the pile of pillows on their bed.

Maybe there was nothing the matter with it. Maybe it was just fine. But it wasn't how things were going to go for me and Jewel. Not if our daddy had anything to say. Not if my father had his way.

But you can't love somebody into living the life that you've been wishing they could have. You can't endear a dream to them just on the strength of how much you maybe think you care.

And, I guess it's true, even before I met Galen, I never did intend to do what I knew my father was expecting me to do. I never wanted to have to leave this place. I couldn't imagine myself going anywhere else. I couldn't picture me living in a school dormitory on the manicured college campus of some little town somewhere. Reading all those books, listening to some old man's lectures, writing down pages of notes, coming up with the answers to complicated questions, taking all the little quizzes and tests. I would not have known how to live in an apartment on the sixty-first floor of a black glass building in Chicago. With windows that don't open and landscape that isn't clear. I wouldn't have been happy at a desk job, going out for lunch with my boss, shopping for dresses in department stores, eating dinners in restaurants with linen tablecloths and silver spoons and china plates.

And, as it turned out, I didn't have to do any of those things. Because there was Galen Wheeler, and then all my daddy's plans for me got changed.

Galen Wheeler came into my life like a falling star, all heat and light and pangs for the hope that my most brilliant wishes could be coming true.

"Don't reach out too high, girls," our mother had warned us. "Take good care that you don't go asking for too many things; don't go looking for too much. Don't make your dreams so difficult that there isn't a way in the world for them ever to turn out real."

And yet Jewel had gone away to Chicago to school. She had a part-time job with Uncle Charlie in his insurance offices, but she came back home to us again anyway. After only her first year there she had met Clayton Jenkins, and then she married him. My sister brought her husband home with her to Harmony like he was a prize she'd picked up at some game of chance, on the midway at the fair.

After I graduated from high school I was eighteen, and the money that Mimi had put aside for me was mine to spend any way I wanted to — whether I chose to do what Jewel did and move away from Harmony and go to school, or no.

"Maybe not right away," I told my dad. "Maybe I'll just wait awhile first." I took a job with the bank here, in the loan department. I was just a file girl, because I knew the alphabet all right and I was pretty enough to look at even first thing in the morning, when the collection men came in and started to make their early calls. I made the coffee and brought in the cart of doughnuts and breakfast rolls. It was my job to keep track of the files, bring them out when someone needed one and put it back again in the right place when they were done.

The men that I worked for had basically three parts to their jobs, and like a wheel spinning around and around, like a dog chasing after the wag in his own tail, one part of the work led to the next part, and then to the next, and then it started all over at the beginning again.

First we would arrange for the bank to give out loans to the families from around here who came in and applied. Sometimes people might be buying a new car or a boat, sometimes it was a mortgage on a house or the financing on a piece of farm equipment, a combine or a tractor or a picker or a plow. Then after a little while went by, usually some of those folks would have hit rough times for one reason or another — not enough rain, a bad storm, some depression in the economy, whatever it might be — there were a million ways for a family's checking account to all of a sudden come up short. And when that happened, whatever luxury had been bought with the loan, well, that was always the first thing to get dropped out of the overall financial plan.

And then the men in our loan department worked as collectors for the bank. They spent hours on the telephone tracking down any person who had missed some payments, or who had been consistent about coming in late with the check. They threatened the repossession of cars and houses and boats and campers.

They did give a sympathetic ear to the excuses they were given, the stories they were told. Everybody understood how it could be for a person who was down on his luck. But business was business, and so after lunch, the men had to leave their desks and go out to collect. They brought back all kinds of collateral — deeds to houses, stock certificates, brand-new appliances, power tools, jewelry, antique furniture, boats and snowmobiles and jet skis. Sometimes if it was a car or a truck that they had taken, they might keep that to themselves for a day of fast driving along the county roads before they turned it over to the attendant in the vacant lot across the alley from the bank.

But no matter what it was that they brought back, still the next morning there these men would be, back in the office again, stirring the spoonfuls of cream and sugar into their coffee, munching on the doughnuts I'd brought them, working to figure out how they might offer these same people the benefit of another small loan.

One of the men that I worked with then was named Wade Roberts, and after I'd been with the bank for almost a year, I started going out with him now and again, for dinner or to see a movie, and even though I didn't really like him too much and the truth was he didn't like me too much either, still we kept seeing each other because Harmony is a small enough town, and there aren't so many people here that you can be all that choosy about who your friends are or what kind of company you think you'd like to keep.

Wade Roberts was a lake kid just the same as me. He was closer to Jewel's age — a plain-looking boy with a bland white face and brown hair and green eyes and not too much imagination either, who still lived with his mother and his older sister in their farmhouse off the main lake road.

Wade said that what he liked about his job at the bank, besides the regular hours and the benefits and the paychecks that came with such reliability every week, was the challenge of manipulating numbers to make a family's income look its very best. He said that the loan department gave him a chance to be the one who could fulfill some people's fondest wishes, make their wildest dreams come true. He loved it that he was the one who made it possible for a farmer to buy that fancy piece of equipment he'd been wanting, or for a young man to get that car or boat he'd always hoped for, a family to begin to make the payments on that camper that they'd had their eye on for a while.

"I'm like a Santa Claus or something in the eyes of some of these folks, Clodine," he told me. "Why, they look at me like I'm a kind of friendly wizard, a person who has it in his power to work miracles for them, reward them with luxuries that they always wished for but never really expected to be able to afford."

But I think that the truth of it was that what gave Wade a greater pleasure than that, what he enjoyed seeing even more than all those bright smiles of relief and gratitude that people flashed over at him across his desk, was their darker, more hidden glance of fear.

Wade's job as a loan officer, like that of any kind of a benefactor, gained him some control over all these other people's lives. What Wade gave them was maybe what they wanted, but they paid for it with the encumbrance of a debt and the threat that they might just lose everything back to him some rainy day. And then Wade Roberts really loved it that he'd been put into the position where he could give out some orders, teach a family a lesson if he thought they needed it, tell a man who was older than he was what he was going to have to do.

Wade claimed that it truly did pain him sometimes to have to come in and take a person's best things away from him, but he argued that sometimes there was no way around it, it just had to be done, for the benefit of everyone involved. When he talked that way I thought he took on the stance and the tone of a domineering parent who is scolding the child who has dared to disobey. Wade Roberts punished people by confiscating all their toys.

It was early in December, and Wade had offered to drive me home after work in one of the luxury cars that he'd taken in that day. It gets so dark so early here at that time of year. The days are so short. We came to the bank in the murk before the sun was up, and went home again at twilight. Almost all the time, it seemed, there was no sunshine, only night.

So, by the time Wade and I left the office together, it was dusk. And then when he pulled the car over off Edgewater Road on the bluff behind the empty fairgrounds, already he had the headlights on, and all around us it was pitch dark. And it had begun to snow.

"We should go home, Wade," I told him.

We sat side by side there with the motor running and the radio murmuring, hundreds of snowflakes tumbling toward us, silently slapping the smooth curved surface of the windshield. It was too dark to see much beyond the beam of the headlights to the lake. And I knew that my parents would be wondering where I was. Mom might stand at the window in the darkened living room, watching the street. Daddy might have folded his newspaper over his knee, listening for the sound of my footsteps on the porch.

The car that Wade had taken that day was a huge gray Lincoln Continental, with leather upholstery on the dashboard, black velvet over the seats, plush carpeting on the floor. Wade leaned toward me. He turned me and pushed my shoulders back against the door. It felt like we were encapsulated there, wrapped together like bugs in a soft cocoon, insulated from the outside world, sheltered from the dark and the cold and the snow that was falling, the wind that blew through the trees beyond the shiny glass windows of the car.

Wade was kissing me. But his lips pressed there against my throat were giving me creeps, goose bumps and shivers, until I thought I couldn't stand the sound or the sense of it anymore. When he wormed his tongue around, loud and wet and sloppy inside the hollow of my ear, it felt to me just like a fish that wound through the rocks and weeds in the shallow water at the edges of the lake.

I was picturing a whole lifetime of me bound up with Wade Roberts. Moving through the rooms of his old house out there in the middle of nowhere, with his mother and his sister shut away behind the doors of their own rooms upstairs. Bringing up his bland-faced babies, holding their heavy bodies like sacks of flour in my arms. Cooking his meals, washing his underwear, folding his socks. Sleeping every night beside Wade in his bed while he savored his own stories about some dumb families who had found themselves so much worse off than us. Driving around these back roads with him in some poor stupid fellow's brand-new repossessed car.

And before I really knew what I was doing, I was arching back and rolling out from under Wade's embrace. I pried his fingers off my arm. I pushed his face away. On my knees on the floor of that car, I was fumbling with the door handle and then I was stumbling away across the gauzy snow.

I scrambled up the ditch to the shoulder of the main road and was caught there, in the glare of the lights from a snowplow as it bore down upon me at a terrifying speed with the roar of a wild animal.

Well, it turned out that was Galen Wheeler there behind the controls of that plow. He managed to swerve around me and pull up to a stop. He hopped down and ran back to me.

His eyes were so blue, they were like ice. And his face was sweet, kind-looking, gentle and nice. He was very soft-spoken, polite, careful of what he asked me, about how much he said.

He hovered near enough to me that I could smell him, the fragrance of his body, and the scent of his cologne. He put his thumb under my chin and tilted my face up toward his. He kicked at the snow with the toe of his boot. When he smiled it seemed like a star had opened up inside his face, bright enough to shine with some warmth and sparkle over onto mine.

When I told him what had happened, he lifted me up onto the snowplow, and together we watched as Wade Roberts came tearing back out onto the road and then skidded off the other way, fishtailing in that big Lincoln so the back end of it waggled, like it was scolding us. The red glow from the brake lights was spilled out like blood against the surface of fresh snow.

And then Galen Wheeler drove me home.

Oh, but Daddy was so mad. I had never in my life seen him like that before, or anyway not with me. He grabbed me by the arm and he shook me, he was that angry. This was something different from when he fought and yelled at my mother. He was grinding his teeth, and he kept slapping his hands on his thighs.

He shouted, "Never pull a stupid stunt like that again, Clodine."

My mother stood there in the doorway, framed under the hall light with the collar of her robe pulled up snug under her chin. Her hair stuck out in tufts around her face, and her eyes were glittery with anxiety and fear.

"We didn't know where you were," she whispered. She reached her hand out and laid it flat against my cheek. "We were so worried. We thought something might have happened to you. When you didn't come home from work, we could only imagine the worst."

When we were alone, later, I told her that I'd never seen my father as furious as that. My arm was bruised and sore from his fingers where he'd held me.

"I guess the truth of it is, Clodine," my mother answered me, "that you really should feel complimented. Because you know the only thing that makes your father so mad is he loves you that much. Don't say I said it, I'll deny it if you do, but the fact is he has always, since you were a little baby, held you special, Clodine. He's loved you the best. And if anything were ever to happen to you . . ." She paused and shook her head, and looked off past me, through the curtains, beyond the window, into the shadows of the night.

"Well, there is just no telling what your daddy might do."

And then I despised her for that. I held my mother suspect for what she had told me. I hated her for trying to make me believe that my father loved me more than he loved Jewel. I thought about my sister, and it didn't seem right, and I knew it wasn't fair. Let him love her best, I was thinking. Let him worry over her. Let her be the one that he gets mad at.

It seemed to me that Jewel always got to do what she wanted, only because Daddy didn't care as much. All I wanted was the same kind of opening so I could go about living my life, too. I never asked to be my daddy's favorite. I only wanted some freedom. I was only asking for him to give me up. I wanted to be left alone.

And so maybe it began to seem that how much my father loved me became a burden then. Something like a handicap, like being blind, or deaf, or crippled, that I would just have to learn to live with — something that I would have to work to break away from or give in and find a way to bear.

I kept seeing Galen after that. First he called me. He found out who I was and where I lived, and then he had a reason to be driving his truck up and down outside my house, along my street.

I was happy just to look at him. His body fascinated me, the way he held himself, the way he moved. His hands seemed graceful and strong, both at the same time. He knew so much about so many different things. I liked the way it felt when his eyes met mine. I was wallowing in the attention he paid me. And I was constantly surprised by the miracle that he was still interested in me, that he might be able to like me just as much right back.

I put my fingers on the hard ripple of muscle on his shoulder. I kissed his throat, felt the blue vein pulsing there. I ran my hands along the hardness of his back. My face bore the sand-papery roughness of his cheeks. His smile seemed like it was a gift for me.

It really did just seem like I couldn't get enough of him. He called me in the morning. We went to the lake for a picnic lunch. He took me swimming in the afternoon. Out for ice cream after dinner. A drive. The movies. Some nights I didn't come in the front door again until long past midnight.

And I guess our behavior then was good for fueling plenty of my parents' arguments after that.

"He's a fine boy," my mother said. "Good-looking, well-mannered, polite. He has a little money. And he works hard, too."

But ever since that first night, my father did not like Galen. Something about him rubbed Daddy wrong. Or something about me, when I was with him.

Galen was working at all kinds of jobs then. He never had known how to stay with one single thing. He didn't like the idea of a person being held down by how he made his living, he explained. He didn't want to be characterized by what he did, like a lawyer or a doctor or a teacher. People were always thinking that they could tell something special about a person just by knowing what his occupation was.

So Galen took whatever work was handy.

"I'm a lineman," he would say. Or "Oh, well, I drive a plow."

And that was true—he did operate the snowplow on the roads in and around Harmony during the wintertime, whenever there was snow. He kept a job with the power company for a while, stringing up the electric wires between poles put up all along the edges of the fields. The Lake Commission hired him to fix fences one year. And he worked for the Fire Department whenever they asked him, helping to burn back a farmer's field or sandbagging the river when it was threatening to flood.

"I'm a fireman," he'd tell one person. "A farmer," he might say to the next.

Galen would take on any job you could think of, as long as it was something he could do outside.

"Just don't try and lock me up in an office somewhere," Galen said to my father with a smile. "I don't want to be tied to a telephone and a desk."

"It'll never work out," my dad predicted.

"Now, Jack," my mother argued, shaking her head at him, pursing up her lips, sucking on her teeth, "how in the world do you think you can tell what's going to work out and what won't?"

"He'll dump her, Maggie," Dad answered. "I know the type. Believe me. He'll get an itch and then he'll move on. He's a drifter. He has no family. He's got no roots. He doesn't know what he wants to do."

"What about your future?" Dad asked me. "What about all your plans?"

"What plans?" my mother asked. "Why can't these be her plans?"

"Maybe you'll have to learn it the hard way," he shouted at me. "But don't come crying to me, Clodine. Don't look to me to pick up the pieces when you fall."

"Don't be stupid," my mother warned him. "Galen Wheeler's a fine catch for any girl. And anyway, Clodine's in love. Aren't you, honey? Can't you see that? Leave them alone. You ought to know better. She's old enough. What you need to do is just let them be."

"And let her ruin her life?"

"Oh, like I ruined mine, I suppose? Or Jewel ruined hers?"

"I didn't say that."

"No, but that's what you meant."

"You just don't get it, Maggie, do you?"

"Where are you going? Don't you turn your back on me!"

"I'll do whatever I goddamn please!"

"Oh, no you won't."

"Yeah? Who's going to stop me?"

"Me."

"You? How?"

"Just try me, Jack."

"I'm trying."

"Don't push me."

"I'll push you."

And he reached behind him, groped for the knob, pulled shut their bedroom door.

But my father would not quit, and he finally got to be so forceful about how he wanted to get me to see his side, that it came to be almost like it was a challenge. He got so afraid of what he was seeing grow there between Galen and me. He could feel the way that I was always waiting for him. How I hung on his every word, wished for the phone to ring, perked up at the sound of the truck pulling into the driveway outside our house. It felt like Daddy was daring me to defy him. Trying to engage me in a battle of some kind. And taking a big chance that I might decide to fight him back.

"Is all of this really necessary, sir?" Galen asked. "Can't we be civil, talk it over, work it out between us, man to man? I love your daughter, Mr. Ferring. And I believe she loves me, too."

Daddy's answer was that I had to start coming in earlier, begin keeping better track of the time, stay closer to home, see more people, make some new friends. Finally he made it that I wasn't allowed to take a step outside the house at all. He left the telephone off the hook. He shouted at Galen. Turned off all the lights in the house. Slammed the door in Galen's face. He hid me away upstairs, locked me up in my room.

Galen and I went out to Lakeside one night when the fair was there. I was wearing a new dress. It was sleeveless blue cotton with white stars printed on it. It had a low neck, and it zipped up the back. I had on stockings and sandals with broad leather straps and thick heels, and a snow white ribbon tied in my hair.

Galen played one game and won a little pink dog. We drove

the bumper cars, threw baseballs at the clown in the dunk tank, let a woman in a shimmery gold dress guess our age and estimate our weight.

When we rode the Ferris wheel around, the operator stopped us at the top, and there was Harmony spread out so far away and small below us that it didn't even look to me like it could be real. We leaned out over the safety bar and watched the tiny people milling down below. The lake glistening. The dead trees in silhouette, like soldiers lined up on the horizon. The twinkle lights made it feel to me like Christmas, never mind how hot it was. There was music and people laughing, voices shouting, but nobody was angry, none of it was mad. There was a thick smell of dust and straw, sweat and burned sugar.

Galen rocked the chair with his body, scaring me. I clasped his arm, pressed my cheek against his chest. He reached over and pulled the ribbon from my hair. He dangled it, waved it, and then he opened his fingers and let it drop. We watched it drift away; caught and lifted in shafts of warm air rising, it wafted, sailing, floating down into the crowd and out of sight.

Later, on the front seat of his truck, Galen unzipped my starry blue dress and pulled off my bra, and he cupped his hands around my breasts so gently that for a while I forgot what it was like to breathe.

Jewel did tell my parents; she warned them. When my father tried to come between me and Galen Wheeler, when he locked me up in my room, when he unplugged the phone and took away the car keys and said that I was not allowed to be with Galen, Jewel cautioned him.

"Don't say that to Clo, Daddy. Don't tell her such a thing. You might just as well be putting your blessing on it," Jewel said, "as to say to Clo the word no. Same thing as making her promise that then she'd have to go and do it, too."

So, now that I can look back over it, put what has happened into some kind of perspective, look down on it like from the top of the Ferris wheel, get a real picture of the way things have gone, how my life so far has turned out, I can wonder if maybe what Jewel was always telling us is in some way actually true. That maybe she's right, and maybe it really was only the fact that Daddy kept saying over and over again how I'd better just not that drove me to run off and get myself married to Galen.

It was in August that we decided we would elope. We drove away, out of Harmony in Galen's old white truck, all the way to the city hall in downtown Harlan, and when we came back home again, we had a piece of paper that said I was Galen Wheeler's wife. I moved out of my father's house, and I quit my job at the bank. I took my grandmother's money, and I bought a cottage for Galen and me to live in together by the lake.

One thing I will say about Jewel, and that is, she does know how to cook. She doesn't make things the way our mother did. What Jewel fixes is not like anything I've ever had before. It's different, experimental sometimes — she likes to say it is gourmet, not the usual pot roast and meat loaf, tuna casserole and corn on the cob. Jewel doesn't buy cookbooks, even. She doesn't follow recipes. She just makes things up as she goes along, using what she finds in the cupboards and the refrigerator and even the back yard. She calls this making do with what you've got.

She keeps a garden, and she gathers fresh vegetables — eggplant and zucchini, green peppers, tomatoes, carrots and cabbage — and herbs — peppermint and wintergreen, sage and parsley and chervil and cilantro and dill — and she mixes them up with lemon juice and brown mustard, sour cream and vinegar and yogurt. She broils a breast of chicken; she roasts a leg of lamb. She adds strawberries to her spinach salad; she garnishes our plates with purple heartsease and yellow nasturtiums, beet greens, sunflower seeds, and nuts.

The dinners that Jewel prepares are always healthy. She makes things that are good for you, and eating it all, every bite, picking up the last bits with the back of my fork, somehow leaves me feeling satisfied but chaste, purified and cleansed.

Emma likes it that Jewel has asked her to help. My little girl stands in the kitchen with her cousins, on tiptoes on the top rung of the step stool and tears big leaves of Boston lettuce into little bits.

"Keep them bite-sized, Emma," Jewel says. "Not too big, but not too small."

And somehow Emma is able to judge just the right compromise between what is bite-sized for her, and what will be bite-sized for Clayton. When she stands next to him, he puts his hand there on top of her head, and it seems to me as if he is pressing her down, holding her in place. She accepts his touch and nuzzles comfortably against it.

Emma is wearing the red polish that Mary Alice has painted on the small pale petals of her nails.

And I'm sitting here at the little table by the window in Jewel's kitchen, fingering the gold confetti flecks in the Formica while she stands at the sink, cleaning carrots and slicing tomatoes.

I'm a widow now. Galen Wheeler is dead. For me, it's all begun to unravel, to fall apart. I feel as if I've come unglued, unhinged, undone. Through a prism of tears, it looks as if my whole life has been shattered, broken into pieces, shards and fragments sharp enough to cut me right through to the bone.

I eye the scar on my finger, from where I hurt it so badly that time, on the sharp metal blades of the fan my daddy had. It's long and thin and white, slightly curled, like a small worm, like a wedding band, and I can see that it rings my knuckle almost all of the whole way around.

7

THEY DON'T wanna have nothing in this world to do with a girl like me, so why should those women expect me to try and make friends with them?"

Lilly Duke was standing in the kitchen of her cabin, bold and defiant, with her shoulders back and her knees locked and her feet apart, toes bare against the jagged holes in the torn linoleum floor. She brandished a long slotted metal spoon in one hand; the fingers of the other were splayed out against her hip.

Lilly had tied a red bandanna back in a vain attempt to hold down her wild hair. Over the summer it had grown, and she had hacked away at it with an old pair of scissors she'd found in one of the kitchen drawers. Big tufts of it stood straight up at the back of her head. She had entwined some of the longer strands in a thin braid that hung down between her shoulder blades, along the narrow ridge of her spine. She was cooking a beef bone in a big iron pot on the stove behind her, and the broth boiled up so furiously that her face was flushed with the heat and her head and shoulders were framed by a billowing cloud of steam.

I had been doing my best to get her to take some of my good advice. I was hoping to convince her that maybe she should work on loosening herself up a little, make an attempt anyway at being friendlier, at least say hello to people, good morning, hi, smile and nod, start a conversation, comment on the weather, the color of the sky. She could let the women look at her baby, curl their hands around his feet, cup a palm against the smooth orb of his head, measure his weight in their own arms, cradle his bulk in their empty laps.

Some of these women — Rena Zurn and Jewel Jenkins, Agatha Pajek, Elana Forester, Gracie Wilson, Nancy Withers, and Ivy Lazelle — they had all had babies of their own at one time. They were mothers; they had raised children; they could be sympathetic in that way.

I was explaining to Lilly that they wouldn't talk about her so much if she wasn't always giving them something interesting to say.

"You don't have to keep yourself so separate," I told her.

"They scorn me, Clodine," she answered, widening her eyes, running her tongue along the sharp edges of her teeth.

Lilly's family had not had the money or the inclination to waste their time on cosmetic concerns. She had never worn braces, and her front teeth lapped over each other slightly, in such a way that her top lip seemed a little swollen, tender and bruised.

"I don't see that I have any other choice except to scorn them right back." She smiled and raised the spoon, waved it in the air, stirred the steam. "Tit for tat."

She claimed that she could actually feel these Harmony women looking — she sensed the heat of their gaze against her shoulders, watching her while she shopped through Pajek's store. She saw their eyes skitter over her; they lowered their chins, studied the floor, examined their own feet, turned and ducked away. Lilly could hear them whispering, hissing behind her back, like snakes.

*

Jewel among them, of course. Jewel was one of the first to start the talking, to tell the stories — about Tim Duke and his crime, about Lilly and how she had loved him, shamelessly, what the papers and even magazines had to say about it, how she went to visit him in jail, at the time of the trial, how they said she wore a skirt and no underpants, sat on his lap one afternoon during visiting hours and conceived a baby that way there.

"A murderer's child," Jewel liked to say, her eyes narrowing with the nastiness of it, the thrill. "Conceived in cold blood." She flared her nostrils in distaste.

Clayton, always serene, always firm, reached for her, brushed her shoulder with his fingertips, meant to steady her with the sureness of his touch.

"Jewel," he would murmur, trying to warn her when he thought she had begun to take it just one step too far.

You could see the pink circles that burned in her cheeks. The cords in her neck stood out, her hands fluttered, restless as leaves, loose in a wild wind.

What fascinated Jewel, even more than the scandal of it, even more than the wickedness, was the ignorance and the innocence, the pure simplicity of Lilly Duke. She just couldn't believe it, she said, that any girl could ever be so dumb as that Lilly Duke. Simpleminded. Stupid. Ignorant. Dimwitted and dull.

"I hate to use the word sin, Clodine," Jewel argued earnestly. "I don't mean to cast judgment. Or blame. Really, I don't. But, honey, look, you just gotta admit . . ."

Here's why. Timothy Duke had murdered a man. Then, right after — the body wasn't even cold yet in the ditch where Tim had dumped it, off a side road in the middle of the cornfields of Nebraska — he latched onto Lilly Vernon, found her at the lunch counter in a five-and-ten-cent store, bought her a Coke, looked her in the face, brushed the hair away from out of her eyes, touched her cheek, put his arm over her shoulder, held her hand, saw the white scars there on her wrists, kissed her on the mouth, and then took her off with him, running as fast as he could from the law that pretty soon was trying its best to catch up with them both. And when the police finally did get their hands on the pair, Tim was arrested for kidnapping and murder. He went to jail, was tried, found guilty, sentenced to death, and still this stupid Lilly Vernon was fool enough to fall in love with a killer, take his name for her own, and then get pregnant and have his bastard kid!

Jewel made the exclamation point with her body, standing on her tippy toes, wrapping her arms over and around her head. She let her jaw hang with her disbelief at the idea of this whole absurd tale. She dropped her arms and lowered her head and shook it.

"Go figure," said Jewel.

She jutted out her bottom lip and whoofed a breath of air out onto her own face, hard enough to make the bangs on her forehead puff up.

"I took one life, but then I saved another," Tim was quoted as saying in the transcripts of the trial. "It's true, I don't deny it, I killed Raymond Pilcher. Kidnapped him in his own car, shot him in the back of the head, three times, and rolled him over, left him for dead in a ditch. But, won't anybody see this, I also at the same time rescued Lilly Vernon? That my coming along actually saved her from herself, from her stepdad, from a life that was leading her down a long slow road to nowhere? Or worse? It was me who kept Lilly from trying to kill herself again. It was Tim Duke who gave her a good reason to keep herself alive. That has to count for something, I would think. Doesn't it? I mean, isn't there some redeeming factor here in that?"

His lawyer had fully expected that the judge would see some mitigating circumstance in this and settle on giving Tim life.

When the death sentence came down, both men were said to be solemn and breathless, surprised, shaken and pale.

━━◇◇━━

Before she met Tim Duke and got her whole life turned around and upside down — started over was how she put it, so she could begin to believe that maybe there was some purpose to it after all, some meaning in it, some reason to go on — Lilly Vernon had been living with her mother and stepfather in a farmhouse on the outskirts of the midsize city of Fremont, Nebraska. A victim of the worst kinds of abuse at the hands of her mother's husband — another ignoramus, Jewel said, judging by the photos of him in the news, his face all puffy and swollen from drink, the way he held his shoulders back, let his belly hang out over the thick brass buckle of his belt, took off the greasy baseball cap and ran his trembly thick fingers through the curly, sun-bleached wisps of his hair — Lilly had quit school twice and tried to kill herself three times before she'd even turned seventeen.

The first time she had swallowed up two whole bottles of aspirin and then had to suffer the awful indignity of having her stomach pumped in the emergency room of the county hospital in Fremont.

The second time she cut her wrists, but she was rescued by a gas station attendant who found her bleeding in the bathroom, sitting on the toilet, just about passed out, with her hands held under the trickle of warm water that was running into the sink, mixing in pink with the heavier flow of Lilly's bright red blood.

The third time she really did almost make it — because one of the girls that she met in the therapy sessions at the hospital after the second time had told her that if she really meant to slit her wrists and do the job right she would have to learn to make the cuts run up and down and not across. The stepfather himself found her that time and, after wrapping her arms up tight in the shreds of his own underwear, he rushed her to the hospital in the middle of the night.

"He just happened to go into her bedroom and check on her," Lilly's mother was filmed explaining to the news reporters after Tim was caught. "I can't say why. Only God knows what made him do it, but he woke up guessing something was not right and he thought he'd better have a look-see. It was like he had ESP or something crazy that way, you know. But of course, he always has been real close to her anyway, even if he isn't her real dad or anything—they have this same wavelength is how he puts it—so I guess maybe he did have some kind of a sense about what she might be up to. Me, I'd quit trying long before. I gave up worrying about her. She's my only daughter, I know, but that girl, heck, she'd done it twice too many times already, as far as I was concerned. And why? For what good reason? Well, by then I was seriously considering the idea that I'd just have to leave her be, let her have her way if that was what she meant to do. The hell with her then, you know?"

The surfaces of Lilly's inner arms were swirled with pale raised scars and thin blue veins. She had hoped to defy her stepfather, answer his lust with her own death. And yet, each time she tried it she had somehow failed, been found, rescued, treated, and released. In spite of her best efforts, Lilly had survived, and Tim tried to tell her that it was fate that was only saving her up, keeping her alive, setting her aside for when the time was right for him.

So Lilly went off to the hospital for the third time and accepted the blood transfusions and the psychiatrist's evaluations, and the therapy sessions, and when she had recovered enough to be let out of the house on her own for a few hours in the afternoon, she rode the city bus downtown and went shopping in the discount stores for some new clothes, shoes, a pretty shade of pink lipstick that she'd admired on another girl, and before she got back on the bus to ride it home again, she took a minute to sit down and relax, have a cigarette and a Coke at the lunch counter at the five-and-ten. It was there that she met Tim Duke. He took the stool next to hers, put his elbows down on the counter, and ordered a meat loaf sandwich. He was already a killer by then, on the run from the law that hadn't even discovered yet the terrible full extent of his crime.

Tim Duke had gone into a car lot in Omaha, Nebraska, and, after looking at several models and makes, he asked to test-drive the black convertible sports car they had on display there in the showroom window. The salesman, Raymond Everett Pilcher, fifty-nine years old with his youngest son still in college and a wife who worked teaching second graders at one of the local schools, had agreed to let Tim take the car out for a spin. His knees stiff and cracking, Raymond stooped and wedged himself into the passenger seat of the little car, where he sat next to Tim with one elbow hanging out over the door, his gold watch gleaming in the broad summer sunshine, wedding ring flashing, and he continued with his pitch, explaining about the fifth gear, overdrive, riding the clutch real easy, the air conditioner, the radio, telling Tim to turn right here, now take a left.

"Feel that torque, son? Notice the suspension? Nice and tight, lithe as a virgin, supple as a teenage girl. Gives me a hard-on just to be sitting here, don't you know? Did you ever in your life take a ride in anything so powerful and at the same time so quiet and so smooth? Like a kitten, she is," he said. Grinning, laughing, he threw back his head and smacked the passenger door with the broad flat of his hand — until they were out on the highway, where Tim could really open her up and let that baby fly.

And then, Tim said later, bewildered by it still, long after it was past, there was something that happened, with the wind in his face and his hair blown back, the engine purring at his feet, the wheel so easy in his hands, the highway rolling out from under him, something so free about the road and the radio, turned way up, blasting — "That speaker system, son, it's state of the art, can you hear how clear?"—something that came down over him, or surged up in him, like a wave, like a rush of fresh air, a tornado blowing so hard through the emptiness of his soul that he could feel its terrible roar. Then the next thing he knows he's slowed down and pulled off onto a dirt road and forced poor Raymond Pilcher out of the car, turned him around and shot him point-blank—boom! boom! boom!—three times in the back of the head.

Tim rolled the crumpled body down into the deep weeds beside the ditch and left it there. He wiped his hands off on the grass and heaved the gun hard, tumbled it up high against the blue sky, over a fence far into the cornfield. He climbed back into the black convertible, and, his blood still humming, hot in his head, he took off down the highway to the Interstate south to Lincoln and then north again on Old Highway 30 until finally, out of gas and tired and hungry, and maybe even getting scared, he stopped in the town of Fremont, where he found his Lillyheart sitting there alone at the lunch counter in the five-and-ten, smoking a cigarette and sipping on a Coke and wondering whatever in the world there could be left for her to do with herself now.

They were on the run for one week. Headed northeast on Old Highway 30, they crossed over the Missouri River into Iowa. Seven days and seven nights, that was all.

"How do you fall in love with a guy in only seven days?" Jewel wanted to know. "Lust, maybe, but love? Uh-uh." She shook her head. "No."

But Lilly called it love, and so did Tim. They were soulmates, he said. She felt as if she had found a long-lost friend, sitting in that car, his arm around her, the fields rolling past, small towns a blur, the radio always on, playing love songs, a background score that made the whole trip seem like it was a movie she was watching on a screen at a drive-in theater somewhere.

They stayed in motels. Ate at coffee shops and diners. Filled up on hamburgers and French fries and Cokes.

"Oh, yeah, we were scared," Lilly said. "I was scared. This was a real adventure for me. The real thing. And I was afraid because there I was, dropping everything, running away. I thought my stepdad might come after me. I wasn't sure how mad he'd be. And I really didn't know then, either, how well I could trust Tim. He was scared for other reasons, I guess. I found out later, Tim had other worries than I did on his mind."

Scared, but alive. Lilly was filled with a terrific sense of her own life. Her own heartbeat, her own pulse, her own spirit and breath. And now it was a life that she could care about. For once Lilly Vernon had a value that had never been recognized by her before. Now she could thank God that she hadn't died those other times.

"Just imagine, Clodine," she said to me, "all the things I might have missed."

Tim made love to her on a creekbed, in a cornfield, one time right there in the car.

"That was how she learned to do it sitting on his lap, I bet," Jewel said, smirking. "It'd be those fancy bucket seats."

They stayed one night in Harmony, in his grandmother's cottage by the lake. Then when Tim was finally caught, outside Des Moines, trying to cash a check in a convenience store, Lilly claimed that she was ignorant and innocent, she didn't know a thing.

"I thought the car belonged to him," she swore, under oath. "He told me we were headed for the East Coast, New York, where he had a job with the company that does those funny beer ads. You know, the ones with the ugly dog?"

"Advertising!" Jewel exclaimed. "Beer commercials! How stupid can you get?"

Lilly was not an accomplice, and during the trial she continued to see Tim, she sent him letters, passed notes to him through his attorneys, visited him in jail.

"I love him anyway," she said, surrounded by reporters on the courthouse steps. "I don't care what he did or didn't do. Besides, I'm used to this. I've always, my whole life, had to settle for taking things marked 'as is.' "

By then she was already pregnant. And although they weren't legally married, she took his name anyway, started calling herself Lilly Duke, spelling it out for the reporters, just to make sure they got it right. And Tim Duke was convicted of kidnapping and murder and car theft and crossing state lines and trying to cash a bad check. And the judge had sentenced him to die.

Lilly kept a scrapbook. She had pasted in its pages matchbooks and menus, the *Do Not Disturb* signs from the motels where they stayed. The letters he wrote to her — *My beloved Lillyheart.* Newspaper clippings. Magazine articles. A note from his lawyer. A valentine that Tim had made for her out of yellow legal paper, folded over twice and torn into the shape of a hollow heart.

She told me she was keeping these mementos for her son. She was hanging on to them so he would see how it had been for her and for Tim. And who knew, she added, scheming, sly, maybe there would be some money in it somewhere, too. Maybe this stuff would have some value in the future. Be worth something to somebody, in the years after Tim was dead.

"It's history, you know," she said. "A part of the past. The American Dream gone foul."

Lilly continued to be adamant about her own innocence in anything criminal.

"I didn't know," Lilly claimed. "I never knew he killed anybody. He never mentioned it. It never came up. I just loved him, that was all. He wasn't anything like a murderer with me. He never tried to hurt me. He wasn't violent or rough or mean.

He wouldn't know how to be cruel. He was nothing at all but loving and gentle and kind."

She narrowed her eyes.

"He's my husband," Lilly insisted. "He's the father of this child."

The baby bounced on her hip, reached up and pulled at the red bandanna in her hair.

And I could only think how young she looked. The freckles on her nose. Her thin fingers, the narrow span of her shoulders, the firm sweep of her throat.

A baby with a baby, I was thinking. A child with a child.

"You imagine we don't know what you've been up to, Clodine?"

Jewel said she was only trying to look out for me. Because she loves me, she said. Because I'm her sister, and we're family, and she owes it to Mom and Dad.

"Even Galen thinks what you're doing is crazy, Clo. He said so to Clayton himself. He told him you've been over to see her just about every day. He put it that the two of you are like sisters. Thick as thieves."

We were having a Christmas cookie exchange at my house. Each woman baked ten dozen of her favorite cookies and then we could all go home with a sampling of every kind.

I had set out my Christmas creamer and sugar bowl set — thin white china with a decorated noble fir painted on the side, its arms outstretched protectively over a tumbling pile of teddy bears and toy trucks, a thin billowing red ribbon trim around the edges, holly leaves fanned like hands upon the lid — but Jewel stood in my kitchen with the refrigerator door propped open against her shoulder, and she poured the half-and-half right from the carton into her coffee cup and then used a spoon with a grinning porcelain Santa Claus handle to stir.

"Clayton's worried, too," she said. "Really he is. He says that you should know she's just another common criminal, like any other one, and probably she'll do something to you sometime that will only make you sorry that you ever let her get to know your name."

She looked up from the cloudy swirl of milk and coffee and laid the spoon down on the counter.

"You know I'm only trying to tell you what I think is right. In your best interests, Clodine. I'm on your side. I'm your sister, kiddo. And I care about you. Really I do."

And I felt the bruises on my leg, tender purple flowers that were blooming on my thigh, above the knee, spread out upon the surface of my skin in the unmistakable shape of the palm side of Galen Wheeler's hard hand.

Agatha Pajek had been saying that, well, at least Lilly paid her bills. Nancy Withers pointed out that the baby was a bastard, no matter what name Lilly used. And if Harmony was going to be famous, in the newspapers and on the TV, she hated to think that it would be for something as disagreeable as this. Ivy Lazelle tried keeping track of what kinds of things Lilly was buying at Pajek's store, and she judged her on her choice of fruits and what brand of soap she used.

And I was beginning to sense the weight of their silence my-self by that time, too — when I came into the store, or at the Supper Club with Galen, how they stopped talking. They turned away to straighten the cans on the shelves; they studied the meat on their plates or the ice in their drinks; they looked at me only after I'd already turned away. Because Jewel had been telling them, of course, that Lilly and I were friends. That I had brought her a bicycle and a dog and chickens and a radio. That I was listening to her story. That I had begun to take up her side.

It is a well-known fact among the women of Harmony that Rena Zurn loves reading crime books and true confession magazines, and she told Jewel and Elana Forester and Gracie Wilson that she could understand how I might find myself fascinated by Lilly Duke even if she couldn't see how a decent person could go as far as I already had by taking any action on it and getting to be the woman's friend.

"Well, I love a scary movie," Rena said. "I like nothing better than when the late show is about murder and crime."

Jewel shook her head.

"How can you watch that stuff, Rena?" she asked. "It just gives me the creeps. Takes away my sleep. Leaves me listening for noises in the night."

The women all agreed that that was because Clayton traveled so much all the time and left Jewel and the kids alone.

Elana shrugged, her shoulders thin and her breasts hanging. She had lost her younger son in the war, and her husband had died early, of heart disease. Jewel said it was because of all the animal fat she fed him—bacon and eggs and steaks and fries.

"I think I could find enough death and sadness in the real world to last me a lifetime, without going looking for it in a book or a magazine or at the movies or on TV," Elana said. "I don't expect that anyone needs much more drama in her life than what I've already had to bear."

Rena laughed. "Not me," she said. "No sir. I love that stuff. Gives me a thrill." She grinned.

Gracie Wilson, her face small and pinched and serious, picked at the ruffled cuffs of her blouse. "Rena only says that because she likes it when she gets the creeps. It's a good excuse to jump into Patrick's big strong arms." She turned to Jewel. "Those things work just like an aphrodisiac on Rena, see? A lot of women are that way. It's not so uncommon. I read about it once in a magazine. Makes a woman feel all cuddly and helpless and small. Like a child again. There's something sexy in that. So Patrick doesn't mind. He'll buy her as many magazines as she wants. Says they make her horny. Tells his friends they turn her on."

Jewel's face reddened with her righteous anger. "I don't see how someone could get turned on by the fact that some poor car salesman is dead. What's sexy about that? And Tim Duke killed him. He said so himself, didn't he? Shot him in the head. Three times. From behind!" She hugged herself and shuddered.

Rena smiled and squashed her cigarette out in the ashtray. "Well, he also claimed to have rescued Lilly Duke," she put in, raising her eyebrows to see how Jewel was going to react.

"Well, now you're just as bad as my sister, Rena. You're as heartless as Clodine. How can anybody make a romance out of that pitiful Tim Duke? He is a killer. That's all. A murderer. Of somebody's husband. Someone's father. That car salesman was some poor woman's son, you know. I don't find that exciting. I don't even find it sad. I think it's sickening, that's what. Nauseating. Disgusting. And I think anybody who tries to pursue it must be sick, too."

"They said her stepfather was having his way with her, if you know what I mean."

"Yeah, well, her mother said she as much as asked for that. Walked around the house at night in her underwear and left the door open a crack when she was in there taking a bath."

"Most likely she enjoyed it."

"She looks to be that kind."

"Plopped herself down on Tim's lap, right there in the visiting room, in front of everybody, as easy as you please."

Jewel stood there in my kitchen before Christmas. She stirred her coffee with a Santa Claus spoon, and she asked me, "How can you stand to be in the same room with her, Clodine? Knowing what you know? How can you bear to even hear that woman's name?"

This was how those women talked. That was how it was. It had never been any other way. Like a swarm of starlings, these women flocked together, comforted by the crowding of their own mass, warmed by the gathering of their own shared heat.

And the truth of it is that what they all resented most was not the waywardness of Lilly Duke. It wasn't the wrongness or the wickedness or the sin.

It was the defiance. The stubbornness in her body, the way she held herself, with her chin up and her shoulders back, refusing to bow down. The look of challenge in her eyes. The resistance that was wrapped around her like barbed wire, menacing and sharp. The fact that she would not speak to them or look at them, that she did not seem to heed their judgment. She didn't want anything, either, to do with their sympathy or their wisdom or their mercy or their care.

And, so, knowing what I knew about these women, seeing how they measured each other, hearing the way they talked, the conclusions they came to, the opinions they held, how in this world could I myself ever have found a way to go to them then? To turn to any one of them, even my sister Jewel, for help? How could I tell them what living with Galen Wheeler was really like? What it meant to love a man as much as I loved Galen and have to hate him, too, both at the same time? With the same heat, out of the same cold flame?

Would Jewel only put her hands on her hips and shake her head and say that Daddy had warned me, he'd told me so, hadn't he? I had no business marrying that man Galen Wheeler, and if I was unhappy now, well then, whose fault was that?

What words could I have found to say to them that would let them know how far I had been wrong? How much of it was a terrible mistake?

Could I show them all the bruises? Have them listen to the sounds of his blows? Let them see the marks?

"You made your own bed, Clodine."

I could imagine my mother's tight face.

"Now I guess you'll just have to go ahead and lie down in it. Just like the rest of us. For better or for worse."

To have and to hold. For better or for worse, for richer, for poorer, in sickness and in health. To love and to cherish.

Till death do us part.

❥⤫❧

So it was winter. December. Christmastime.

Mom and Dad had begun preparing for their move to Florida, which was to take place in a few weeks, after the new year. They had already sold the house, and a young couple with small children was making its plans to move in. Mom had begun to distribute the furniture and the other things they thought they could definitely do without.

"Accumulations," was what my mother called them. "Like layers of dust on the windowsill, things do begin to build up."

"Lightening the load," Dad said as he filled up the back of his car with boxes of broken picture frames and lamps and old magazines, gadgets he once had sold — orange peelers and lettuce dryers, facial masks and barbecue brushes — to be dropped off at the Baptist Church to be given away to whoever wanted them, if anyone ever did.

He had put his deposit down on the condo, and he was trying to get a promise out of all of us that we would visit them sometime in March, when, he knew, the weather here might be particularly cruel, when we might be wanting to maybe get away and see some sunshine and some warmth.

"Don't bother buying any presents for me," he told us. "Save your money. Just tell me that I'll see you."

He smiled and touched my cheek. "That's all I want for Christmas, Clodine, the promise that you'll come."

When we were little, Jewel and I made crayon-decorated pamphlets that we gave to our parents. They were filled with coupons made of colored construction paper, pledge books we called them, solemnly lettered — "I promise to shovel the walk"; "This coupon is good for one free table setting, clearing and dish washing"; "I hereby guarantee that my father's shoes will be shined every day for a month."

Of course, my sister Jewel was always true to her word. She kept her promises, but mine weren't worth the paper they were written on.

Jewel also made orange pomander balls. She would sit, hunched over at the kitchen table, for hours and hours, poking cloves into oranges until there was a definite rough callus on the edge of her thumb. She tied these up with red and green ribbon. You could hang them in your closet to keep your clothes fresh. The smell was extraordinary until the oranges went soft and, after a while, began to rot.

"Of course we'll come visit you, Dad," I told him. "Won't we, Galen?"

Galen smiled.

"Sure, Mr. Ferring," he said, lighting one cigarette off another and flicking the butt into the roaring fire. "Absolutely. Why not?"

He was drinking clear, cold vodka from a crystal Christmas glass.

Jewel was hunched over on the floor, in a nest of colorful gift-wrap paper, putting the finishing touches on the packages she had wrapped for her children and her friends. She tied each of them with a length of ribbon, and asked me to put my finger on the knot while she tied a fancy bow.

When I reached out, then my sister saw the ragged mark that had been burned into the soft skin on the inside of my arm, from where Galen had grabbed me and held my wrist out over the white column of steam that billowed, screaming, up out of the spout of the teakettle on the stove. The scald was a seething, angry hole, red in the center, blackened along its edge, seared flesh.

"Ugh, what is that?" Jewel wrinkled up her nose and tucked in her chin, backing away. "Jesus, Clodine, that really is nasty. Daddy, did you see this?"

"Oh, I burned myself," I said, shrugging, pulling my arm away, holding it by the wrist in the palm of my other hand. "An accident. On the stove. Stupid thing."

My father lowered his head, and he eyed me over the tops of his glasses, puckering his lips, frowning, smoothing out the newspaper on his knee. Well, he had some ointment he could give me if I wanted it. But, really, they all agreed that the best thing would probably be just to let the sore breathe and heal over on its own.

I felt Galen's eyes skimming my face. He walked over to the window and stood there, one hand in his pocket, his back to us. He was smoking. He looked out at the cold gray sky.

"Maybe it will snow," he said, turning in toward the warmth of the room again.

He glanced over at my dad. He smiled at my mother. "Yes, a snowfall would be very nice."

The streets of Harmony had been decorated and made festive with silvery tinsel, feathery green garlands, and huge red bows tied to the tops of the lampposts along Old Main. The big fir tree in the middle of the square was strung around and around with wired twinkle lights and topped with a blazing blue plastic star. The figures in the Nativity scene were huddled, frozen in familiar tableau, beneath the ragged roof of a wooden crèche on the street side of the square. Joseph gazed upward with a look that seemed at once bewildered and crafty. A cow grazed with its neck bent, nose down in the snow. A sheep tilted its head, and its glass eyes shone with curiosity. The kings' glacial expressions were convincingly regal. Mary's face was fixed with worry as she reached for her swaddled babe. His blankets seemed flimsy and inadequate for our winter freeze. His cheeks were flushed and fevered-looking; his smile was pensive and sweet.

Bundled in our parkas, muffled in our scarves and mittens and hats, our boots scraping on the ice, we trudged along the shoveled walks, between the rising drifts, and joined in the caroling with the clusters of church choirs. Jewel was there, her nose red and her cheeks pink, a bright handmade scarf wrapped around her neck and thrown back over her shoulder, so long it hung all the way down below her hips in rows and rows of almost every color of yarn you could find to buy. She stood with Peter and Mary Alice, huddled there in among some of the other women on the courthouse steps, singing, "O come all ye faithful . . ." and "All is calm, all is bright . . ." and "Hark! the herald angels sing . . ."

Peter stood on his tiptoes, craning for a better view of the street. Mary Alice was holding on tight with both hands to the folds of her mother's skirt, and she sang along loudly with the rest.

Finally Peter got a glimpse of what he was looking for, and the singing was interrupted, overwhelmed by another wave of sound, a siren's wail rising and falling, first from far off and then louder as the fire engine rounded the corner into view, its red lights maniacally flashing, sparking wildly off the drifts of snow, the shriek and blare a deafening thrill.

It was Santa Claus, coming into Harmony as he has every year since I can remember. When Jewel and I were little, we and our friends had all crowded around this bearded man in his red suit and big black boots, hoping for the usual gifts of candy and toys. He clambered awkwardly down from the back of the truck as the siren sound died down and faded away, replaced by the squeals of the children who mobbed him on the courthouse steps.

It was a huge Santa that year, a giant dressed in enormous, baggy red pants and a wide red shirt with black buttons down the front, his big hands in white gloves digging into the burlap bag he carried, pulling out the candy canes and whistles, licorice ropes and tops and yo-yos and passing them over into smaller, grasping palms. His beard, long and wavy and pure white, was as shiny and silken as angel hair. It had somehow got pulled askew on his chin, so I was able to recognize Clayton's face there underneath it. He was sweating, grinning at all the kids, laughing — "Ho-ho-ho!" — and reaching out to pat a blond head, touch a rosy cheek, wrap a smaller hand in the warm slab of his own.

I had seen that Lilly Duke was standing off there to the side of the crowd, and she had C.T. cuddled in her arms. His face was slick and chapped-looking, his body bundled up so thickly in his snowsuit and coat that he was hardly even able to turn his head. He stared at the crowd and the lights and the fire engine and the Santa, his eyes as round and black as coals. Lilly was looking on quietly, taking in the whole spectacle, her own eyes dark and her face pale. Her breath was a thick cloud. She was hatless, and her hair was uncombed as usual. It poked out around her head all scraggly and wild.

I was considering how I ought to go on over to her, right then and there, say hello, Merry Christmas, take the baby's hand, get a candy cane from Clayton and give it to C.T. to suck on, talk to the two of them right out in public, like that, just to show Jewel, to spite those other women. Let them know that I was not so unforgiving as they could be. Let them see that Lilly Duke had at least one friend.

I had already been planning to bring her a ham for her Christmas dinner. And some gifts that I had bought. A stuffed rabbit for the baby. A plastic truck. A wool coat for her. A hat.

But, then, just when I had decided, determined that yes, in the spirit of Christmas, I would go up and talk with her, that was when I also saw that she was not altogether alone.

Because he was there, behind her, sidling up next to Lilly, slipping in and out through the crowd. I saw his hunched shoulders and how he had his hands stuffed down into his pockets. The hood of his parka was pulled up; the fur trim framed the picture of his face. He had stepped in closer, was pressing up against her. Their shoulders touched, and she leaned away.

The choir had begun to sing again.

"Joy to the world!"

And Lilly was turning. The twinkle lights were shining in the branches of the tree. The star on the top radiated its glow like magic, into the pitch-black, moonless winter sky. Lilly was hugging the baby's head up close to her body. She held its cheek against her shoulder, and she turned, leaning toward him now, smiling, lowering her eyes, then raising them to face him, her look solemn and thoughtful and shy. She spoke; he smiled; she laughed. There was a crowd gathered; people pressed forward, bumping Lilly's body closer against his. He touched his finger to her throat; he ran his thumb along the line of her jaw; he put an arm around her shoulders and jostled her with a friendly hug.

"Let every heart prepare him room . . ."

That was Galen Wheeler bending in there toward Lilly Duke. He was leaning forward over her, his face so close to hers. His whisper was in her ear; his breath was in her eyes; his hands were in her hair.

～✕～

My parents' house was empty, and it sat abandoned by them, left behind. Mom and Dad had gone off to start up another kind of life way to the south of here, in a place where they didn't have to work, where they could relax, where the weather would be warm. What furniture they'd left behind for the new family moving in was enshrouded in old sheets. Chairs and sofas huddled together in the silent rooms, as if the windows had been left open and the house had been filled up with drifting snow.

Dad had given me the key to pass on when the new family was ready to move in.

Galen and I kept our gifts unopened until after Christmas

was over, after everyone else was finished, when everyone else was gone. There was a red flannel bathrobe for Galen. A blue sweater for me. A can of wildflower seeds. A brass ice bucket. Crystal candlesticks.

He bought champagne, built a fire, brought glasses, lit the candles that glowed, yellow as butter, lunatic shadows surging on my parents' four bare bedroom walls. I wore my sweater, opened his bathrobe, pressed my palm against his chest, ran my fingers across the quivering rippled surface of his stomach, cupped my hand against his cheek, kissed him, listened to him whispering my name.

"Clo-dine . . . mmm-mmm . . . Clo-dine . . ."

And here, where my parents' raised, angry voices still seemed to echo in my ears, Galen's murmur seemed like it was just the softest, the sweetest, the dearest one of all the Christmas songs.

～✕～

Winters in Harmony, after the new year, can be so silent and so cold, so hard and so still, the air so crisp and sharp that it bites right through your quilts and your sweaters and your skin and holds on like mean teeth to the very marrow of your bones.

The fields are blanketed with snow and the lake freezes over, granite hard. The whole world seems colorless, black and gray and white, like an old photograph in a family album, distant and dim. Frost glazes the barren trees; the sheen of ice on the highway glistens, bitter and fierce.

Galen, a shadow hulking in our darkened bedroom, hovers over me, yanks back the quilt that covers me, exposes my curled body, rips into the fabric of my sleep, drags me groggy, drunk with my dreams, up out of the bed.

I'm crying out, "What? What?"

He's twisted off all my buttons. He tugs at my cuffs, yanks down on my sleeves. The flannel nightgown drifts off my body, and it collapses at my feet, limp, useless, mere cloth.

I've begun to tremble. I can't keep still. Galen throws back the casements on the two full windows in our bedroom, and then he has me standing there, bare-naked in the open air— two below, ten below, and sometimes, when the wind is blowing hard, snow swirling, even more. I clasp my own elbows, my arms are squeezed across my chest. My stomach muscles heave and quake.

The wind seems like it is a live thing, wild and angry. It rattles the branches of the barren trees. It whistles down to tangle my hair and suck my breath away. I shudder and moan, gasping, lips drawn back, teeth clicking and bared. I think that maybe I can even feel the thin film of tears that freezes over across the smooth white insides of my eyes.

Picture the fish trapped beneath the frozen-over, icy surface of Harmony Lake. They drift and float through the chill water, somnolent, slivers in glass. They are dozing there in that cold, hard, solid dark, senseless and stupid and blind.

8

AND THEN I was pregnant, two months, no cramps, no spots, no periods, a fullness in my belly, a soreness in my breasts, a rolling nausea in my stomach that made it difficult to eat or cook for Galen or even drag my body up out of the bed at all some days.

Galen drove me in the truck down to the clinic in Harlan for a visit with a doctor, but it was the nurse who took blood out of my arm and had me pee in a cup, and then she meant to send us home. She said she'd give us a call when the results came in from the lab.

And Galen picked that time to make a scene. Why couldn't she just tell us right now? he wanted to know. Why wait?

He pushed past me into the hallway and stood, turning, hesitating, undecided, his hands reaching, fisted, and at the same time I could see he was restraining himself. He was afraid to go too far, he wouldn't open any of the closed doors of the examining rooms. Behind them were other women waiting, their bras and underpants hidden under a nest of clothing in the changing rooms, crisp cotton hospital gowns tied in bows at the backs of their necks, their naked bottoms flattened against the protective tissue paper on the tables, bare feet dangling, ready to be raised up into stirrups, warmed by the focus of the doctor's lamp. Their faces would be turned away, or they would stare up hopefully at the ceiling, over the doctor's shoulder as he probed.

"Why all the secrecy?" Galen was demanding to be told. He wanted to know why a doctor didn't need to take a look at me right then. He was asking, shouldn't somebody be doing something to make sure nothing was wrong, that everything was going along the way it was supposed to and I was normal and healthy and strong?

And where were all the doctors, anyway? Galen craned toward an empty office down the hall. Why couldn't one of them talk to us?

The nurse was kind with Galen. But firm. She laid her hands down on both his shoulders and she turned him around, steered him along, down the corridor and through the swinging door, out into the waiting room again. The other women peered at us over the top edges of the magazines that they held propped up on the mounds of their big bellies.

"Why, you don't even know for certain whether your wife is pregnant yet, Mr. Wheeler. Please, be patient. I know it's hard, but first things first. Even if she is pregnant, and I'm not saying she is, you understand, well, you'll have to be especially patient then, won't you?"

She was talking to Galen as if he were a child, and I could feel myself cringing; I expected him to shrug her hands off his shoulders, grab her, and shake her hard. But instead he only stared, his mouth partway open, the vein at his temple pulsing, gentle, steady, slow.

"And," she went on, her face bland, her gaze unfaltering, "when the lab gives us the results, I'll call you. Right away. First thing, I promise. I won't wait a minute. Then Mrs. Wheeler can make an appointment to see the doctor." Her voice was a whisper, a hiss, even and orderly and calm.

Another nurse was leaning out the door and calling over Galen's shoulder, "Mrs. Hudson?" and then a young woman who seemed to be almost as thick and wide as she was tall, struggled with both elbows bent to push herself up from her chair, stand and walk, waddling, her stomach thrust out ahead of her. The T-shirt that she wore was so tight you could see the knob of her belly button pressing through.

"Excuse me," she whispered, her eyes downcast. I could see that her feet were so badly swollen she wasn't able to tie the laces of her shoes. A red splotch of broken capillaries had sprouted on the tip of her nose.

Galen stepped aside, quickly, as if he were afraid she might reach for him and touch him, and I took hold of his arm and leaned against him; I pressed my whole self into his side, so he could feel my presence and my weight.

"It's only a couple of days, Galen," I whispered. "We can wait."

He let me draw him away, out of the waiting room, into the hallway, down to the elevator, across the parking lot, over to our truck.

"Well, of course you are pregnant, Clodine," he was saying, closing the truck door after he had helped me climb inside. "No doubt about it. You definitely are."

He shook his head and laughed, not with amusement exactly, but with satisfaction more like, as if what he was always telling Clayton, his belief in the fact that the rest of the world was a whole lot stupider than Galen Wheeler, had been, once again, unquestionably, confirmed.

He drove back to the cottage with great caution, going along so slowly, and that know-it-all smile stuck on his face like it was frozen there. He watched the road carefully, braking on the curves, stopping full when he came to an intersection with the highway, making a big point to look both ways, more than once, back and forth and back again, before he pulled out onto the road, even though it was plain to see that there wasn't another car in sight. We hit some ice on the bridge, and for one breathless minute the truck lost traction and was skidding, ready to spin. Galen clenched his teeth and gripped the wheel hard in his fists, and he was somehow able to keep control. When he looked over at me afterward and nodded, it was as if he meant to let me know that I was in good hands now, he'd take care of me, of us, all three, make sure everybody's needs were seen to and nobody got hurt.

And, sure enough, two days later that nurse called me and over the telephone she told me that my tests had come back positive, the answer was, as Galen had predicted, as he had promised me, yes.

When I had my appointment with the doctor, and I went in to be weighed and examined and have my blood pressure taken, that same nurse from the first time looked at the scratches on my back, and she raised her eyebrows, but she didn't say one word.

I had one bruise that was like a big black and purple flower on my leg from a time when Galen had pinched me, grinding the muscle and fat of my flesh between the vise grip of his thumb and finger, twisting it while I howled, and I told the doctor that I had backed into the sharp corner of the kitchen counter and wasn't it funny how some places on the body seemed to bruise a whole lot easier than others, it was just a good thing that this one was where nobody would have to see, it was so ugly.

The doctor sat behind the broad mahogany expanse of his desk—a clock, a blotter, a pencil jar, a pile of patients' files, a triptych of framed photos of his own kids waving from the back end of a boat—and he brought a little round plastic calendar from out of his drawer, and he turned it in his hands, his lips moving as he calculated the weeks. He took off his glasses and folded them carefully and slipped them into the breast pocket of his white coat. He rubbed the bridge of his nose and stretched his legs out under his desk. And he told me that

I was about three months along already, and we could expect to have a baby around the last week in October, early November.

He gave me a prescription for vitamins, said any bleeding, any cramps, any swelling, anything unusual at all, you call me. All hours, somebody will answer. Try to keep your weight down, eat good food, fruits and vegetables, plenty of protein, but don't fill up on sweets, bread and cake and noodles and ice cream, like most mothers he knew. Once you put that weight on, he told me, it's almost impossible to get it back off.

He would want to see me once every month up through the end of summer, and then every week until the baby came.

And then he sent me home.

At night, I lay there next to Galen in our bed, and I dreamed of furnaces. Of coal chutes and incinerators, basements and boilers. A web of sweating steel pipes, clouds of steam, the clank and whistle of hot water churning, warm air blowing. Brown braided hemp rope and a twisted silk handkerchief. A body swings, toes brushing the slick surface of the scrubbed concrete floor, hands hanging, eyes wide, mouth slack, head bowed, tongue thick and swollen, speechless and black. A heavy smell of excrement and wet wool, urine-soaked, sweat and fear and bottomless despair.

～✕⌒

When I rolled up the sleeves of my sweater, Lilly saw where the burn on the inside of my forearm had healed and left behind a rosy splash of scar tissue on the otherwise smooth, white surface of my skin. She took my hand in hers and turned my arm this way and that under the light.

"Does it hurt much?" she asked, raising her eyes to meet mine. She wasn't asking me how it got there. Or maybe she already knew.

"No." I pulled my hand away and spread it on my belly, caressing the smooth, hard swell.

Lilly pushed back her own sleeves and rolled her fists. She stretched them out toward me, her thumbs curled over her bent fingers, her arms side by side, elbows touching, pressed up against her chest. Lilly's scars were so much meaner-looking than mine. Self-inflicted, they looked more desperate, ragged and raised, entwined like vines with the pulsing blue branches of her arteries and veins.

She touched her finger to her tongue and then reached for me again, pulling my arm out toward her, outlining my scar with her moistened fingertip. The nail had been gnawed down to the quick; the skin around the cuticle was frayed, sore-looking, pink.

"I knew a girl in my high school," she said. "She would take a lit cigarette and lay it down lengthwise, like this" — she pressed her finger straight along the inside of my arm — "down between her own bare wrist and a boy's."

Then they allowed the cigarette to burn down, slowly, smoldering, for as long as both of them could stand it, while each stared into the well of the other's eyes, unblinking, held fixed by the pain. Until it became too much to bear. Until one or the other gave up, she or the boy, and pulled away, sucking in air between his teeth, tears rolling out the corner of her eye, nostrils flared against the smell of seared skin, singed hair, burnt flesh.

"See, it was like a way to tell whether a person really was in love," Lilly explained.

She lit a cigarette of her own and plopped down cross-legged on the bed. She squinted up at me through the gray haze of smoke.

"It was how you could prove to each other what kind of strength you really had. How far you were willing to go," Lilly said. And then the scars came to be like an award, a prize or a trophy, a medal of courage, a badge of honor, a symbol of love.

I took in the sight of her unmade bed. The bottom sheet was

wrinkled and stained, the comforter rumpled and bunched into a clumsy pile, the pillows wrestled down to the wrong end of the mattress. The picture of Tim that she kept in a frame on the bedside boxes had fallen over, or been turned face down.

Lilly's baby Chance was squatting on the floor nearby, picking at the craters in the cracked linoleum or fingering dust balls or slamming a spoon against the wall, banging and pounding with his face full of serious intent, drool slathering his chin.

✧✕✧

The lake was all ice, a great flat black disk with lozenges of snow along its edges, powdery and blowing in gusts and whirlwinds, as delicate as sugar, finer even than sand. The trees stood trapped, like wounded soldiers, hunched, bent, frozen in the grimace of their worst defeat. Their trunks were black with lake water; icicles dribbled down from the thick edges of their mangled limbs, glittering in the sunshine, trickling, sharper, longer, frozen over when the temperature plunged again at night. Groups of young people went out for skating parties on the lake. They built warming fires in rusted metal barrels along the shores and set up hockey games with brooms and black rubber pucks.

Everyone was warned, and we all discussed the dangers in skating out too far, falling through a patch of thin ice, into the killing cold water at the deepest center of the lake. When the ice did begin to melt, the terrible rumble of it came cracking across the lake with an echo and roar that sounded just the same as the far-off warning thunder of a springtime storm.

The water on the boulders of the spillway was frozen as quickly as it fell, captured, like a photograph, motionless, fixed and held there in midair.

Galen went out skating by himself one afternoon, and he came home again at dusk all covered with snow, from head to toe — it was as if he'd fallen down a hundred times. His face was flushed red and sweating with the effort of it. But he laughed

and dropped the skates that, tied together by their laces, he'd
slung over his shoulder. He brushed away the snow from his
arms and legs. Stomped it out of the treads in the bottoms of
his boots. It was stuck in his hair and his eyelashes and on the
fur around the hood of his parka, inside the cuffs of his gloves.
His nose was so cold against my neck, I shivered and jerked
away.

I fixed him some hot milk and brandy and filled a big pot
with warm water for soaking his frozen feet. I built a fire and
wrapped a blanket over him, stood behind him with my arms
around him, my hands on his chest, my cheek pressed up next
to his, and I recognized the flutter and the flurry of the baby I
was carrying, as it quickened within me for the very first time,
and let me know that it was real, with a life and a being all its
very own.

Lately Jewel has been sewing a quilt for her baby that's about
to come. Clayton, overcome with paperwork, is holed up in
his office all day long, writing out the insurance company's
investigative reports.

Emma sits here with me in the kitchen, kneading colored
bits of clay between her fingers. Her laughter ripples in the air.
It rolls around me like warm waves.

Peter pokes a stick into the fireplace; he is fascinated by the
flames. Jewel is winding curlers into Mary Alice's fine blond
hair.

Everyone all over Harmony is shut in for the winter. The
women read thick novels, write letters to distant friends, sip cups
of broth, stand at the window with the curtains pulled back,
and stare out into the cold and the gray snow. Their husbands
come home early from work; they listen to the radio, drink beer,
watch television, get fat.

Lakeside Acres in the wintertime isn't anything more than a
fenced-in, flat, empty field. Gone are the whirly-loop and the

Ferris wheel, the bumper-car cage and the game booths. Chains and padlocks secure the iron gates. The wind whistles through so it sounds almost like maybe the calliope is still playing somewhere. The tree branches rattle overhead. When it's clear, the starry sky hovers, seems close. In the daytime, with the sun buried behind clouds, the place is gray and forlorn, abandoned. The snow lies thick and untouched except for bird and squirrel tracks, the footprints of a rabbit, sometimes deer. Tall poles rise up out of the snow, purposeless now, the twinkle lights and banners and streamers all gone.

There is a sled run built into the bluff above the river. The kids drag their toboggans through the streets, up to the top of the hill. They pile on, three or four at one time, each holding tight to the one in front, who steers, grits his teeth and squints his eyes, and they scream, hair flying, and they tumble off at the bottom, rolling every which way in the snow, laughing, breathing hard.

I can remember the feeling of reckless speed, of the wind so cold on my face, snow spilling down the collar of my shirt, inside the cuffs of my jacket, into my socks. My skin raw and burning, reddened, chapped and chafed.

Galen grabbing me and rolling me, turning me over and over, away from the others, apart from the rest. He hovered above me, pinned me on my back in the snow with his own weight pressing down upon mine, his breath hot in my face, his hair hanging, tickling my nose, his teeth nibbling my lips.

And now when I look at Emma I can see the shadow of Galen's face there, buried under the full baby fat of her cheeks, a skeleton lurking beneath her flesh, Galen's bones. I recognize his eyes in her look.

Emma makes me miss him, in spite of everything that's happened, never mind anything he did. The truth is, I can't help it, I loved him anyway. I did.

I'm older now than Galen was then. Before long I will have

passed him right by. I'll have grown more sure of myself, become more set in my ways. Emma already thinks that I know what I'm doing, that she should do what I tell her to, take seriously the things I say. She won't be able to believe that I could have been young at one time, too. She'll have trouble imagining how it was for me with Galen. I'll show her the pictures of her father's handsome face and she'll compare that with the aging that she'll think of as a weakness in my own.

Then won't there come a time, too, when even Emma, baby Emma, our daughter, our little girl, is older than Galen ever lived to be? Even as all these years go by, still there Galen will be, set in my photographs, constant in my mind, a fixture there, never aging, never changing. Forever and ever Galen always will stay the way he was—youthful and beautiful and wild.

⌒✕⌒

"You be careful now, Clodine," Mom warned me, over the phone. Her voice was strained by the distance between us, her tone seemed thin and uncertain and vague.

Dad said, as if he were accusing me of something, "You've got more than just yourself to think about now, Clodine."

Jewel was telling me the same thing. And I knew exactly what it was that they both of them really meant. They believed I'd always been too selfish and self-centered. Without a thought for anybody but myself, for anyone's wishes but my own, for anyone's feelings but mine. And now the time had come. I was about to learn how to give. Know what being a parent means. How sad, how painful, how difficult and disappointing and hard. Get my own heart broken, just like maybe I broke his.

And what about the promise we'd made at Christmastime to visit my parents on their island in Florida? I had said again and again to Daddy that I would. We all had told them so.

Jewel and Clayton were as good as their word, and they actually did go. I remember that we got a postcard from them, with a picture of two lazy alligators, snoozing, motionless as logs, in the sun.

But Galen said absolutely no. "Visit your parents?" he exclaimed to me in disbelief.

Live in a condo with them? Trapped like rats, on an island? With absolutely no way out, no means of escape. Morning, noon, and night, sit there in the sunshine and listen to them talk? He said for me to go ahead, if that was what I wanted, but he wouldn't think of it, not in a million years.

"I was glad when they moved away, Clodine," he told me. "You know that. What a relief."

So I told my mother it was impossible. I said I was too sick all the time. That my doctor had advised against travel, especially to a place that was hot.

"I have to be careful about things like edema, Mom. Water retention. You know. Sunstroke. And swimming isn't any good, either," I explained. "Especially in the ocean. There's so much bacteria. So many germs. It could hurt the baby, I think."

I said all this to her as if I thought she'd never been pregnant herself.

"I'm not thinking of myself. It's just that times are different now, Mom. You must know that. Doctors are so much more careful. The infant mortality rate is way down because of it, too, believe me. You read about it all the time. How mothers do better and their babies, too. But I'd definitely come and see you, if I could."

"Well, you did promise him, Clodine," Jewel was saying. She sat in the front seat of Clayton's car, her lap full of maps and guidebooks and a bag of needlepoint that she was taking to keep her hands busy on the long trip down.

Peter and Mary Alice had been buckled into the back seat with their books and crayons and toys.

Jewel squinted up at me with such an accusation in her eyes

then that I felt I had to turn away. "He was expecting you. You can't blame him too much if he's mad."

"Well, don't get lost, anyway," Galen said, interrupting us. He leaned in toward the window, wrapping one hand around my elbow to hold me and maybe, if he had to, pull me back. "Just remember, Jewel, the sun comes up in the east. It goes down in the west. If you wait long enough, it'll move one way or the other, up or down."

"Drive careful, Clayton," I said.

He leaned over and kissed me on the cheek. He reached out and shook Galen's free hand. Then he walked around to the driver's side and opened the door and folded his big body in behind the wheel.

"You take care of yourself, Clodine," Jewel kept on, like she didn't really want to go away, wasn't sure that she should let go. She looked at Galen and waved back at him as Clayton turned on the car and began to pull away. "Take care of her," my sister was calling. "Make sure she stays okay."

∽⟩⟨∼

Lilly seemed to be keeping pretty much to herself that winter. She stayed all those cold months holed up with her baby inside Tim Duke's cabin by the lake. It seemed like she never went out at all, except to gather some more wood or collect her mail. Not that she had any way of getting anywhere even if she had wanted to. She still didn't have a car, and she couldn't very well ride the bicycle through the snow into town. She didn't like taking C.T. outdoors. She was overworried, was what I thought. But she didn't want him catching cold or getting a sickness of any kind.

"What would I do if I needed a doctor, Clodine? How would I get him in to see one? Who would take me there?"

"Well, I would," I told her. "Of course. I would."

Lilly dressed herself and the baby, too, in layers, sweaters and T-shirts and turtlenecks, long johns and blue jeans and two or three pairs of socks. She always kept a fire burning; smoke billowed from the chimney, making the place seem homey and welcoming and warm. In spite of the boarded-over windows. Never mind the peeling paint or the sagging porch.

I sent Galen out there to chop up some wood for her. He cut down two trees that had been felled by lightning bolts the spring before, and he spent at least a week splitting the logs, which he piled up in a pyramid along the walls of her porch outside the back door.

The dog I'd given her had stayed, but she didn't seem to need that kind of protection anymore. Nobody had threatened her again. No one came out there, even to visit, except me and Galen. No one cared how she was doing. The women hardly even talked about her much after a while. Jewel was gone, and the gossip in the grocery store had slowed accordingly. The mailman brought Lilly letters that bore a postmark from the prison in Nebraska. The story of Tim's crime and trial and imprisonment was all old news, wrapped up in the red tape of the judicial system, entangled in a complex web of appeals.

Lilly told me that the winter made her want to curl in upon herself, bundle up and sleep, like a bear hibernating. She napped and read the magazines and paperback books I brought her. I took our truck into town to do her shopping. She ate vegetables in cans, fed the baby beans and peas and eggs and cheese.

Her bed was always a mess.

How long was it, then, before I first started to suspect? When did I let myself see what was going on? Was it as early as that night in December, the beginning of Advent, when they lit the lights on the Christmas tree in the square? When I saw her turn and smile, watched him leaning over her, his breath warm on her neck?

When did I begin to notice the rosy, self-conscious flush in her cheeks? Recognize the moony look that she was getting, the way her sentences drifted, broken, trailing, her eyes filming over as she stared off, thinking, imagining . . . what? His touch? His words? The way he looked at her? The way he held her? The way he pushed her down upon her back against the floor? The way his hands got tangled in her hair?

When did I admit it? That Tim Duke's Lillyheart had fallen in love.

Again.

There was the picture of Tim Duke, turned over on its face on the boxes by the bed. The rumpled sheets. The pile of letters that she never opened, that she left unread. Her lethargy. The way she lounged against the pillows. The smell — of yeast and sour milk, vinegar, sugar, and sweat — that rose up like a cloud from the tangle of her sheets. A vodka bottle, frozen outside, buried in the snow. Cigarettes piled in the ashtray, some of them left unattended, forgotten, to burn all the way down to the filter, unsmoked.

It was easy for me to see them, to imagine what they were like, the two of them, together. How Galen would be with Lilly. And how she would be back to him.

The baby toddling around the kitchen, or curled up between them, while they slept, while the winter wind blew outside the windows of the cabin, and the fire roared in the hearth. She would fix him a meal of biscuits and soup. Fill him up so that by the time he came home again to me, he wasn't hungry for anything that I had to give him at all. He poured himself a glass of vodka, and he sat in front of the television, staring at the flickering images on the screen.

And wasn't there some relief in this, after all? Well, at the very least, he wasn't hitting me anymore. Surely I could have some gratitude in me for that. Even as much as I loved him.

So, whatever jealousy I might have been feeling then was tempered twice, once by the fact that I was pregnant, self-contained, self-absorbed, my sight turned inward on myself.

And then again because at least I had some comfort in the fact that Galen wasn't taking any of his anger out on me now. He wasn't holding me to blame. He didn't grab me, and he didn't yell. He didn't sneak up on me, pounce upon me suddenly, from behind. He didn't call out for me, singsong my name, he didn't accuse me of hiding from him, he didn't reach for me. In fact, he hardly touched me or looked at me at all.

So, was he hitting Lilly Duke instead? Was she the one who bore the brunt of his fury at that time? Well, I never did see the signs that might indicate he did. I never saw a burn on her arm or any scratches on her neck. There were no marks or bruises on her face.

If he was beating her, I didn't know. If he knew how to hurt her or what might make her cry.

I had other things to think of then. I had more to worry about than only myself, just exactly like my daddy had said.

～✕～

On the way back home to Harmony from Florida, Jewel crocheted a sea green afghan for my baby. Their car was loaded down with a beautiful collection of seashells that Jewel used for decorating lamps and shadow boxes, and making paperweights, doorstops, and ashtrays.

And the weather had begun changing some toward spring. There weren't any more storms and the snow that had already fallen turned gray and the drifts were dwindling, worn away from the sides of the roads so the gravel showed.

There was no wind and no rain, only the steady cold, so the air felt like it was hollowed out, drained and emptier than ever in the night.

And all that time my baby, Emma, was growing there, steady, cell by cell in my belly. I went to the library and brought home books about what was happening, so I could begin to understand. I practiced breathing exercises, swallowed vitamins, went in to see the doctor every month.

Her heartbeat sounded just like a panting dog. Galen seemed almost embarrassed when he heard it. He closed his eyes and turned away, as if he felt he had intruded upon somebody's privacy, invaded another person's mystery, burst in upon the secret, hidden life of someone else.

Lilly was happy to tell me all about her own pregnancy with Chance. How she just got fatter and fatter. So fat that at the end none of her clothes fit her anymore and so she just quit going anywhere and stayed put inside. It was hard to think of Lilly Duke as ever being fat. Difficult to imagine her more than skin and bones. She was living in a room in an older woman's house in Lincoln at the time. It was a way, she said, for her to stay close to Tim, even though they didn't allow her any visits with him — she couldn't actually see him. But she did have a good view of the prison from the front steps of the house where she was staying, and she could feel that he was there, thinking of her, breathing the same air as she was.

"We were connected, Clodine, no matter what."

She didn't have a car, so she just walked down to the corner market sometimes, for cigarettes or a sandwich or some milk.

I listened to her tell me this, and I was noticing how dirty her feet were. She was wearing long underwear and a sweater, too big for her, with a hole in the sleeve. She wasn't looking as pretty as she had, I thought. Her skin was pasty white, unhealthy looking. She wrinkled her nose and narrowed her eyes as the smoke from her cigarette wafted up into her face. Her lips looked thin and hard, her teeth crooked and yellowy. Big pink plastic earrings were hanging off the lobes of her ears. The freckles on her nose were sprinkled so they made her face look almost dirty, smudged.

And then, she went on, putting out one cigarette and lighting another, when she finally went into labor and started to have the baby, well, the doctors gave her gas. They knocked her right out. Easiest thing in the world, she said to me, smiling, childbirth when you're asleep. She was unconscious for the entire thing. She missed the whole show. When she woke up finally, everybody was smiling and one of the nurses handed her this baby, all squirmy and red, and told her she had a little boy.

Her hips were narrow, and the baby's head had been quite big. They broke Lilly's tailbone when they pulled C.T. out of her, but she wasn't aware of it until later, when the pain began to seep from the base of her spine up into her back.

"Sometimes even now," she told me, "when the weather's so cold, I can still feel that awful ache."

Tim talked to some friends of his, got some money, and arranged everything so she could move in here. With enough money to last, well, a while anyway.

I was wondering whether it had begun to run out, her stash of twenty-dollar bills. And what she was planning to do about it when it did?

She laughed. "Do?" she asked. She touched her baby's hand, held it in her own, wrapped its fat fingers around her thumb.

"I don't know, Clodine. Do?" She shrugged. "Well, that's one thing for sure that I don't know."

I gave her two ten-dollar bills, and she stuffed them into the rolled-up cuff of her sweater sleeve.

"Thanks," she whispered, "you're a real pal, you know that? A real, true-blue, down-and-dirty friend. I'm grateful to you. You're okay."

❧✕❧

And then it was the first real warm day, too early to be true spring, but too late for a lasting winter either. It was April, when it can be warm as summer on one afternoon and snowing or throwing down handfuls of hail the next.

And Galen was there, at the cabin, visiting with Lilly. I watched him drive off, and I knew where he was going, but I didn't care. I was pregnant. I had other things on my mind. I was out hanging clothes up on the line. Enjoying the feel of the warm sun on my back. The punch and kick of the baby I carried. The smell of growth that I imagined was in the very air.

And so I believe it's true, fair enough, that Galen was the reason that Lilly wasn't minding her child like she should. Galen distracted her, you could say. And she took her eyes off the baby, wasn't watching him, she didn't notice when he left, didn't hear him toddle out the door and down the steps to the yard, didn't hear his laughter or his squeals of delight at his sudden freedom, the wonder of the landscape that was opened out for him then, grass and trees, dirt, gravel, piles of snow, puddles, dripping icicles, birds and squirrels.

A whole, huge world to be explored.

And Lilly, held by Galen, moaning in his arms, off in a trance, experiencing the pleasures of another universe all her own, didn't even sense that the kid was gone.

How long? One hour? Two?

Later Lilly, frantic, wringing her hands, pulling on her hair, biting her lip, squinting into the trees, said it couldn't have been more than ten minutes, maybe fifteen.

Lilly Duke scrambled up out of the bed.

"Oh, Jesus!"

She held the sheet up against her chest and ran from the kitchen into the bathroom and back out again, calling him. "C.T., honey, don't you hide from me. Come here, sweet pea."

Galen sat back against the pillows, lit a cigarette, closed his eyes.

She looked in the closet.

"C.T.?"

Stepped out onto the back porch.

By then the pitch of her voice had risen, carried on her panic like a wave, cresting when she screamed, "Ce-e-e-e! Te-e-e-e!"

But the baby was gone.

Galen got up and put on his pants. "Relax, will ya?" he told her. "He's probably just out in the yard there. Maybe in the trees."

Together the two of them walked back and forth across the lawn, calling, "Ce-e-e-e! Te-e-e-e!"

She was imagining his look, hoping for his face. She was seeing how it would be, how she would come upon him, find him sitting in a pile of leaves, or in a puddle of melted snow, splashing mud, his face suddenly solemn when he saw her tears. Lilly would snatch him up and hold him, squeeze him, scold him.

"Never, never. Do you understand me? Never."

But they didn't find him.

Galen took the truck into town and got the sheriff.

"I only turned my back on him for a second," Lilly said. "It wasn't very long, I swear. Just a few minutes, that was all."

She had put her sweater on inside out. She was standing in the snow in her bare feet until someone brought her out some shoes.

"Calm down," Jewel told her. "Why, he's only a baby. His legs are short. They just can't have taken him off very far."

But by the time that Lilly noticed he was gone, there was just no telling how far off he might have wandered. Into the woods? Out to the road? All the way down to the lake?

By afternoon the sky had begun to cloud over again; a chill lingered in the air, hovering, with a threat of rain in it. The wind was picking up again, riffling through the trees, whistling cold.

The lake had begun to soften around its banks; it was slushy and wet for several feet in. The spillway had thawed and was flowing free. In a few weeks the snow on the hillsides around would melt and the lake water would begin to rise.

People from town had drifted out to the Duke cottage as news of what had happened spread. Men brought flashlights and dogs. The women carried blankets, and they busied themselves in Lilly's kitchen, full of curiosity for the way that she was living there, whispering to each other, exchanging glances, fixing a pot of coffee, standing on the porch, hugging themselves and swaying on their feet.

And then it began to sprinkle, sleet and freezing rain. At first it was only a few sparse drops. People put their palms out, peered at the sky. Shook their heads. Lilly stood shivering in the yard until it started coming down harder, cold and needle sharp. Then Agatha Pajek took off her own coat and slipped Lilly's arms in through the sleeves and zipped it and pulled the hood up over her head. Lilly's face was stricken, white. Rena Zurn shook out a blanket and threw it over Lilly's shoulders. Nancy Withers brought a mug of coffee and placed it between Lilly's palms.

⌒✕⌒

Rising lake water rushes over the boulders of the spillway, cascading down to the riverbed below with a deafening roar. I raise my arms, like wings outspread, for balance; my feet slip on the slick rocks—I stumble, catch myself, one hand on my belly; my coat flaps open, the freezing rain splatters in my face, my hair is wet and plastered back.

I can see the yellow beams of the searchers' flashlights bobbing through the trees.

"Take my hand," Jewel had said. And she brought them all together, got them to stand side by side, made them all hold hands. Rena Zurn and Agatha Pajek, Nancy Withers, Gracie Wilson, Ivy Lazelle, Elana Forester, and Lilly Duke—Jewel strung all of these women, her friends, together in a line that wavered like a ribbon over the yard, across the field, into the woods, as they paced the property off, step by step, so that not one single inch of it was missed.

Not me. Not Clodine Wheeler. I'm not down there with the others, outside the cabin, standing in the yard. I'm not among the crowd of curious onlookers that's gathered there. I've not become one of the links in Jewel's human chain.

No, instead I'm here, by myself, balanced on the boulders at the top of the spillway, and from where I stand I can see what they've all been looking for. Below me, the poor dead body of Lilly's baby, C. T. Duke, Chance. It floats with the pull of the current, and turns. Its face, battered by the rocks, is buried in the river; the red corduroy jumpsuit billows, bright in the seething foam. One bare foot is exposed, the head bobs, hair fanned like seaweed, arms outstretched. The body catches on a branch, pulls loose, circles, dips, moves on. The dead trees hover overhead, stark against the threatening glower of the sky.

And I've cupped my hands around my mouth, and I'm shouting. I'm screaming and I'm calling. I'm hollering until my throat aches, but my voice is weak, remote, nothing, feeble and thin. It's carried off on the wind, drowned in the thunder of the water, muffled by the continued fury of the rain.

⚬✕⚬

Later Lilly would stand in her kitchen with the other women gathered around her. They hovered protectively, touched her shoulder, wrapped their fingers around her arm. They wiped her cheeks with the back of a hand, pulled her hair away from her face. They whispered to her, hummed condolences, held her, rocked her, moaned.

"If only we'd thought of holding hands sooner," Jewel said, gazing out the doorway into the gray, dark rain.

Like that, Harmony Lake had become a perilous place, full of danger, a thing to be feared. Everyone agreed that there must have been other people who had died in it before. Children, babies even.

Some folks could remember one man who had tied a rock around his neck like a locket and drowned himself. One time a boy dove off one of the bluffs and broke his neck.

But these were not people that any of us knew. It was no one we had ever met. They were only tourists, visitors, passersby, vacationers here who, Jewel said, would have been better off if they'd just stayed put in the first place, never come here, never left their homes at all.

BABY DROWNS IN HARMONY LAKE, the headlines read. CONVICT'S KID ACCIDENTALLY DEAD. NATURE'S JUSTICE? DEATH ROW INMATE MOURNS LOSS.

They laid his little coffin down in the cemetery up on the hill. People floated flowers there on the rising waters of the lake. Lilly Duke was taken in by Harmony, and it was here that she decided she would stay.

9

RIGHT AWAY then it started to look like just about everybody else in Harmony except for me had all of a sudden turned out to be nothing less than Lilly Duke's best and closest friend.

The black cloud of their spite and their disdain was dissipated, dispersed, melted in the heat of their compassion like the mid-morning sun burns off the blanket of mist that lifts up from the surface of the lake. All of them became kind and generous and sympathetic. They rallied together, gathered around her, circled her, enclosed her in a tight, protective, feminine embrace. Even my sister Jewel Jenkins joined the parade of women who took casseroles over and offered Lilly lifts into town, drove her to the church and back, made the funeral arrangements, jockeyed for a place near her when the newspaper and television cameras came out to cover the story of the murderer Timothy Duke's baby's drowning death.

Rena Zurn managed to get her picture printed in one of the magazines that they keep on the rack beside the cash register in the grocery store, and she bought ten copies of it for herself, and she still, even now, keeps these in a fireproof metal box in the basement of her house.

"Well, for posterity," she could be heard explaining. "This is history, after all. It's America. It's news."

She meant to leave one copy of the magazine to each of her grandchildren when she died, she said. Never mind that Rena didn't even have any grandchildren then. Her oldest daughter was only seventeen, but Rena was planning babies for her already, and a house and a husband, expecting that these things would certainly one day come, like snow in winter or rain in the spring, a permanent part of the natural order of things.

"Well, I guess I never really realized that Lilly was so very young," Jewel said to me. "I don't know why. I never thought about it, I guess. Maybe because that Tim Duke was older. Why, looking at her now, it's easy to see that poor girl's really not much more than a child herself."

Jewel shook her head and looked at me, her eyebrows wriggling with concern.

"And she's been through hell, Clodine," Jewel sighed. "Pure hell."

It was as if now that these ladies could somehow look at Lilly as a girl, a child, a daughter, rather than as a mother or a woman, she wasn't anymore a stranger to them, to any of us. Now Lilly had become a victim, a casualty, an unfortunate creature who could be pitied more deeply than she ever had been suspected or feared.

As helpless as any of the strays that Jewel took in. As in need of repairs as any of the projects that she undertook. She was like a special bit of junk that had washed up on the lake shore after a storm. Some small treasure that Jewel had found and was hoping to restore.

What my sister had in mind then was that she could in some way work to set poor Lilly straight. To make her right. Clean her off and fix her up and get her running smooth again.

"Lord knows, she may never recover from the loss of a child, of course," Agatha Pajek said, nodding into the faces of the others who had gathered around.

They put together boxes of food and blankets and clothing for Lilly. They assembled little care packages from the things they found on the shelves of Agatha's store.

"But at least we can offer her some solace. Show her how to have faith. Make sure she keeps on having some reason to go on living."

"She tried to kill herself three times!" Rena said, looking up from the magazine article, amazed at the depth of Lilly's desperation as well as at her astounding ability to survive.

And Jewel expressed her fears that Lilly might just take it into her mind to go and try again. And that this time she could very well succeed.

"Hey, we don't dare leave her alone for a minute, now do we?" Jewel asked, leading Lilly by the elbow into her own house, dragging Lilly's things up the stairs, fluffing up the pillows on the guest bed in the sewing room, setting an extra place at the table for Lilly Duke.

Jewel counted out the sedatives that the doctor had prescribed for Lilly. She made sure there were no razor blades handy in the bathroom. No scissors. No aspirin. No ropes.

Except for Jewel and her friends then, once her baby had drowned, there wasn't any reason anymore for Lilly Duke to be living here. My sister had become Lilly's most tenuous connection to our town.

She could have sneaked away. She could have slipped out of town, taken off and lost herself in the gray shadows, skulked off like a thief in the middle of the night. She could have packed up a few of her things—a jacket, some clothes, the framed photograph of Tim, the scrapbook, any pictures of the baby that she had. She could have filled a pillowcase with the bits and pieces that were left of her life, and slung it over her shoulder like it was her own special grab bag of gifts. She could have crept away out of here, as quietly as she had come, under the cover of the dark.

Maybe she would have found her way to the highway again. Stood out there by the HARMONY sign, her thumb out, her bag at her feet, one hand on her hip, and hitched a ride with a truck driver who would have been happy for the company, would have been pleased as punch to give a girl a lift. There would have been no baby awkward in her arms then. No child, no infant to raise difficult questions. Just a girl on the run, escaping from an unhappy home life, a ruthless stepfather, a mean mother, abusive brothers, a boyfriend who beat her. Lilly Duke could have come up with a million of these kinds of stories to tell.

She might have stopped to slit her wrists in a public bathroom. Or to throw herself off the railing of a bridge. Who would miss her? Who would care if she ran out into traffic on the Interstate and was mowed down by a semi roaring to Chicago with a trailerload of groaning hogs?

I could picture her perched on a padded leather stool in a coffee shop somewhere. I could see her picked up by a stranger there. A man with a car parked outside in the lot. A rail rigged up between the windows, across the back seat of his wide black car, hung with a row of his crisp dress shirts, his dark, woolen jackets and his folded slacks. I could imagine Lilly Duke latching on to anybody else, living any other life. Not sure of where she was going, never once revealing the truth of where she'd been.

Like a cat with nine lives, Lilly Duke could have found herself saved and saved and saved again.

But that wasn't how it happened. That wasn't what she chose to do. Lilly didn't go. She didn't move on. Instead, my sister had persuaded Lilly Duke that Harmony was where she belonged. We were her family. This was her home.

In 1891, there were one hundred blackbirds that were brought over from Europe to New York City, and they were set free in Central Park. These starlings had no enemies at all, and nothing killed them, so by now their population has grown and grown, and you can find them anywhere you might decide to go, in almost every single state.

They've given the starling the nickname of the interloper, because it will build its slovenly nest in just about any place, it doesn't care where. In the crook of a high tree or on the ledge of a tall building. Up high or down low. The starling is the very dirtiest of birds, and the noisiest. It scares off all the better birds, the prettier ones, the downy woodpeckers and the fly-catchers, the bluebirds and the flickers, by annoying them. It just drives them crazy. It imitates their calls, and it takes away their nests.

Out beyond the city limits of Harmony, past the thermometer population sign, farther than the Supper Club and the fair-grounds, over across on the far side of the lake, some of the old fields have been left to grow up from the prairie into what's become almost one hundred acres of hardwood trees and tangled brush. The area all around these woods is open farmland, fields plowed and planted, some of it pasture land. Besides the farmhouses that huddle in the midst of these acres, an out-cropping of more modern, well-kept homes has been scattered here and there along the back roads that lead up into town.

We call this area of the county Baxter's Woods, named after old man Baxter, whose family had at one time owned all that land for miles and miles around. He let most of it grow over. Sold some of it. His children made a fortune when they developed what was left, after the time when the lake was made.

You can go out into Baxter's Woods at dusk and watch while the air around you comes alive with the roiling thundercloud of the starlings' flapping, chittery dark shapes. They come soaring across the skies toward their roost here in an endless, un-broken stream, thousands and thousands and thousands of blackbirds. The flocks swirl down into the trees and they settle there, ready to spend the long hours of a winter night huddled together, warmed by the shared body heat of their own great swarm.

And almost the whole way around the edges of Baxter's Woods you can find the ground and the underbrush spotted with the splattery white droppings of these wild black birds. In some places you might stumble over a feathery high pile of dark corpses. Look up and you could see some of them caught, with their wings outspread, snared there in the net of leafless branches that arch out overhead. Everywhere it seems like, there are the cold, dark little bodies of hundreds of thousands of the blackbirds that the farmers have found a way to kill. Redwings and cowbirds, starlings and grackles. The nearby fields are littered with the spent casings of the men's shotgun shells.

It was the starlings, Galen said, that were the worst. Because there were so many of them. And they all of them were smart.

❧✕❧

I did go out to visit at the Duke cabin, before Emma came. Lilly had left Jewel's house and gone back to live there on the lake all by herself again. She'd gone home to pick up the pieces, to reassemble the puzzle of her life. All the talk seemed to have pretty much died out. The television cameras were focused elsewhere, their attention turned away to other people's stories, different tragedies, fresh disaster, more immediate news; the photographers and the reporters had all left Harmony. Everybody else had gone on home.

And I found Lilly left to herself, surrounded by the many gifts that all her sympathizers had sent. Blankets and clothing, food and furniture, religious pamphlets and videotapes and books. There was even a fund begun at the bank, where interested parties could send their donations for the support of that poor childless child, Lilly Duke. She had a bank card and a checking account both set up for her there in her own name.

Someone had donated a beautiful black wool coat, long with high padded shoulders, thick buttons, rich fur trim. Lilly put it on to show me. She shrugged her arms into the sleeves and turned the collar up against her throat.

"Isn't it something, Clodine?" she asked me. "Tell me, what do you think?"

That old mongrel dog, Hero, was sprawled on his back across the foot of Lilly's bed. Useless to anybody, he hadn't even noticed when C.T. went off. His tail thumped the mattress when I walked over and sat down near him, his nostrils flared, he sniffed, but he didn't bother to get up.

The old bicycle lay abandoned outside behind the house among the tall weeds.

All of C.T.'s blankets and sleepers, the little mittens and the jacket, the stuffed rabbit I had given him, the plastic truck, every bit of it had been boxed up and taken away.

"Out of sight, out of mind," Jewel said.

She believed it would be better to remove the reminders of the child. Easier for Lilly, she meant, if she didn't have to all the time be confronted by the absoluteness of what it was that she had lost. Give her the relief of not having to sit down and sift through the meager accumulation of his things.

Some of the men came in because their wives asked them to, and they fixed up the broken glass in the windows of the cabin. They tore down the boards that Lilly had hammered up. They laid some sheets of new linoleum. They patched the broken shingles on the roof. They had a telephone hooked up for her, so that if she ever needed anyone again, for whatever reason at all, this time she could have a way to call, to keep herself close, within easy reach, in touch.

Someone had donated some pieces of old furniture. There was a table now next to Lilly's bed, instead of the cardboard boxes overturned, and a lumpy sofa, two wobbly-legged wing chairs. An old refrigerator had been plugged into the kitchen and its constant low hum had become a comfort to her, Lilly said. Leftover casseroles and plastic tubs of Jell-O and tuna salad, egg salad and fruit were piled up on the shelves inside.

A Bible lay open there on the table by the bed, next to that framed photograph of Tim.

When Lilly looked at me I could see the tears that were brimming up in her eyes. She took the coat off and hung it up carefully from an iron hook on the wall beside the front door. She had buttoned her shirt, yellow and blue plaid flannel, demurely all the way up to the collar under her chin. The cuffs were pulled down on her arms and buttoned firmly at her wrists. The blue jeans that she wore were stiff and bore a crisp crease ironed in down along the front of each leg. On her feet she was wearing a bright, multicolored pair of woolen slippers that I recognized as having been crocheted for her by nobody else but my own sister Jewel.

Lilly had boiled a pan of water and brewed two cups of a pungent herbal tea for us. She held hers between her palms, up in front of her face, and she shut her eyes against the rising steam. To me her hands looked so childlike and small. She'd filed her fingernails and painted them a soft pink. Her hair was growing out longer, and it hung down over her forehead, into her eyes. The skin beneath the splatter of freckles across her nose and cheeks was smooth, softened, and pale. I would have called her pretty then. She looked cared for, in a way that had not belonged to her before.

"I'm thinking about going to work, Clodine," she was telling me. "Mrs. Pajek says I could have a job clerking there in her store. What do you think? It would be a way to make some money. Enough anyway to get by. To live respectable. Be normal, like everybody else. Just go on day to day, that's all I can expect to be able to do, I think. Don't you?"

On the wall Lilly had hung a dull blue and gold butterfly, mounted and framed, and from where I sat it looked to me just like it was a bruise spreading out against its snow white cotton mat.

Lilly was watching me, and then she looked away.

There was a murmuring of voices that kept rising up from

the television set on the counter in the kitchen. Someone had given Lilly a videocassette player, and she'd been looking at an old movie in black and white. The grayish figures moved back and forth across the tiny screen like shadows, indistinct and dim. The wind outside had begun to pick up some, and it ran its fingers through the trees, brushing the branches up against the shingles of the cabin roof, fondling the walls and windows with the softest whispery sound. Lilly's stone fireplace sat cold and empty and unused.

What was it then that I had been hoping I would hear from her? Did I think that Lilly Duke was going to turn to me and tell me she was sorry? Was I looking for a shadow of shame to fall across the features of her face? Did I believe that she might be feeling some regret, that she might have found herself obligated to explain to me how it all had happened, how one thing had led to another, but now she was sorry, she wanted me to forgive her, to understand her, to forget? Did I expect her to be embarrassed, humiliated, ashamed? After all that had already happened to her? When she had just lost her baby? When her only child had been taken from her, had wandered off and drowned?

There had been some murmuring in the beginning about a man, but that rumor was quickly denied by Lilly and dispelled by Jewel, so that later there was no word, not a hint, in any of the reports, in anyone's conversations, in any of the telling and retelling of what had happened. No one ever mentioned Galen. No one seemed to know or want to admit that he'd been there. His name was not in the papers. As far as Harmony was concerned, the connection between Lilly Duke and Galen Wheeler had never been made.

Lilly told the sheriff, "I don't know what happened. I was tired. C.T., poor thing, he had a cold. He'd been up all night fussing with it. It was after breakfast, and I was watching him playing with the pots and pans there, and then I guess I must have closed my eyes. Just for a second. It couldn't have been very long. I fell asleep. When I woke up again, well, my baby was gone. You all know for yourselves the rest."

And people looking at her pale face, the dark circles under her eyes, her freckles, the thin bones beneath her skin, her bad teeth, her crazy hair, the people who saw Lilly all believed her. It was easy to picture her childlike body at rest, sleeping, exhausted, curled up against the pillows, cuddled under the blanket. They could imagine Chance wandering off, unnoticed, untended, out the door and into the yard and down the path to the deep, icy waters of the lake.

No one was thinking then to place anyone else there next to Lilly in that cabin that day. No one pictured a man, Galen Wheeler, lying with her in that bed. No one but me was able to imagine their self-absorption. Only I could conjure up the harmony of their whispers, the flavor of their mingled sighs, and the nature of their moans.

On the floor beside the bed were the letters that had been sent here to her from Tim. Unopened, they lay scattered carelessly about, like fallen leaves.

I picked one up and turned it over and over in my hand. Lilly's name and address were written in tiny, smeared letters on the front. The postmark was Nebraska.

"What if he's sent you more money?" I asked her. "Don't you want to open them, at least? To see? Shouldn't you take a look?"

"He hasn't sent me money," Lilly answered, her eyes level, facing me, steady and straight. "And I already know what they say."

I raised my eyebrows. "What?" I asked. "What, Lilly, what do they say?"

"They say he wants to kill me now," she answered. "He writes about how much he would like to see me dead."

I could imagine then what must have been the searing white

heat of Timothy Duke's helpless rage. His only baby boy was dead. Drowned. Had he saved Lilly from herself, for this? Because without the child, what else in the world did Tim Duke have? Lilly had betrayed him in a way much worse than what she'd done to me. Because she had squandered his last hope. She had dashed his final dream.

I could picture the fury of his fists pounding against the steel bars of his cell. His face would be twisted up with anger.

"That bitch killed my kid," he would be crying. Screaming out, until the other inmates hollered out for him to shut up.

"He says I'm just as much a murderer as he is," Lilly told me. "He wants to know why I shouldn't be the one who ought to die."

I struggled awkwardly up off of the edge of Lilly's bed, unbalanced by the gravid bulk of my belly and the extra weight of my limbs. I went into her bathroom. I stooped, hunched above her rust-stained porcelain sink, and I splashed warm water on my face. It smelled like metal, iron and rust, gravel and mud.

Lilly's medicine cabinet door hung open above the sink. I saw the three or four brown plastic bottles — prescription doses of sedatives and sleeping pills — overturned there on the grimy glass shelves. It would have been Jewel who came in and took them all, emptied them into her own hands, afraid that Lilly might get depressed and try to kill herself again. I closed the mirrored door, and when I looked up into the cracked, scratchy glass, I could see that Lilly had followed me, and she was leaning in the doorway, watching me. Her face hovered, moonlike and pale, afloat there in the air behind me, and it seemed like it could just as well have been the ghostly reflection of my own.

The water was running hot then, and I thrust my hands into the angry, seething cloud of steam that billowed up, fogging the mirror, blotting over the two of us, erasing us both, entirely out.

Lilly had pushed herself away from the door frame and taken

a deft step forward, toward me, and she had grabbed ahold of me by my shoulders, hard.

"Clodine!" she was crying out, but her voice seemed thick and muffled by the rushing sound of the water that was running into the sink.

Her strong fingers dug down through my sweater and into my skin as if she might be able to mold me into some other shape, like I was made of mud or clay. She yanked and pulled, turned me, hauled me stumbling backward and away.

Lilly had freed my hands from the boiling fierce cascade of scalding water in her sink. I waved them, and they flew around my face like two bright red birds, throbbing, shrieking, bright shrill screeches of stinging, burning, purifying pain.

❧✕❧

By the end of that autumn, then, I was as big as a barn and not quite sure about how in the world I was going to make it all the way through without my insides dropping right down and out the bottom of me, like a soggy paper sack, I felt so heavy and so bloated and so big. The doctor at the clinic reminded me that I was supposed to be watching what I was eating, and I told him that I was, but that was a lie, because the truth was I was eating all the time, pancakes and eggs, grilled cheese sandwiches, frozen cakes and brownies. I slathered stalks of celery with mayonnaise, then quit with the celery and just slurped up spoonfuls of mayonnaise all by itself while I stood there at the refrigerator door, in the middle of the night, in my bare feet, in the dark. I gobbled cartons of ice cream, whole packages of bacon, bags of potato chips and cookies and bread.

When the baby kicked, so hard you could see the ripples across the stretched tight skin of my belly, I asked Galen if he would like to see. I offered to let him touch me, then, but he was afraid, and he didn't dare. He looked, and I took his hand and placed it there on the swell of my belly, but he snatched it back against himself just like he might have been burned. His eyes were wide, and his face was full of shock.

And the fan there in the window of our cottage turned and turned, humming, a whirring, silvery, flashing blur of blades.

Then on the night when I went into labor with Emma, Galen wasn't there, and it was Clayton who answered the phone and Jewel who came out to the cottage and helped me into the back seat of her car and drove me down Old Highway 30, past the lake and the trees, through town and beyond, between the fields, bouncing in the potholes so I had to cry out because it all, everything, every little bit of it was hurting me so bad, all the way to the hospital in Harlan where they strapped me to a table and tied my feet up in high stirrups, covered me with blue sheets and shone a bright light up warm against my skin.

There was meconium, like black mud, floating in the amniotic fluid, a sign of fetal stress, they told me, whispering, their brows furrowed, eyes frowning and filled with worry and concern. And so the doctors came in and laid a black rubber mask down over my mouth and I went to sleep while they cut me open to take my baby Emma out.

"Clodine." I heard the voices of the doctor and the nurses calling out for me, rousing me from the lake of ether that I'd been drowning in. They bent over close, and they called out my name. A bouquet of bland flat faces, pressed in close above my own.

"Wake up now," they were whispering. "It's all over. You have a daughter. Everything's just fine. You have a girl. A beautiful baby girl."

My hands were limp, as weak as wilted flowers. My body was an empty basket, hollowed out and still. I was shivering, flushed in a film of freezing sweat. Blood whispered. It seeped. It seemed to pool and thickly drip, into the sheets and through to the mattress, a blossoming, bright red stain.

They were holding Emma up for me to see. Her body was so perfect and so small, so pink and smooth and calm, her eyes squeezed shut, her mouth pursed. And when I closed my eyes again, it felt as if I was with Emma one person, the selfsame thing. As if I was Emma and Emma was me, we were one single being, one connected circuit, one whole essence, one creature, one thing. I could feel her body as if I was right there on the inside of it, looking out. I could hear her breathing; I knew the fearful flutter of her heart. I lay there all alone, in the darkness, in my hospital bed, my belly cramping, blood seeping, my hands tucked up under my chin, and I felt as if I had only just then been born, just that very minute come to life, myself.

A woman, a mother, a daughter, a sister, a girl. At the mercy of the boys that I might meet, the men that I might one day get to know—the fathers and the brothers, the stepfathers, the husbands, the lovers, and the sons. How all of them would come to me for something—they would turn to me, ask me to give them whatever it was that they thought they could not live without.

And I was thinking, oh, Jewel, please, come closer, touch me, hold me. Mother, take my hand. Cradle me. Gather around me all my friends, stay with me, don't you dare look away, don't you walk off, don't duck, don't lower your eyes, don't bend your faces down, don't drop your chins, don't turn your backs.

"If we had only thought of holding hands sooner."

That was what my sister Jewel had said.

"Then maybe her baby could have been saved."

If only she had reached out to touch Lilly Duke. If only Lilly had reached out for help from her.

And the other women picked it up; like a refrain this phrase was repeated and played through Harmony, over and over and over again. It was a lullaby, a song, a litany, jingle jangling, humming, winding around and around, a river running, a cur-

rent coursing, up and down the stairways, along the tangled
hallways, in and out the shadowed rooms of all the deepest of
my dreams.

So after it was all over, there was still Galen. It was raining,
and that was when, finally, he came to me. He brought the
truck in, headlights careening, tires skidding and screeching off
the street and into the hospital lot, humping the speed bumps,
rocking over the parking curbs, and he drove it right up onto
the sidewalk and left it there, with the one headlight gaping and
the motor running and the door hanging open, the radio howling some wild love song out into the night. Like a boat run up
over the shores of the lake, up onto the solid slope of the beach.

Galen staggered in through the double emergency room
doors, scaring the nurses, flinching at the harsh, accusing stares
of the other people who had huddled there. He stopped and
teetered, his fingers splayed on the wall for balance, suddenly
unsure, blinking in the harsh bright hospital corridor lights. He
lunged for the front desk and gripped the lip of the counter with
both hands, holding on for dear life, gasping, breathless, "My
wife . . . my baby . . ."

Well, my husband, Galen, was drunk. He smelled like cigarette smoke and vodka and green olives and sweat. His shirt
was wrinkled—he'd buttoned it up wrong so the tails hung
lopsided. The back seam of his jacket was torn, and his shoes
were sopping wet—they squeaked along the hallway as he
walked, and they were caked with mud. His hair was soaked
and plastered to his head.

"Well," said Clayton, steering Galen by the elbow, leading
him into my darkened room, drawing him up close to the bed
where I lay with our baby nuzzled up next to me, sucking blindly
at my breasts. My belly tightened, jerked and cramped, a deep-
seated ache that began way far down and then spread.

"See here, Clodine," Clayton said, "will you look at what
the cat dragged in."

Oh, he did look terrible. Jewel said that he looked like somebody who'd fallen into the lake. He looked like a man who'd been dredged up from the bottom, like a person who'd come this close to being drowned.

To me Galen's face looked like it had begun to melt; it shifted and sagged, and his cheeks were flaccid under a bristly growth of beard because for so many days now he hadn't shaved. Shadowy circles of exhaustion smudged his eyes, so blue they cut right through me, and I had to turn away.

"Oh, Jesus, Clo. I'm sorry."

Galen's hands were trembling. They shook as he reached for me. He tucked them under the baby's body and lifted her, oh so easily, up and away. Emma Margaret Wheeler. Galen held her, he cradled her there, balanced her in both his hands.

"She's so pretty."

He turned to Jewel and Clayton and shook his head, and he grinned. "God, she's beautiful."

He laughed. "Clodine?"

But I couldn't help it — my hands were fists, curled up and flailing out. I pounded Galen. I clawed at him; I tore at his clothes, pulled at his shirt, groped for his hair, tried to scratch out his eyes. I couldn't stop myself. I didn't know what I was doing. Jewel and Clayton each had grabbed hold of my arms. They pinned me there to my mattress. I was no match for them. With their combined strength and weight, they held me down.

And all I could do was scream and scream and scream.

❧✕❧

"I won't go back home with him," I said to them. Clayton had handed me one of his embroidered handkerchiefs, and I was wringing it, twisting it around my fingers, pulling it, snapping it tight between my hands. "I just can't."

"But it really does seem like he's trying, Clodine," Jewel answered. "Maybe you could just give him one chance. Find

it somewhere in your heart to . . . I don't know . . . forgive
. . . forget."

"Jewel's right, Clodine," Clayton said. "It does look like he's
trying to make this up to you. I mean it does seem like he's
sorry. For everything."

Clayton had taken Emma from me, and he held her body
cupped in his hand, pressed against his shoulder as he circled
around and around, rocking her, back and forth across the room.

I had come to them after they let me out of the hospital. I
had been living in this guest room of their house, the same
room where Lilly Duke had slept, for two weeks already by
then.

"At least, he does seem to be making some sort of an effort,
Clo," Clayton said. "I don't know, maybe you owe it to him
. . . to let him take you, both of you, back. Why not at least
give him a second chance?"

And I could picture what it would look like, our little cottage
by the lake. The china stacked in the cupboards, crystal sparkling
on the shelves. The laundry neatly folded in the basket at the
bottom of the stairs. Fresh flowers — baby's breath and rose-
buds — arranged in a glass vase in the living room; a Thanksgiving centerpiece of walnuts and small pumpkins, shiny green
and gold and orange gourds in a basket on the dining room
table. Our shoes lined up side by side on the floor of the closet.
The pillows snug beneath the smooth folds of the quilt on our
bed. The crisp white railing of the crib in Emma's nursery. The
ducks and chicks marching across the wallpaper; the sunlight
spilling in, puddling on the floor.

All of it, including Galen, there waiting for me, patiently,
biding time, breath held in anticipation of the moment of my
return. He would have kept the place picked up, everything
would be sparkling, like new, clean and neat. The refrigerator
filled. The bathroom counters scrubbed. There would not be
one thing left out of place.

"The house looks just beautiful, Clo," Jewel told me. "Really, it does. And I don't think he's been out at night one time. He isn't drinking anymore, I do know that. The least that you could do, Clodine, is do your best to meet the man halfway."

"A little forgiveness—" Clayton began.

And then there was the sound of Galen's truck in Jewel's driveway, timed perfectly to interrupt this conversation we'd been having. Clayton and Jewel looked at each other and smiled.

He left the motor running, as if he wasn't expecting anything else but that he would stop in for a second, gather up our things, and take us home. The exhaust from the tailpipe was billowing, a white cloud in the cold air outside. I stood at the window and watched him walk up to the front door. He clapped his gloved hands together. He hunched up his shoulders and hugged himself against the terrible cold.

"Don't let him in, Jewel," I told her, but too softly. She didn't hear me when I warned her, begged her, "Please don't let him come in."

And so Jewel opened the door, and Galen was standing there, his hands clasped behind his back, a ridiculous-looking red-checked hunting cap with a long front brim shading his face, and earflaps that had been tied together up over the top of his head.

I had backed away into the living room, and I sat down on the sofa there, with my hands folded in my lap. Quickly, I ran my fingers through my hair. Moistened my lips with the tip of my tongue. Wondered were my cheeks too pale, my face too fat, my eyes too red, their circles too ugly and gray?

And my heart was fluttering in spite of my resolve.

I listened to the sounds of their feet as Jewel led Galen in and pulled shut the door. Her slippers skimmed the carpet. His heels were heavy on the hard wood of the hallway floor.

Their voices reached me, Galen's rumbling soft and low and Jewel's a murmur that rose and fell almost like it was a song. I listened to the secret whisk and brush of their whispers beyond the open arch of the doorway, and then Galen was there, a black shadow, a silhouette, framed by warm bright light.

Jewel, behind him, ducked away. She took Clayton's elbow and turned him, led him off to the kitchen, Emma still cradled in his arms.

"We'll just leave the two of you alone."

So maybe it wasn't that I couldn't have helped myself. Maybe it was, in the end, that I didn't want to. And never had. Maybe it was the way that he was watching me. The way he moved, painstaking and slow, like an old man, like someone who's been injured, nurturing a soreness, favoring a wound. The way he stopped and held his body still. He hovered over me, so close that his knees touched mine. He looked down, lingered patiently, as if he could wait for me forever, and he would.

When I stood up and tried to turn away, he reached for me. His hands were warmer than I had expected them to be; they were soft where he touched me, they were gentle and smooth, but strong.

And it felt like I was falling.

And I had no other choice, then, but to give myself up to him, to let myself go.

Jewel is sitting here in the room where I've been sleeping. Her back to me, she is hunched over her work at the old sewing machine. Her shoulders move as she carefully guides the heavy folds of fabric along. She is stitching together a blue watch-plaid wool maternity dress that she's designed for herself to wear. Her foot is pressed down firmly upon the black pedal on the floor, and the needle jabs in and out, flashing with efficiency, a businesslike whir. She wears a red pincushion bracelet on her wrist. The hair at her temples is damp.

Morning sunlight streams in through the small dormer window and bathes Emma's body with the comfort of its warmth and yellow glow. She is on the floor, coloring in a book, lying on her stomach with her feet up in the air, heels thumping, toes curled.

And I am perched here on the edge of the bed. My knuckles are white because I've been holding on so hard.

Clayton has had to go off on one of his investigations again. We had another phone call from Daddy last night, and Mother is still asking me why don't I bring Emma and come away and stay awhile there with them.

Outside, in the park across the street, the children are calling to each other. An ice cream truck idles by, its speaker blaring out the tinkly notes of a nursery song.

"This old man came rolling home . . ."

"Jewel, did you ever wonder what he really does?"

"Does?" Her mouth is full of pins.

"When he's away, by himself. Clayton, I mean."

"Well, he works, of course. He talks to people. Interviews them. Takes statements, you know. He has to ask a lot of questions. He has to know which questions he should ask."

"But what about at night?"

And even as I start to say it I realize how unlikely what I am thinking is. How impossible it is to imagine Clayton striking up a conversation with a girl. Letting it get any more than brotherly or fatherly. Clayton, like a dog, everybody's one best friend. Because, first of all, he's just so large. I just can't get a picture of him leaning over someone like that, touching her hair. His big hands on her body, thumbs groping up under her shirt, tucking into the waistband of her skirt. I see instead his fleshy earlobes, the wide flare of his nose.

"Did you ever have a reason to suspect? I mean to maybe not trust him? Not believe what he said?"

And Jewel has turned to face me in the sunshine. The pins between her lips bristle.

"Are you serious, Clodine?"

I'm shaking my head. My hands, gripping the edge of the mattress, have begun to ache. Frozen, clenched. If I move them, I'm afraid that they will crack, splinter, and break.

"Don't the two of you ever argue, Jewel? Do you ever have a reason for a fight?"

She smiles.

"Of course we argue," she tells me. "Yes, we fight. Why, just last week, oh, I was so mad at him, I remember, because he hadn't bothered to fix the faucet on the kitchen sink yet and every time I turned the damned thing on, well, God, it sprayed water all over me, so by the time I finished with the dinner dishes I'd have to change my clothes, they'd be all sopping wet."

"Do you throw things? Do you slam doors? Do you run from him?"

"Finally I had to go in and fix the damn thing myself."

"But has he ever hurt you, Jewel? Did he ever hit you? Have you ever had to find someplace where you could hide?"

Emma has put her crayon down, and she's rolled over onto her back to get a better look at me and judge the expression on my face. She squints up to see me through the sunshine so bright that it blinds her eyes.

Jewel has pulled the fabric out of the machine and she is folding it over and over and over again in her lap.

"No," my sister says to me. "No, Clodine, of course not. Never. No."

After Galen and I were married, and we had moved into our cottage, we went out shopping together for the things we would need. We bought some furniture — a sofa, chairs, a table for the kitchen, a bed — and linens — towels and sheets, a flowery gray bedspread, pillows, place mats, tablecloths, napkins, and rugs. We picked out appliances — a washer and dryer, a dishwasher and refrigerator and a stove. We filled our kitchen drawers and cupboards with knives and forks and spoons, ladles and spatulas, pots and pans and drinking glasses, a wooden salad bowl, a pewter soup tureen, a silver gallery tray, a cut crystal vase.

But we never could settle on which dishes we should buy. We couldn't agree on the right china pattern. This one was too formal. That one was too frivolous. This one too plain.

"You'll only get tired of it," Galen warned me. "Imagine having to eat breakfast off the same plates every morning, every single day."

Finally what we chose was just a few pieces of each kind.

We had one place setting that showed the white and blue fronds of willowware, another the many-colored blossoms of Royal Doulton. Our shelves held plates of fragile bone white Worcester, bright gold and purple Palmyra teacups, pink and lavender Cornflower bowls, stately Wedgwood saucers, a flock of exotic birds perched together in a line along the rim of a Spode tray.

And so it was these plates that Galen and I threw at each other. The dishes that he smashed to pieces on the tiles of our kitchen floor. The cups and saucers that I lobbed through the glass window in the dining room, in those months that came then after our baby girl Emma had been born.

Afterward, I got out the broom and the dustpan and I swept away the colorful puzzle of their mingled chips and splinters and shards. I went into Pajek's store and I bought all plastic this time, without ornament, plain white.

10

WHAT HAPPENED to us then was this: Galen came to Jewel's house to take me home after Emma was born, and when I knew that he was coming I did my best to tell them, but I didn't find any way that I could say no to him, so I allowed him to take me and the baby both back home, and then we honestly did begin to make a real effort to start all over again, brand new, this time as a family, together, the three of us, Galen and Emma and me, in our pretty little cottage there on the shores of Harmony Lake.

That was November, at Thanksgiving.

And from a distance, where Jewel and my parents and all the other women who watched us stood, the life we had must have seemed like it was almost picture perfect. A dream come true. Galen Wheeler was just so handsome, Rena Zurn had been heard to exclaim. And so friendly, Nancy Withers said. Jewel agreed, and added, he's an interesting man, thoughtful, very smart.

I began to lose all the weight that I'd put on and my hair was taking back its shine. I was happy to be busy, wholly occupied, with all of the things that it was now my job to do. I washed diapers and bathed my baby in warm soapy water at the kitchen sink. I cooked simple meals for me and Galen. I washed our clothes and ironed his shirts. I sat in the rocking chair by the window in the front room with Emma sleeping peacefully in the comfort of my arms. I lay in our bed, on my back, wide awake in the middle of the night. I brought my baby up to nurse at my breast. My husband was sprawled out next to me, his hand on my leg, his eyes fluttering with the visions of his dreams.

I hummed, "Hush, little baby, don't say a word . . ."

I studied the moonlight that spilled in through the window and bathed Galen's face in the pooling of its broad, white beam.

And Emma was the most beautiful baby anyone had ever seen, they said.

To me, she looked just like Galen.

Mother and Daddy came up to see Emma and to visit us for a week over Christmas. I suppose that they had figured out by that time that it was highly unlikely we would ever be traveling down to Florida to stay with them, no matter how bad the winters got to be here. Galen didn't care for travel, I explained. He had obligations here in Harmony, and he couldn't just pick up and leave. He had been hired to drive the snowplow again that winter. He worked the asphalt roads between the farms, the narrower concrete streets, private driveways, public parking lots. He shoveled snow and broke through ice, sprinkled salt, spread sand. Neither one of us had any reason in the world then to want to go away.

And it seemed like Daddy finally had found a way to accept that fact. Or anyway, he told me that he did. He came up the front walk to our cottage, grinning at Galen; he put a hand out, and the two of them shook hands with brisk and hearty father-and-son good cheer on the front porch, outside the door. It seemed then as if the two of them had come to some kind of an agreement, reached an understanding, buried the hatchet and, for my sake and for Emma's, too, I suppose, they decided they could find a way between them to come to terms. Mostly Galen's terms, but anyway they were terms.

It was as if Daddy had said to himself, "Well, if Clodine loves him, then I guess that'll just have to be good enough for me. I won't stand in her way. If he makes her happy, well then, that's all that matters here. Nothing else in the world counts."

Mom slipped her hand into the crook of his arm and she beamed at me, all smiles, like a person who has just won the latest battle in what has been a long, hard war.

Jewel had been stopping over to visit with me just about every single day then, and she always brought something with her, cookies or casseroles, little things she'd made. Mom had used the time in the car driving up here to knit a baby sweater with tiny painted porcelain buttons. She'd also made a Christmas stocking with Emma's name across the top and Santa's face rosy and pink under a fluffy white Angora beard.

Mom and Daddy both were so helpful, and so generous, so tickled, really, to have another grandchild. They just loved to hold my baby.

"Isn't she just the sweetest little thing?" Mom said, hovering behind, watching over Dad's shoulder, leaning in to straighten Emma's blanket or retie the laces of her booties.

Peter stood in my kitchen and methodically bounced a small rubber ball against the wall with a noise that was as maddening as the constant plunk and tap of a leaky faucet dripping water in the bathroom sink. Mary Alice was crouched on the floor eating a red and white striped candy cane that Jewel had given her. She turned it around and around, in and out of the puckered kiss of her reddened lips, until she had sucked its end into a long, sharp point.

Later, when Daddy and Galen and Peter had all gone off into town together and Emma was napping, I came out of the bedroom, and I overheard my mother and my sister with their heads together, whispering between each other at my kitchen table. I caught Mary Alice staring at me, in wonder, with wide eyes.

"Do you really think she's all right, Mom?" Jewel was asking. "I'm not sure that I could tell anymore. I mean, I worry so much about her sometimes. Do you think she's going to be, you know, okay?"

"Doesn't she look fine now?"

"Well, I guess she sure does . . ."

"Jewel, Clodine has had a very bad experience. She's been through a lot. Imagine if you were pregnant and then found that baby drowned like that. Why, that's enough to give anyone the willies, I'd say."

"But Mom," Jewel was saying.

She leaned in closer, across the table, and lowered her face so her hair fell forward and hooded the greedy gleam of pleasure that I imagined would be lighting up her eyes.

Because there is a part of my sister Jewel that relishes the notion of upset. She will revel in that swampy murk of scandal that sometimes messes up the otherwise clear waters of another person's being. Her heart might sing with the sounds of a disturbance dredged up from out of anybody else's life. A part of her that thrives on the gossip, on the examination of what might have happened, what didn't happen, what did, what was planned, what wasn't, on the telling of what has gone wrong. A woman like Jewel might cherish the fact of the story itself, without caring whose it is.

"There's some more to it than just that, I think, Mother," Jewel began. "What I mean is, well, Galen . . ."

And when I heard her saying his name like that, I moved from the doorway, cleared my throat and walked deliberately through the kitchen, over to the sink. They both of them looked abruptly up, stopped, reached for the sugar, poured more coffee, stood too fast, turned too quickly away.

"You're happy, Clodine, now aren't you?" my mother asked

on the night when she and Daddy left to go back to their warmer Florida home. "You have everything you want?"

I said, "Don't be silly, Mother. Of course, yes, I am. I do."

And who in her right mind wouldn't be happy? Who wouldn't be content? In my situation. With all the things I had. A beautiful new baby, and a sister to look after me. A mother who cared very much about me. A father who had always loved me best. What reason in the world could a girl like me find for being so sad?

Well then, that was it. Why wasn't I happy? What was it that I wanted? What did I expect? What possible purpose was served by my not finding a graceful way to let it go, to give it up and move on? Why couldn't I let things be? I might have expected we could find a way to go on like that forever. I could have worked harder to keep things calm and quiet between Galen and me. I might have waited for those bad times to pass us over, for the bruises to fade, the wounds to heal, for the pain to go away, for the three of us to grow. The worst things were in the past, all of it behind us now, the most terrible parts over with, molded into memories, more distant and, over time, turned into something even vaguer than a dream. I didn't have any need to dredge up the toppled framework of our old quarrels, or sift through the ruins of what had already been said, or resurrect the remains of what was already over and done.

Except for this. There has always been this naughty place in me where I must keep on picking at things. A part of my heart where it seems I have no control, where there is an urge, a compulsion, that just will not be satisfied to leave well enough alone. I will worry a loose button until it falls right off in my fingers. I'll fiddle with the frayed cuff of a sweater until the whole thing has come unraveled in my hands.

So what I did was—and even while I was doing it I was aware that I was wrong to be doing it, that I could have found some way to restrain myself, that I should have looked for the strength to hold back—I started in provoking Galen. I picked at him. I poked at him. I pushed him here, and then I pulled him there. Just like I was needling him on purpose, just like I meant to make him strike back at me; it seemed as if I could not keep from doing the things that always brought it out of him. I couldn't stay quiet. I had to push and push, and poke and poke, just like you roll your tongue over and over a sore spot inside your mouth, testing it, touching it, almost relieved in some way when you discover the reliability of how it continues to cause you the same expected pain.

Like that game we had played, when I was little, nestled in my father's lap, and then he told me, he said, "Clodine, don't you touch my nose."

So that then I just had to. And I couldn't stop myself. I couldn't help it. I took his words to be a challenge. It was a dare. It was a temptation that I never was able to resist.

Well, I guess, then, the truth is, it was me. I was the one who was always urging Galen on toward whatever violence and cruel things he felt he had to do. I just about came right out and asked for him to hurt me. Begged him for it.

"Hit me, Galen," I whispered. "So I know that you still love me, same as always, like before." Burn me. Freeze me. Bruise my arms and legs; claw my back; tear my muscles; crack my bones.

And what I thought then was that all of them, including my sister, especially my sister, and her friends, had found some talk in what they thought might have been going on between me and Galen and Lilly Duke. I could picture how those women might huddle up together around the table in my sister's warm kitchen, spinning out their stories, seaming together one another's observations and opinions and points of view to make what they could of the whole tale. And Jewel Jenkins right there in the middle, at the center of it all, while the others craned in closer to hear her better when she talked, her hands moving fast, face reddening with the effort, her eyes bright with the wicked thrill.

"Well, and then he burned her, that's what."

"He never."

"Yes, he did. She as much as told me so herself."

"Well, why in the world then does she ever stay?" Agatha Pajek would be turning away in disgust.

"He slapped her. Pinched her."

"No!" I could imagine Rena Zurn's hand flying to her face when she gasped. Goose bumps would have popped up to tickle the skin on her arms.

"Oh, my." Nancy Withers's eyes would have widened with wonder.

"And then, you know, there is more to it even than that. There is also Lilly Duke."

And I know now that I had begun to think too much about Lilly and Galen, how he was maybe going out on me all the time, leaving me behind and attaching himself to Lilly Duke instead. I pictured them meeting up after dark at the Supper Club. I could imagine how he took her out into the parking lot and eased her down there on the cracked leather seat of our truck. How they drove off together, cruising the back roads, with one headlight broken, the other beaming, passing other cars while other lovers cried, "Padiddle!" and fell into each other's arms. How he glided down into the fields and spread a quilt out over the grass. How he took her hands and walked her along to the edge of the lake. How he pulled up her skirt and pressed her back up hard against the thick, rough bark of a tree.

"Don't think I don't know what you're doing, Galen Wheeler," I told him. "Don't believe that I don't have the kind of eyes it takes for a person to see."

"Know what, Clodine? See what?"

That he was with Lilly whenever the notion occurred to him,

driving her off one place or another, renting motel rooms, following her into her cabin, taking her there in her own bed, with Tim's photo face down on the table, the TV babbling dimly in the other room.

"You've slept with her, Galen Wheeler," I screamed at him. "And I know it for a fact that you have!"

Galen picked his napkin up off his lap and laid it on the table by his plate. He took a sip of water from the crystal glass. I watched his throat moving when he swallowed. He looked at me; he sucked on his teeth and he licked his lips with such deliberation, as if he were considering, weighing the possibilities, the pros and the cons of what he might decide to do next.

"What you know is nothing, Clodine."

He pushed his chair back, cleared his throat, stood up and came around, across the room, until he was standing behind me. He put his hands on my shoulders, laid them there, like weights, a burden that would keep me down. He clenched his fists against me; he dug his fingers in deep.

I could feel the sting of his nails cutting through my sweater and into my skin. The ache of his thumbs bruising me. The pain was almost like a relief, then, when he brought me up to my feet and pulled my hair back so my throat was opened to him. I held my breath and let my body sink into his.

And all that time Emma was screaming in her room, howling in her crib, gasping.

"Let her cry," Galen shouted.

He slammed me back against the wall. He tore down my jeans and ground himself into me while I whimpered and groaned. Milk rushed down into my breasts, hard and fast, prickly and warm. It squirted out; watery and thin, it leaked through the layers of satin and lace; it soaked into the cotton and the wool fabric of my clothes. It bled right through the weave of Galen's own shirt, sopped all the way down to where it cooled like sweat against the bare surface of his skin.

*

And then it seemed like what had happened was that the pain of it all just got to be too big. It began to spread too far. At first it had been like a bruise, flowering, so ugly and so slow. But now it had become something else, rolling along so fast and so far that it seemed like pretty soon it was going to be too late for anyone to do anything to save us, too far gone for either one of us to stop.

"You have more than just yourself to think about now," my mother had warned me.

And when I looked at Emma, I knew that this was all that was important. This was what was true.

It was summertime again. There were the flowers that bloomed in the fields along the edges of the woods. There was the heat. A threat of rain. Lightning sent its shivery fingers groping out across the blackened sky; thunder pounded the air, smashing it like glass.

I went out in the afternoon to cut the wildflowers that I would arrange in a crystal basket on the table by the door. I left Emma napping in her crib, and I went out walking through the meadow behind our house, above the lake.

Herbs for the meat were growing wild on the mounds beyond the woods. I snipped small bunches of parsley, dill, tarragon, and thyme.

In the summertime like that, the heat would be conscious and oppressive; it bore down. Galen was expecting rain, he had told me. I kept hearing the thunder rumble; it was a distant, angry roar.

Before I saw them, I heard them. There was the murmuring of their mingled voices, as steady and as soft as the song of water flowing over rocks. There was the quilt spread out upon the grass, a patchwork of color, a rainbow of patterned squares. Galen's arms were folded over his chest. Lilly lay on her stomach, with her knees bent and her feet wriggling in the air. She was wearing white leather shoes. Galen's shirt was undone, his skin was damp, and the hair on his body gleamed. The heat bore down, a weight, a shawl, as sodden and heavy and shapeless as wet wool. Ice chimed in their glasses. There was a thermos of cold lemonade; a plastic bottle of tea.

"Lilly," Galen was saying.

Her earrings glinted a message coded by the sunshine. Her face was hidden in shadow, bent down over the opened pages of a magazine.

"It was on a cross-country flight," she was telling him. A birth in a bathroom. "A teenager is what it says here." The father was from Georgia. "My God, Galen, my God."

He was cracking the ice between his teeth. She shivered and kicked off her shoes.

A teenage mother had stuffed the newborn in under her sweater and smuggled it off the plane. She'd hurled it into a trash bin, and then she slipped away. She left a trail of blood. Like a snail's slime. Like the crumbs dropped by a child in the forest, lost.

"Galen," Lilly was whispering. She leaned over closer to him. She hooked her hair behind her ear. The bracelet on her arm was a gold snake with emerald eyes, wound around. It spit. She rubbed his stomach. He closed his eyes.

Galen and Lilly lingered there on the quilt in that heat. Her head was cradled in his lap; his head was tilted back. Eyes closed, they drifted and dozed. She was dreaming; he snored. Her lips slightly open, she drooled; saliva gathered, spilled over, a rivulet down her chin. My arms were full of wildflowers; I was invisible, soundless, a ghost. I haunted them, but neither of them knew me out there while I watched them, when I was passing by.

When I got back to the cottage, Jewel was there in my kitchen, waiting for me. She had brought a basket of tomatoes from her garden. A head of lettuce, some peppers, zucchinis, and eggs. She was standing at the window with her hands in the warm dishwater in the sink.

She turned when she heard me come in.

"Clo?"

She must have seen the stricken look in my eyes. My hands were clammy. I felt faint and dizzy. My face must have been so pale.

I opened my arms and the wildflowers I had gathered spilled away from me; they lay strewn and broken across the kitchen floor, their brittle stalks bent and their fragrant blossoms crushed. The crystal basket at the edge of the table bounced and teetered as my hip knocked against it, and then it fell. It crashed, exploded, shattered; the hard shards and sharp splinters of broken glass glinted like chips of ice, hidden in the deep pile of the green rug beyond the door.

Jewel lurched toward me. "Clo?"

Her foot came down on a thick chunk of the broken glass. Its edge was so sharp that it sliced right through the rubber sole of Jewel's thong, into the soft, fleshy pad of her foot. Jewel's blood was slimy and warm; it ran through her fingers, seeped into the white fabric of the dish towel and bloomed there like flowers on snow. Her blood was like a finger painting on the floor.

⟩⟨⟨

"It's all for the best," Jewel had whispered to Lilly. "I know that it's hard, but you'll have to find some way to use your pain to give you strength. Somehow this was God's will. A punishment maybe. Retribution. Divine justice. Do any of those phrases mean anything to you at all?"

Outside the church, standing together, the sharp heels of their shoes sinking into the grass and soft soil of the lawn, the women had stood together, circling Lilly, as their husbands carried Chance's bitty white coffin down the steps to the yawning maw of the waiting hearse. And my sister had touched Lilly Duke, she had held on to her shoulders and looked into her eyes, jostling Lilly as if she meant to rouse her from a dream, to shake her into wakefulness, open her eyes, make her aware.

"Are you listening to me, Lilly?" Jewel hissed. "Do you understand? Can you hear?"

But what I knew was that these were also exactly the same sorts of phrases that someone else might have offered as a comfort to Raymond Pilcher's family after Tim had murdered him. This was what the people who convicted Tim and sentenced him to death believed. That somehow a person must and will be made to pay for what he owes the world. That there is a price for sorrow, a payment to be made in exchange for the pleasure to be got from inflicting pain upon the helpless, beating up on the defenseless, bullying those who are too small or too weak or too stunned to fight back.

"There's no such thing as a free lunch," my father told me, reaching for his belt.

"You won't get away with this," my mother said, grabbing a hairbrush and yanking down Jewel's shorts. "I love you too much not to do something. You have to be taught. I'll drum it into you until you can tell the difference between what is right and what is wrong. You've got to be told. But it does hurt me a lot more than it will hurt you. Believe me, I do this for you. For no one's good but your own."

And my sister understood what our parents were telling us, and she tried offering this same way of looking at the world to a girl like Lilly Duke. Jewel really did believe it when our mother told us that all things, good or bad, comic or tragic, healthful or hurtful, these things that happen to people can be seen to have had some other purpose beyond their pleasure or their pain. Some scheme at work that transcends the accidental and turns it into reason, gives it sense.

"Everything is useful," our mother told us. "Even misery. Even sorrow. Even pain."

When good things happen to you, Jewel believes, well, no doubt you've somehow earned them. You've kept your chin up. You've made the best of a bad situation. You can laugh your afflictions away, if you really do believe strongly enough in your own basic goodness. You can put off death itself if you're armed with enough good cheer.

Or, to turn it all around backward, you can draw disaster down upon yourself. You can create catastrophe out of your own unfounded dread. You can attract sickness and disease like a magnet of ill will. You can catch your stepfather's eye and tempt him with your own unspeakable desires; you can use your obsessive love to make your husband crazy and push him into violence against you; you can slit your own slim wrists; you can stick your own small finger in between the sharp turning blades of the fan.

In the following series, the fifth number is omitted.

56 . . . 35 . . . 20 . . . 10 . . . ___ . . . 1

Which is it?

2?   3?   4?   5?   6?   or 7?

And if I tell Jewel that the answer to this question is 4, would she ever be able to understand why? Would she see that there is more than one operation involved? Could she look beyond the first level of adding and subtracting to discover another difference, a different sequence, a secondary sense? Will she know to look deeper, to take more steps, to go further? Will she get it that there are more layers than what she is used to being able to see?

No, if Jewel wants to understand the pattern in this, she will have to work it out backward. She will have to take the numbers and try them all, to see which one is correct, to figure out which one fits. And when I tell her it's a 4, she'll have to answer, "But, of course. I see that now, Clodine. Really, I do. I should have known."

Because that is exactly the way that Jewel went about interpreting what was happening to Galen and Lilly Duke. She had no trouble in the world seeing it as an inevitable outcome of an already unstoppable series of events. That a baby should have died. That an infant should have drowned that way. Face down in the water, red jumpsuit billowing, circling, turning, tiny arms outstretched. Jewel told me then that there is no such thing as a second chance when you're talking about a murder.

It was divine justice, she said. Retribution. Revenge.

Once her baby was dead, Jewel reasoned, well, then Lilly Duke was in a position where she might after all be saved. She could be taken into the fold. Slough off her markings as an outsider here and begin to consider herself one of us. She had a history. A tale to tell that might begin to define her, that might seam her own life in along with the patterns of the rest of ours. Lilly Duke could be absolved of all her crimes this way. She could be pardoned, vindicated, forgiven, and even, in a way, loved.

When I tried to tell Jewel otherwise, maybe I did get overly upset. Maybe I raised my voice. Maybe I grabbed her by the shoulders, dug in my nails, shook her. Maybe I screamed in her face, spitting, "No! Please! No!"

But it was only because Jewel was refusing to see what I knew was the truth; she would not allow herself to grasp it, or to try and come to an understanding of what was really real. Jewel had no honest hold on what had happened, or what I knew still was going on. She couldn't comprehend even the smallest part of the whole thing, either the beginning or the middle or the end. My sister had no way to even try to conceive how complex it all might be. How one thing might imply another. How having faith in one idea could only lead to believing something else.

That Timothy Duke had murdered a man named Raymond Pilcher—for no better reason than the thrill of a ride in a very fast car — and that Tim then went a long way toward redeeming himself by saving Lilly Duke — who would surely have died without him; who most likely would have killed herself sometime if he hadn't loved her enough to take her with him, fill her with his dreams, pump her full of his false hope — and that between the two of them they had conceived a baby and made a child, only to let it go, only to lose it again, let it toddle off for no good reason, topple into our lake, sink and drown in our water, its small, short life smothered, like a flame, by Galen's selfishness and Lilly's carelessness and my laziness and Jewel's spitefulness and Harmony's heartlessness and Tim's crime.

And that anyway Tim is still there on death row, waiting, and that he will die there, too — that we will murder him right back, strap him into a chair and let a thousand volts of electricity go pulsing through his body until his heart bursts with it, lurches and sputters and, finally, stops — and why wouldn't it have been better all around if only Lilly had been left alone, if only she had succeeded in killing herself that one first time, with the aspirin, before there was any blood, before there was a baby or a friendship or an adultery or a drowning? Before any of us here in Harmony ever became involved.

Because — and this was the real what for of it, this was the part that was making me crazy, this was what had me shaking Jewel, screaming at her, spitting at her, filled with fear and panic and dread — hadn't Galen Wheeler, my Galen Wheeler, hadn't he, by loving Lilly, by distracting her, by taking her away, hadn't he murdered that baby just as surely as Timothy Duke had shot Raymond Pilcher? And wouldn't Galen Wheeler, my Galen Wheeler, somehow, just as surely, in some way have to pay?

"Well, Clodine, now isn't it true she already tried to kill herself at least three times before?" Jewel was asking me. She had pulled the glass out of the bottom of her foot and wrapped a white dish towel around and around. She stood now, in the bathroom, leaning against me, her weight supported by mine. I could feel her warm breath like a breeze rustling in my hair.

I nodded. Yes. Lilly had swallowed a handful of aspirin the first time. Twice that I knew of, she had tried to slit her wrists.

"And so the chances are pretty good, don't you think, that some day she's going to wake up and decide she wants to try it again?"

Jewel had wrapped an arm around me, and she pulled me close. Her body, smaller than mine, was soft and warm. She rocked me back and forth. I could see that the blood from her foot was still seeping into the towel.

"She'll be depressed, wallowing in grief for her lost baby, sorrowing after what she thought she might have found in Tim, mourning for her miserable childhood, her wretched stepfather, her neglectful mother, the ugly squalor of her whole messy life."

Set out on the white tile countertop in my bathroom, a small tin box. The face of a smiling man with a long, curled mustache painted in black and yellow on the top. Six double-edged blades spread on the tile like an opened fan.

"Of course, we have no way of really knowing for positive sure whether Lilly will ever have a need for them, Clodine. But when that time does come, if those kinds of thoughts ever do cross her mind again, if something happens that pushes her over the edge, if she decides to, if she thinks she can't bear it, if she wants it, well, it'll be there. She'll know what to do. That's all. It's like an opportunity. A chance. A way out for her. Think of it as an offering. Look at it like it was a gift. A wish fulfilled."

Jewel picked up the box. She held it between her finger and her thumb, and she turned it, as if examining it under the light. It seemed like the man with the mustache was leering at me. Daring me. Winking, grinning, urging me on.

I wrapped my arms around my own body. I held myself,

hugged myself, doubled over with apprehension, my panic and my pain, because I knew then that I had come apart. I could feel myself splintering. And I knew that I would shatter, like thin glass, that I was exploding, into a billion little pieces, a million bright sparks. Like the stars in the sky above the lake on a moonless black night. Like fireflies adrift in an empty far field. Like the twinkle lights scattered through the branches of a tree.

"You're just upset, Clodine," Jewel told me, narrowing her eyes.

She laid an arm over my shoulder, and she hugged me, squeezed me up close. She kissed my face. She nuzzled my neck. She hummed, whispered, murmured, comfort and peace.

She touched her lips to my forehead; she brushed her hands across my hair. She reached and picked each blade up carefully with the tips of her fingernails. She slipped them back into their box, and she pressed it into the pocket of my opened palm. She folded my fingers down over it, patting my knuckles, holding my fist in the nest of her own small, useful hands.

And in the nursery, then, Emma had begun to cry.

Sometimes now I'm thinking about Galen, about how it was before Lilly came to Harmony, how it had been with us. I might find him out on our front porch, sitting on the steps with his knees drawn up, and maybe he was staring off into the shadows between the trees, but I didn't try to guess what it was he thought of then, whether he was longing for something that he couldn't have, whether he was wanting something else. I didn't know what was in his mind, and I never had, and I didn't ever want to, either.

I take a seat down there beside him on the step. I lean up close to him, let my head rest on the solid smooth ledge of his shoulder, feel the crisp cotton fabric of his shirt sliding up against my cheek. I let my hand lie there on his leg. My thumb follows the raised double stitches of his pant seam. I am smelling him; I'm breathing him in.

There are swarms of fireflies that skitter in and out among the high weeds along the path down to the lake. The rumble of the motorboats rising up from the distance is a low, comforting growl. Crickets whine; a chorus of frogs chirps and sings.

"We go on," it seems like they were telling me, over and over and over again. "We go on. We go on. We go on."

That summer the cicadas came crawling up and out of their tunnels underground, and they left their contorted, hollow husks clinging to the bark of every tree.

But in all this time of my whole life, all the years that I've been living here in Harmony, I have never that I know of even one single time seen a real live cicada. Only those empty shells that they leave behind. And I am guessing that the creatures themselves are nothing at all in the world like their shells. I am imagining that they are beautiful, feathery and huge, with wide-spanning, glimmery, many-colored wings.

"They're not birds, Clodine," Jewel tells me. "They're insects. That's all they are. They're not even butterflies. They're bugs."

And in Lilly Duke's bathroom, on a cloudy glass shelf of the medicine cabinet, behind the cracked mirror on the door, there were the empty pill bottles, brown plastic, as useless and hollow as the abandoned shells of the cicadas that clung with such tenacity to all the trees. And there is where I put the razor blades that Jewel had found for me. I left them like a message, a treasure, a secret gift that Lilly Duke would someday, when she thought she maybe needed them, find.

~✕~

Galen was thundering, "Shut up! Shut up! Shut up!"

But Emma wouldn't quit crying. She was hungry; she was

lonely; she was wet. She had a tummyache, an earache. She'd had a bad dream, been frightened or frustrated or hurt. She was a baby. She couldn't help it if she cried.

She wailed and wept and screamed. Her breath was hitched with sobs that heaved her body like a rainstorm shakes the trees. Tears gathered and rolled down her cheeks.

I tore Emma out of the angry grip of Galen's hands. There were bruises on her arms. A trail of marks, across her shoulders, down along the middle of her back.

Then Galen wasn't coming home to me at night anymore. As if he was fearful of what might happen, afraid of what he might be capable of, scared of what he might be driven to do, Galen chose to stay away. He went out one morning, early, while Emma and I were still asleep, and then he didn't come back. The phone might ring in the middle of the night, jarring me awake, dragging me up out of my dreams, but when I answered, he never spoke to me; it was as if he was too far away for me to hear him anymore, like there never was anybody there. Just the deep, steady wheeze of his breathing rising up out of the darkness, humming over the wires, hovering above me, blowing like a wild wind into my head before he hung up and then the emptiness and the lonely silence of our cottage yawned.

I might look out my window and see the pale, wall-eyed ghost of his white truck, the beam from its single headlight grazing the edges of the lawn, the metal grille leering, motor running, constant and soft, like the surly low growl of a wary dog. I could just make out the red glow of Galen's cigarette as he lifted and lowered it, rising and falling there in the murk beyond the windshield, inside the cab. The next morning when I went out I might find an empty vodka bottle in the high weeds beside the driveway, glinting, winking in the bright sunlight.

Jewel said she'd seen Lilly Duke riding her bicycle into town and back again by herself almost every day. The basket on the handlebars would be empty. The dog Hero might lope along after her, his tongue hanging, ears flat, tail wagging. Ivy Lazelle told Jewel that her husband had seen Galen's truck parked there outside the Duke cabin more than once. Agatha Pajek said that Lilly had come in and asked to cash one of Galen's checks, endorsed on the back to her.

"Just be patient, Clodine," Jewel was whispering, rocking my baby in her arms, curling Emma's tiny pale fingers over the thicker knuckle of her own. "If it's meant to be, then he'll be back. That's all. And, well, if not, then that's what's for the best. Believe me. Have faith. Just wait awhile and see."

⟿✕⟾

"And if that looking glass gets broke . . ."

I was holding Emma, rocking her, asleep in my arms, so warm against me, the edges of her curls darkened, damp with sweat. The weight of her head against my arm had numbed it, put my fingers to sleep. I sat in the chair by the window, looking out from the living room at the dusky sky. I didn't bother turning on the lights. I let the gray light accumulate, covering us like a blanket, rolling in over us like a cloud.

Jewel and Clayton and the kids had gone out to the Supper Club to eat. They had asked me to come along, too, but I said no. Maybe this was the night when Galen would change his mind about things and decide he could try coming home. There would be plenty of people at the fairgrounds, eating popcorn and cotton candy and hot dogs, soaking up the smells of sawdust and grease, animals and mud, taking in the sights and sounds of the carnival as if it was something wonderful and unique, as if it didn't come back again the same as always, every year. Boys winning stuffed bears for their girlfriends. Holding hands on the Ferris wheel. Stepping away from the midway, into the shadowy corners for a kiss.

Maybe Galen was out prowling the back roads in his truck, with the windows rolled down and the radio on. Maybe Lilly was sitting in the dark like me, waiting for Galen to decide to come to her.

Emma's eyelids were fluttery with dreams. I could almost hear the hammer of her heart, that's how quiet it had got. Her lips moved, sucking. Her hands worked, clenching and un-clenching fists.

And then that was when the phone rang. I hoisted Emma up into the crook of my elbow and fanned my hand out across her back. Sensation pricked my deadened fingertips — a burning rush of feeling, a maddening, far-off itch. Emma's head lolled on my shoulder. Her drool was slithery, a trail, wet and shiny on the smooth surface of my bare skin.

"Hello?"

But that wasn't Galen calling me, changing his mind, hang-ing silent on the other end as if there might be stretched between us a wide and empty, airless vacuum of regret and unhappiness and doubt. That wasn't Galen Wheeler. That was Lilly Duke.

Her voice was a whispering in my ear, breathless and hushed. "I'm sorry, Clodine. Whatever happens next." She wanted me to know that one thing. "That's all," she said. "I only wanted to tell you." She wanted me to hear it straight from her, before they all of them started talking, before they changed it with the way they decided it should be told. So I wouldn't believe one thing otherwise, so I wouldn't think anything else. So at least I'd be one who knew what the truth was, which was that Lilly never did mean to hurt a soul. She didn't mean any harm. It wasn't her intention for any of it to go along the way it had.

"If I could somehow find some way to make it up to you, Clodine," Lilly said, "I guess you can believe it that I would."

Emma's weight was like lead in my arms. They ached with the heaviness of her.

"Okay, Lilly, it's okay," I was saying. The receiver was pressed hard between my shoulder and my chin, cramping my neck. "Just wait a second . . . okay? Let me just . . ."

I would go and put Emma down. I would sit again in the

chair there by the window, watch for Galen, let Lilly tell me whatever she thought she had to say, hold her there on the telephone, keep her talking, keep her connected to me, distract her with the drone of her own voice, until someone came. Galen or Jewel.

"Hold on, Lilly, please? Don't hang up? Let me just . . . I'll be right back, I promise. Don't go away, hold on."

Well, because what I was thinking then was that she was telling me, in her own way, with her own words, that that was all, she'd had enough, she wouldn't go on, couldn't. She'd do it now, this time for sure, and then that would be the end of it.

I was thinking that Lilly Duke was going to kill herself. And that even if she didn't use the razor blades that I had left for her, she'd find a way. And it would all be my own fault. Even if she didn't slash her wrists and bleed to death and die. Even if she only put her head into the oven. Or tied a rock around her neck and walked off into the deepest waters of the lake. Or hanged herself from a pipe with a scarf. However she did it, if she did it, still it would be my fault.

Or Galen's. We would be who was to blame, even if nobody else ever figured it out, even if it was only Jewel who knew, even if all of Harmony and the whole world, too, believed that Lilly Duke had it coming—nobody in the world to blame but her own self—still anyway I would always know that it was me.

What else could I have thought?

When she was saying to me, "Whatever happens next, Clodine, I just want you to know, I'm sorry."

"Hang on," I told her. "Wait."

I dropped the phone and let it swing and dangle above the floor while I stumbled upstairs and laid Emma down gently into her crib. It didn't take long. No time at all. A second or two, I was that quick. But anyway when I came back, when I picked up the phone again, there was no voice, no urgent whisper, no confession, no apology, no warning, no sign. Only the dial tone, humming back at me, steady and mean.

Lilly Duke was gone.

Emma came awake quickly and without a whimper when I plucked her up again out of the crib. She didn't cry, only snapped open her eyes and gazed at me, her face so solemn and her lips pursed thoughtfully, as if she knew that whatever it was we were up to that night, it must be important. I bundled her in a blanket and carried her on my hip down the stairs, through the kitchen, out the back door and into the yard. I was in my nightgown. I was barefoot. I hadn't bothered to dress. I had forgotten to put on shoes.

To get from our cottage by the lake to the old Duke cabin near the spillway, you can climb the short cut up from the meadow, follow the path that winds through the hovering shelter of the woods, and then step out into the dirt of Edgewater Road that circles the long back side of the lake and then curves in and out around the steep bluffs that rise up in some places higher even than the trees.

All around us, the night had thickened. It seemed like the clouds were waving in the sky, passing over us like the shredded fabric of torn flags. There wasn't any moon.

I was hoping that if I hurried, maybe there would be time to stop Lilly. Maybe I could save her, just this one last time.

I struggled along the path, bruised the bottoms of my feet on the small rocks and sticks, scratched my leg against the sharp thorns of a raspberry bush. Emma bounced, head wobbling, in my arms as I shifted her weight over from one hip to the other. I slipped on the grassy rise and staggered to my knees. Clawing at the earth with one hand, I pulled myself forward again and scrambled up out of the ditch and into the road.

The lake on the other side, below the high bluff, was black as ink, and perfectly still. I squeezed Emma up against me; she reached with her hand and grasped at a fistful of my hair. Like a monkey, she clung to me. For dear life, she held on.

What you can picture is this: me in my nightgown, a thin, shapeless dress, loping along barefoot through the dust and ruts of Edgewater Road. Emma bounces on my hip, her head bobs, her face is tilted back and she gazes wide-eyed at the murky sky, the spray of stars, and the shreds of the clouds as they move past. My hair is wild, tangled, blown back away from my face. My jaw is clenched, teeth grinding, chin out. I'm gasping, breathless from the effort of running with Emma's weight so solid in my arms.

And now I can hear the rising whine of a truck's motor as it moves along from a distance, toward us, following the curving course of the road. And I can glimpse it, white, a flash that ducks like a secret, in and out between the trees.

And by now I can see that this is Galen's old white pickup truck that barrels along toward us. The tires have raised up a wake of billowing dust.

And then I've taken one long step sideways, over into the middle of the road, and I've raised my arm and I'm waving, and Emma has turned and her face is just skimmed by the light of that single skewed headlight as its hobbled beam passes over her and past, scanning the roadway, the rickety line of the guardrail, the drastic edge of the bluff. A wanton shimmer on the flawless surface of the lake. A reckless flicker along the low-hung branches of the trees.

And by then the truck has come in close enough, and it is still moving closer, and I can just see Galen's face there, white beyond the windshield, behind the wheel, turned away, toward Lilly Duke. It's Galen and Lilly, side by side, in the white pickup truck, and they're laughing, or singing with the radio. She has her knees bent and her feet up on the dash; his one arm is wrapped around her and he is steering with his left hand;

there is a bottle of vodka that they've been passing back and forth between them.

Lilly Duke didn't kill herself, and she never meant to.

"Whatever happens next," she told me. "I'm sorry," she said.

But she hadn't been about to slit her wrists that night. She hadn't meant to apologize to me because she'd decided she would die; she was only saying she was sorry because she had found a way to live.

And so it isn't only Galen that I'm seeing there in the cab of our white truck, it's also Lilly, snuggled up beside him, pressed against him. And I'm there in the road, with my baby wrapped up in a blanket in my arms, my thin nightgown clinging to my legs, my wild hair, my bare feet, and it's as if there has been some kind of a trade made between us, Lilly Duke and me.

And Galen, turning away from Lilly then, looking back again at the road as they come into the curve where I am standing, sees me, finally; his eyes meet mine with a shock that seems to stun him, so when he recovers, it is too late. He's yelling—I can see it in his face, I recognize the syllables moving in his mouth, I hear his cry even over the rising roar of the truck's motor and my own blood screaming in my ears, I can hear him howling my name.

"Clo-*dine!*"

But it's as if I'm frozen there, snagged. I can't move. My legs are crippled, my feet are stuck.

Galen slams on the brakes and wrenches hard against the wheel, fighting the pull of the road's sharpest curve, so that now the truck is skidding and bucking over the ruts. The single headlight ogles the road, and then the truck has begun to spin, a graceful, fluid loop, and it careens, bounces up onto the narrow shoulder, splinters the battered guardrail and crashes through, over the edge. It rocks down into the emptiness that looms up from between the jagged trees.

Together, Galen and Lilly have left the last solid safety of the ground. The white truck is flying. Its engine rages, bellows; roaring with a furious, deep, helpless anger, it revs uselessly; the truck sails. Airborne, it soars. It hovers there, frozen for one fleet second, and then it begins to fall. It circles, dives, tips gently, nose first.

And smacks the surface of the water with a huge, resounding *whoomp!* And, turning then, it begins to sink.

And what I'm hearing now is the echo of Galen's mother's screams as they are carried off by the wind, across the dazzle of the snow, like the screech and cry of a hundred thousand wild birds. The night is filled with their dark forms; the sky is blackened by the flock's hectic swarm.

Galen's body was thrown forward in the impact, and his head was slammed up hard against the windshield, with enough force to shatter the tempered glass. He was knocked unconscious. A broad gash was cut into the fair skin of his brow.

Icy fingers of water probed the sockets of Galen's eyes and slid up inside his nose; they groped down his throat and strangled him. The lake reached out for Galen; it pulled on his arms and his legs, grasped his hands, caressed his body, yanked at his hair, embraced him. It held him, it drove him — the weight of the water pinned him down.

Well, I have kept this memory of Galen now. And I can cradle it here like it was a treasure, a gift, a flame that flickers in the cupped shallows of my palms. His hands moving over me. His eyes watching me. His voice calling out my name.

His shirt, soaked through, clinging to his body, shaping his muscles, molded to the outline of his bones. His hair flattened, wet against the curve of his skull. Water streaking off his cheeks like tears.

I pounded on his body with both my fists. I bruised his chest; I broke his ribs. I pressed my mouth against his and tried to thrust a breath back down into his lungs, to wish a pulse back down into the awful stillness of his heart.

They had to pull me off of Galen. They had to pry my fingers open and lift and carry me away.

The autopsy report said that Galen Wheeler's blood alcohol level was three times higher than the legal driving limit. And that Lilly Duke, trapped in the cab of the truck, had drowned, with a six-week-old fetus curled like a shrimp there in the still, dead waters of her womb.

Convicted murderer Timothy Merriweather Duke was executed by electrocution early last Wednesday at the Nebraska State Prison in Lincoln. Duke, 33, was pronounced dead at 5:52 A.M., after having been denied a stay by the Supreme Court only hours before.

Tim Duke's cabin has been left abandoned, and it seems to sag farther under the rain and the low gray sky. A summer thunderstorm brings hard winds in and blows branches down on the roof. A bunch of teenage boys have broken in and ransacked the place, looking for the money, hoping that she might have left something of value or interest or importance behind. They picked up the old TV set that I'd brought her and hurled it off the porch, left it smashed and broken, like a blinded eye, in the middle of the yard.

Finally, Clayton and some of the other men went out and boarded up the place. They put signs on the trees around it that say NO TRESPASSING, and they have had the property condemned.

I remember Galen out at the lake one night in the summer, many years ago, before Emma and before Lilly Duke. His blond hair had been bleached out almost white by the sun, and the skin on his face was smooth and tanned brown. His eyes were hidden behind the wide reflective lenses of the sunglasses that he wore.

We were out on the diving float in the middle of the lake. A group of shivering wet children, girls and boys both, had gathered around Galen, and they gaped at him in wonder and awe. There were some bigger kids hanging back, suspending their own approval—snickering, even, some of them—nudging each other, arms folded, belligerently protective, across their chests.

And there was Galen, all dressed up, completely out of place, curiously unsuited to the situation, there on the water, at dusk, on a worn wooden platform in the middle of the lake. He wore dark slacks, perfectly pressed. A blue-and-green-plaid sport coat. A starched yellow oxford cloth shirt, button-down collar, silver cuff links, paisley tie. His hands were wrapped around the handle to a ski rope tow. His feet were bare. I noticed the stiff cuff of his shirtsleeve against his wrist, the serious pale face of his watch, the fine curl of hairs on his fingers and his toes.

Someone set down a wide, heavy pair of skis, and Galen slipped his feet into their rubber casings. He turned and flashed a grin over his shoulder at me, and then he waved with one hand to Clayton in the boat that idled out beyond. The motor revved and whined, and the boat veered out, splashing up a high wall of spray in its wake. The tow rope came to life, picked up, tightened, and pulled against Galen. He straightened his arms and stiffened his back, flexed his legs, bent them gently at the knees. He glided off the dock as gracefully as a kite takes off and rises into the wind. His skis kissed the surface of the water with a gentle smack; he wobbled, caught his balance, and then he was gone, flying, his necktie flapping, his pant legs fluttering, the coattails of his jacket blown back flat.

Galen rode the water. He was balanced there, held against the surface of the lake on a pair of skis, circling gracefully, arcing out, bobbling wildly back and forth across rugged troughs of the boat's wake. The mirrored lenses of his glasses glinted a reflection of the reddened sky. His hair was slicked back by the wind against his head. And as I stood watching him, he diminished into the distance, finally lost among the grappling branches of the dead trees that rise up into the sky on the far side of Harmony Lake.

⌒✕⌒

One day those trees out there in the lake will begin to topple. One by one, all of them will rot, deteriorate, and fall. They'll drop and disappear beneath the placid surface of the water, like the first Harmony, demolished, forgotten, drowned.

I have my father's leather packet of maps. Emma and I have gone over and over each one of them. We've unfolded them and spread them out on my bed. We've followed the lines of the highways and Interstates and back roads. We've traced the courses of the rivers with our fingers. We've touched the mountain peaks and pointed out the places where there is a reservoir or a lake. I call out the names of the towns.

"Kirksville, Alliance, Liberal, Pratt. Silver City, Independence, Ketchum and Kalispell, Clovis and Christmas Valley."

I sing these words to Emma, letting their syllables roll off my tongue as if they were the verses to some ancient prayer.

And we are on our way away from here. Together, Emma and I, we're leaving Harmony.

Jewel stands in the driveway, with her hands on her hips, her children pulled in close, her belly huge beneath the flowered pastel cotton fabric of her dress. Clayton hovers behind with one hand on her shoulder, the other shading his eyes.

As we round the far side of the lake, it almost seems as if the trees are reaching out for us, as if they would hold us back and keep us here if they could.

But then we are past them. We've gone beyond the circle of their grasp.

Emma and I, just the two of us, we're free. We have no plans, no expectations, and no dreams. We have no connections. We are loose in the world.

And Old Highway 30 continues to unwind; the road rolls out before us, a ribbon of possibilities, as if we just could be making this whole thing up, right here, as we're going along.